Tales of the Green

DARK CITY

Tales of the Green
DARK CITY

ROBERT F. JONES

ASA PUBLISHING CORPORATION
AN INNOVATIVE OUTSOURCE BOOK PUBLISHING HYBRID

ASA Publishing Corporation
25 S. Monroe St., Monroe, Mi. 48161
An Accredited Publishing House with the BBB
www.asapublishingcorporation.com

Book Title: Tales of the Green *Dark City*
Date Published: 11.06.2023 / Edition 1 *Trade Paperback*
Book ID: ASAPCID2380875
ISBN: 978-1-960104-33-5
Library of Congress Cataloging-in-Publication Data

This book was published in the United States of America.
Great State of Michigan

To Hellen,

You keep me going. Keep shining, girl.

To Dad,

My biggest critic. Miss you.

About the Author

Robert F. Jones, a US Army soldier and mechanic, and a renown published author who is known to enjoy writing in his spare time. He is married and has a newborn daughter. His previous written novels are *Tales of the Green: The Black Priest*, *Little Destiny* and *Dimmer.*

The author enjoys writing his novels in horror, dark fantasy, and Lovecraftian fiction genres. Mr. Jones likes to weave in real life problems and events that are affecting the world, including problems with racial relationships, gender empowerment and equality, political division, and drug abuse.

He tries not to write about people with special destinies or chosen ones, instead, making his heroes ordinary people with ordinary problems in supernatural situations.

Robert's influences include Stephen King (aka, Richard Backman), Neil Gaiman, and Joe Hill.

We hope you enjoy his latest novel,

"Tales of the Green: Dark City"

Table of Contents

Chapter 3

Chapter 4

Chapter 5

Chapter 12

Chapter 13

Tales of the Green

DARK CITY

ROBERT F. JONES

Prologue

The priest walked across the courtyard, seeing a battalion of the golden army drill. The men, all dressed in gold breastplates and helms above red tunics and britches, held swords and shields, spears and arrows, and maces and clubs. So devoted they were. So loyal to the Golden Lord. So arrogant. So stupid. The Black Priest wished that these soldiers saw what he saw, the suffering the Golden Lord caused. People were dying, being raped, tortured, and starved just by his whim. Ever since he joined John's resistance, his eyes had been opened to his sire's corrupt ways. He wished he was back with other resistance members and their freer way of thinking. But that was too risky right now. The resistance was lying low at the moment, having lost dozens of members to Kal, his brother. They had to wait, or risk exposure.

The Black Priest entered the throne room. On the outside, he showed nothing, almost believing his own external body's lie. On the inside, he hid hate and fear for the being he was going to meet.

The Golden Lord sat on his throne, as if carved from stone,

covered by a golden cloak from head to foot. Underneath was something monstrous and evil - a vain creature who seemed only to live to make humans his . . . his playthings. Next to him was the Dark Queen, one of the Great Old Ones. She had a terrible beauty that one both wanted and feared to look at her. She sat, arrogance on her face, only eclipsed by that exuding from the Golden Lord. Horrible stories surrounded her, as with all the Great Old Ones, but she was especially terrible, involving draining young women of their blood and bathing in it.

"Come, my son," said the Golden Lord.

The Black Priest walked forward and knelt before the Golden Lord, who stood and said, "One of my mistresses has gone missing. Do you know anything about this?"

'Yes,' thought the priest, 'Yes, because I freed her from your horrid clutches. I freed her from the hell you put her through, and I am proud of it. I wait for the day when your days are numbered, and you and the Great Old Ones will die at the hands of those you have oppressed and have forced me to oppress. Then I will reveal myself to you as not your servant, but as your enemy.'

"No," he said out loud, "I know not, my lord. I was in the castle offering prayers for those who need it."

The Dark Queen turned her eyes on him. They were dark eyes, like black holes that sucked you in. In fact, the priest swore that those eyes dimmed the light in the hall if you looked into them. Horrible, but you could not look away.

"Two of the guards were killed. How could such a thing happen under our noses? I doubt that woman had the strength to kill such men, weak as she was."

'Putting up with you,' thought the priest, 'She had more strength then either of you could understand.'

Out loud, he said, "My Queen, I fear I have not the answers you seek. I am a mere priest and must bring hope to those who ask the Golden Lord's favor. And if she did escape, she must be in the Green. In all likelihood, she is dead."

The Golden Lord stood, tall and imposing, then walked to the kneeling priest.

"Blaine," he said, "I know she is still alive, for she carries my child."

The priest looked up, shocked. "How do you know this, my lord?"

"All who I sire I can feel, if they live. I felt your brother, Kal, die at the hand of one who used weapons banned here in Etam. I can feel each of my children and their descendants. And now, I feel two outside my lands. One is far in the land I sent Kal to. That is his child. But the child still carries my blood, so I can feel it. The other, not as far, but not as close as I'd like."

"Do you know her location exactly, my lord?" asked the priest named Blaine.

"Not exactly, but I can still feel them. But these children must be brought to Etam. If they grow without proper indoctrination, their powers could be used against me. I tell you this, for I know you are a loyal servant and will do all to accomplish their retrieval."

"My lord," asked Blaine, fear now rising in his blood, "Can you know their exact location?"

"As I said, the land I sent Kal to was far, but I know the general location due to Kal keeping in contact through the Fire Lord. However, this other girl, I cannot tell where exactly she is. Not as far as my grandchild, but still, far from my lands."

Blaine felt fear, but he would worry about that when he left. Right now, he had to get as much information as he could.

"I need you to retrieve the children. But first, we must deal with these northern dissidents. Another one of my priests, Shaldon, has found a great city. It is walled but is home to millions. Millions in need of saving. Prepare 5,000 of the golden army to take care of these lost souls and bring them to the fold to be saved."

Seeing how to use this to his advantage, he said, "Yes, my lord. I will also dispatch 50 men to these northern lands you spoke of to look for the child. The other can wait, as if she is not too far, she will be easier to find. But we must take care of the lost souls in the North."

The Golden Lord nodded, and said, “Go my son.”

Blaine stood. Leaving the hall, he headed to the field where he saw the soldiers drilling. No, not these, but there was another drill field not too far away. He headed there. His head reeled from what he’d learned. Not just how he could sense those who were sired from his blood, but also about the city. Millions. Millions. He had thought only Etam was in the millions, but now . . . now he had proof that there were other lands where people lived free in large numbers. This information was good to pass on to the resista . . .Oh god, the resistance.

If the Golden Lord, however vague the connection could be, could feel him, then every time he met with the resistance, he put them at risk. He couldn’t do that. He wouldn’t do that. He needed time to think, but right now, he had to pass on the information.

He found the field and saw Sergeant Slavern. He was a large man, hard and almost forty. He had trained soldiers all his life. Now, he secretly fought to free Etam from the Golden Lord. But he never recruited those he trained. As a freedom fighter, he was ready to fight to free Etam. But as a teacher, he never would risk his students. Though harsh in his methods, he was never cruel, unlike other instructors, and would do anything for his men.

Slavern saw Blaine and yelled, “Reverence.”

The company of one hundred soldiers knelt. It was custom

when meeting a Black Priest.

"Great instructor, I must speak to you on an urgent matter."

Slavern looked at Blain and said, "Stay in prayer, maggots. I'll return and know who didn't pray to the Golden Lord."

He left with Blaine to an empty courtyard, and there, Blaine told him all that had transpired between him and the Golden Lord.

After a few moments, Slavern asked, "So, he can sense you?"

"Yes," said Blaine, "But it's only general areas. I don't think this is common knowledge among my order, but this does bring new risks for the resistance."

"And to our long-term plans for finding allies," said Slavern, "We have to act fast. Where are these children?"

"One is in a land far to the north, the other is closer, far, but . . ."

"Keep knowledge of the closer one to yourself," said Slavern, "The closer one is ironically safer for now. The Golden Lord believes she is closer, and with that belief, he won't feel an urge to find her as fast. However, the city and the child are a much more urgent matter, so that has to be our priority."

"Do you have men you can trust that can help find this child?"

"I have got a hundred in the main army that I can gather on short notice to find this girl."

"Good. I have no control over the force going to the spoken

of city. But hopefully they will have defenses. I can keep them away from the land I sent the other girl to."

"I'll get started. And I'll warn the resistance," said Slavern, "You best stay away from resistance members for a time. If you can, just bring as much information to me."

"Wise for now," said Blaine, standing. "Find this girl and keep her safe. And while you are there, convince the people there to help us find freedom. They killed a Black Priest. That is no small accomplishment."

"An ally we want," said Slavern, standing, "Good luck."

"You too," said the Black Priest.

1 On a Barge from Sugar Island

The old man whistled, the fog from his breath coming in the morning chill. The barge was both home and work for the old man, and his only company was that of his apprentice and granddaughter, Nala, and his passengers. His son was long gone to work the timber in Sault Saint Marie, an eastern, small colony which was now given the nickname of Asian Town. Chinese, Korean, Japanese, Thai, and many others colonized it, while sculptures of dragons, pandas, and many other animals lined the streets.

The colonies were not the old man's interest, though. His

wrinkled skin and gray, thin, beard, belying his ancient Korean descent face, had familiarization with only the stretch of water and the islands he brought people to.

His passengers today were two riders: one with white skin, spiky black hair, and a leather jacket, the other a tall, muscled Black man with a leather vest, white shirt, and yellow bandana. He had picked up both from Sugar Island, the home of the Sisterhood of the Roads. Strange women he found them, tattooed and fouled of tongue, but they held great knowledge on that which was Michigan. The old kept the records, the young traveled, but the island was their home. Some had families, some children, but all traveled.

The man knew not what the two riders had gone to do there, but his guess was actually a good one. They came to him at about six in the morning. He woke early every day so he could eat breakfast in peace, on the deck of his barge, as he had done for almost sixty years. His granddaughter, Nala, was sleeping in the cabin. He would have eggs and bread ready for her when she woke up a few hours later, for she was young and the young needed sleep. The elderly, like the man, did as well, though he did sleep less than his granddaughter. The riders came up to him about ten minutes after sitting. Riders were not as common around Sault Saint Marie, but he had seen them throughout his life, and transported a few, so seeing the two was not a great shock to him. They parked near the dock he tied his boat to and approached him.

"Hail Riders," said the old man, raising a hand, "Fair day on the road."

"May your travels be as fair as the day, as well."

It was a traditional greeting here in Sault Saint Marie, but to be honest, it was not a great day. It was cool, gray and overcast, and still dark out, the only light cast by the wood burning stove in his barge's cabin.

"We need a ride to Sugar Island," said the dark-skinned man with a yellow bandana.

"Ay," said the old man, "Kinda early, though, don't you think?"

"It is," said the man with the black spiky hair as he pulled out a large, gold coin from his jacket pocket. "But I think this should cover the early hour."

He flipped the coin at the old man, who caught it and looked at it. It was solid gold and large as his palm. The old man's standard fare was seven silvers for a one-way trip, but this would cover months of small repairs that the old man needed, and he could even add that new composting toilet he had an eye on in town. Going over the side at his age was dangerous nowadays at best.

"Ay," he said, putting his eggs on the bread and turning it into a sandwich. “Let me just get my granddaughter. Oy, Nala, come here.

The man with spiky hair, Doug, and his friend and companion, Thug, had traveled to Sugar Island to pick up the maps ordered beforehand by their leader, Barthalamulal, and landed in Homestead, the only town on the island. They left their bikes on the barge, for there were no roads to travel on in the town. The people here were humans, regular mostly. No Otherkins were in the sisterhood. It wasn’t forbidden, they just had no interest. Otherkin had a far better sense of direction than humans.

Ignoring the houses and the few shops the two riders made their way to a large building, the only one not remade, for it was an original building, built after the green. It was large, made of white wood, and could fit the whole town inside. Five spires, each topped with a torch on top, extended far above the green. The door was flanked by two riders, a Skin Changer, and a Goat-Type Otherkin, both on racing bikes and armed with Uzis. They nodded to the fellow riders, and Doug handed him the seal of approval they needed to enter. The Otherkin took it, scanned it, and nodded.

The two riders entered the citadel. The inside was a grand entrance hall, lit by a large, crystal chandelier, where the riders were met by a woman with purple hair. She had a silver circlet around her head, and silver bracelets on her wrist. She wore a black tank top, a purple wrap around her waist, and black sandals. Her arms had several tattoos on them - an iron bar, a bear and berry, a bridge with twin cities, and so many more. She smiled and said, “Welcome riders.”

“Sister Rhea,” both Thug and Doug nodded their heads in reverence, having great respect for this woman.

“Come, what you seek is with sister Andrews.”

They followed her up the stairs. They passed many of the tattoo-armed women, all talking or carrying or thinking. They walked and walked until they reached a hall with three doors. The door was made of Oak wood, and it was opened. A woman, no older than nineteen, her arms covered in tattoos, more than the others, stood there smiling. Her hair was red, and she was very pretty, and her breasts were high, firm and large.

“Hey boys,” she said with a seductive drawl that even attracted Thug for a moment: “I got what you need. But before I give it to you, you know what I need.”

Doug pulled out a letter from a rider in training named Lance and handed it to the girl. Andrews smiled, opened the letter, and a golden ring landed in her palm.

“My word, I’m as happy as seeing a pawpaw. Boy is going to finally make me a proper woman.”

“Congrats,” smiled Doug, “Now . . .”

“Yep, got your map. Here you go. Why the Mitten, though?

Riders rarely go that far south."

"Business," explained Thug, curtly.

"You riders are too strict and need to loosen up. Well, all but my Lance. That boy, oh my god, when he is in bed, that man becomes a god, I'm telling you, the way he just fills . . ."

"Ok," said Thug, his mind going to him being with his lover, Chang, as she spoke, "I get it."

"So sensitive," chuckled Andrews, "Anything else you boys need?"

"Maps of the old USA. If you got them."

Andrew frowned and said, "A got a few, but they are hundreds of years out of date. The Green fucked up things here and we had to redraw thousands of maps. Those maps might not be of any help."

"They're all we've got."

Rhea, who was standing in the background, finally spoke up.

"You're attempting to get past the Green that blocks us from the rest of the world, aren't you?"

The two riders' silence was answer enough, so Rhea continued, "Well, we will give you the map, but the best place to get that information is Detroit."

"Why Detroit?" asked Thug, not mentioning they were going there anyways.

"Because the Mitten is their land, and the Rabbit is ours. They have more knowledge of the south than we do."

The riders nodded as Andrew came back, carrying a map in her arms, and spoke up again.

"How many of you goin'?"

"A few. We are the scouts; the real party doesn't come down for a while."

"Jesus," said Andrews, "so serious."

"Thank you, sisters," said Doug.

The sisters bowed and led the two riders back out, and they walked back to their ride.

The old man's guess was close to that. And soon he would pull up to the Bridge town with these two, and they would meet up with several other riders, and this in the end would not affect the man. He would, in the end, sail to a port, sleep, wake, eat, then start his day again, not knowing he had just transferred two warriors who would be instrumental in keeping Marquette and the Colonies free.

Chapter 1

Across the Bridge, Five Days Later

1 Forming of Ice

Jack filled the water skin off the shore of what was once called the City of Mackinaw. There was an island called Mackinaw, far out into the water, where people still lived. But this city was all but abandoned, save for a few houses on the coast used as fishing lodges and fisheries for those who lived on the island. The Green hit this city hard: trees coming out of buildings, roads in poor repair, and sand going beyond the beach into the city, covering them in hard grit.

Strange folk lived on the island, though Jack reflected that those who were not from the Lands of Marquette, or as the Islanders referred to it as, Northern Michigan, were all strange.

But to him, the island had many strange costumes and laws that were strange even to a culture that worshiped the roads.

Jack smoked a cigarette while he filled the skins. Down the road, Kshea, a master tracker, thin, pink-haired, and tattooed, was setting up a fire to help boil and sanitize the water, ensuring it was safe to drink. Several skin bags were piled next to their motorcycles which were being attended to by Kato, one of the truck clan members assigned to this journey to Etam. He was a dog--type Otherkin, an Irish setter. Humanoid, his head was that of a dog, and his body covered in red fur, a tail sticking out of his blue jeans. The human--like parts of him were covered in this thick, shining fur. Even his hands. His hands, like that of a human, still retained something of a dog, his fingers ending in not fingernails, but thin claws, flattened down to help with his work. The bottom of his hands had the paw structures seen on the bottom of a dog's feet, that hard flesh meant to protect the dog. He wore gloves over them, so as not to get his fur caught in anything, with his black leather jacket protecting his arms.

They were all wearing leather jackets, for winter was coming, and already ice was forming in the water. Soon, the lake would be covered thick enough to walk across and be covered in tents the Island people used for ice fishing.

But none of this was the rider's concern. Their concern was making sure they had enough water to get to Etam. For in truth, they did not know its location; they'd only been theorizing that it was south. Kal, the Black Priest, had never said the direction. In a few months, the riders would send out more parties, but until then, they had to do their best to find the Land which Kal spoke of. But not tonight, for soon it would be dark, and it would be too dangerous to travel through the Green. It was best to stop here, so as not to worry about their travels until tomorrow. And this part was extremely dangerous since it was covered in Pines, their needles sharp and ready to cut flesh. On the bright side, they made good tea.

Soon, Thug and Doug joined the others. Thug, a large, well-muscled man of African descent, and Doug, a man of European descent with black, spiky hair, rode on their bikes, masters of their wheels. Like the other three riders, these riders were in their leathers and bandanas. Jack greeted them by waving his hand, his cigarette in the corner of his mouth, smoke swirling in the wind. Ash blowing off, revealing the hot cherry beneath it.

The two riders stopped behind Kato, who looked up and smiled in that strange way Otherkin did and said, in a growling, barking voice, "You need me to look at them too?"

"Nah," said Doug, "We are good, thanks, Kato."

Kato nodded and went back to work on Kshea's bike.

"We found shelter for the night," said Thug, "A house before the Green. The Makinawians don't use it and it's in relative tack."

Jack and Kshea smiled.

“Good,” said Jack, “Does it have a fireplace?”

“Yep,” said Doug, “We will be warm tonight. The others are setting up, so we should head there soon.”

Kshea and Jack looked at Kato, who said, “I just need a few more minutes.”

The others collected the waterskins and broke down Kshea’s fire pit and pot. Soon they were packed and on their bikes, Kato in Jack’s side cart. His own bike was on his truck, strapped down and being driven by Miko, a friend of Thug’s and like Kato, a member of the Truck Clan of the Riders.

The riders drove down the badly maintained road and got to the house Thug and Doug found. It was old, white, and mostly intact, save for the garage which had a large tree growing out of it, its root, long bending the metal door and cracking the remaining cement. Two female riders named Samantha and Tricks were standing watch on their bikes outside the house. But the main body of the house was safe, and the riders entered. Dinner was already cooking in the fireplace. Sausages and potatoes were wrapped in tin foil, put into the hot coals, while apple and cheese hobo pies cooked next to them. The fruit and dessert cheese were crushed between two pieces of bread using irons. The other riders also set up sleeping mats and bags, close to each other so they could use their body heat to stay warm. A male skin-changer with red, green, and brown patterns shifting on his skin, cleaned weapons in the corner, another of the truck clan named Grenn.

The Pathfinders and truck clan sat round, shooting the shit as they ate, drank, and smoked. Soon cards were brought out and a few games started. All but Jack, who sat in the far end of the house, sitting on a root that worked its way through the garage and into the laundry room. He sat smoking, staring at a picture of his wife.

About three years ago, he found a camera while looking at a site for colonization in Marquette. The area was deemed too hazardous, but Jack found this camera and got it working again. He took that picture. Her face with a smile so wide, it made his heart heavy. In the picture, she was hugging the then puppy, Brute, a large Bear Dog, who had been their companion for almost five years. Like Niki, his life was taken far too soon by that bastard, Kal.

Kal, the Black Priest. So many shots he took, so hard to take down, and yet, when Jack did, he didn't get the satisfaction that he had hoped for. He didn't get any form of closure from his death.

Smoke gathered around Jack's head, remembering, remembering how Kal's body was slit and warped by that beast, the Golden Lord. So much power he felt that night. So much fear of the being who had changed so much. Not just his world, but the perception of the world he had once believed was a product of nature and a divine being which he knew not the name of but figured had to exist. Now he had seen a higher being and knew nothing but fear and contempt for it. He also learned about the existence of magic. Magic, the force of nature that had apparently existed from the time when men lived in caves and trees. Those magic users who paraded themselves as the old gods, who then birthed regular humans with powers in the form of witches and warlocks. Learning that Marven, the hermit in the shack in Iron Wood, was the Merlin from Arthurian Legends, and was responsible for cutting off the world from magic hundreds of years ago. So many questions he still had. At night, he would spend hours talking to Watu, Merlin and his bear and companion, asking all he could about the history of magic. But those things he didn't discuss with other riders, for he feared that they would think him mad. Magic was in the world of children, they would say, not a force of the real world. But he had seen magic. He had seen it when Merlin showed him the history of the world through his own eyes. He heard it when Watu spoke to him with his mind. He felt it when the Golden Lord tore apart Kal's own body to make a vessel to which he could communicate with Jack. The conversation was brief, but it was powerful, and dreadful for Jack.

He told the others none of this. He wished he knew why this was. But at the moment, the memories of fear, hate, and loss were about to overwhelm him. He put the picture back in his jacket pocket. He lit another cigarette and started smoking again.

He supposed such feelings were natural, but he had never learned how to handle them. His father had never taught him. He wished he had listened to his mother more and was able to handle these feelings instead of suppressing them deep in his soul. But it was all he knew how to do. He looked out the window. The sun was setting, and had a guard shift tonight at two am. So he grabbed his sleeping bag from the room containing all the riders without emotional problems, went to the laundry room, closed his eyes, and slept. He had no dreams that night, mainly because he wouldn't be asleep for that long.

2 Watu's Rage

Thug played a few hands of Texas Hold'em with Kato and Grenn until he decided he had enough and walked outside, as thoughts of Chang caused him to lose to Kato's bluff while he had a full house. He had a cigarette in his hands, and he was thinking of Chang. Chang, his love, fell fighting Kal to the end. The memories came flooding back, so he decided to take a walk outside. The backyard was close to the Green, so he walked into it. The oppressive foliage seemed to want to swallow him up. He gritted his teeth against the feelings that came over him. God damn it, he was a rider for god's sake, not a little girl.

He looked back at the broken city through the trees. He saw buildings that might have been impressive at one point, but now were dwarfed by the pines. He remembered telling Chang they would find a city that outgrew the trees, and they would live in one of the tall buildings, looking down on the Green instead of being surrounded by it. He felt a pang in his heart. A pang of sadness. He thought about talking to Jack about this, as he had lost his wife, but he felt he'd be less of a man if he did. He felt alone. He felt . . .

A sound made him whirl, drawing his Glock as he did so. In the branches of a tree, twenty feet away, something sat in the tree. It was large, almost as big as him. It had a gray, feathery body, folded wings, like that of a bat, and its head was like that of a predatory lizard full of bared, sharp teeth. It had a long tail too, which ended in a point, like depictions he'd seen of the devil. A wyvern. Shit, this was not good.

The two, man and monster stared at each other, Thug with a gun, the wyvern with teeth and talons.

"Easy buddy," said Thug, backing up slowly so as not to provoke the animal, step by step, as slow as he could: "You don't want me. All muscle, not fat. You'd just choke on me."

He got forty feet away from it when his left ankle stepped on a small stick which cracked under his feet. The beast roared, spreading its great wings, lifting itself off the branch, and flew at him. Thug didn't hesitate and put three rounds into the creature's head. It flew, then fell, sliding dead, only five feet away from him. 'Back to the house,' he thought and turned.

"Rawwwww. Rawwww."

The high-pitched roars came out of the forest and four more Wyverns awakened. They took to the air and went to their fallen brother, and began to eat it, like vultures, ripping chunks of flesh off the dead creature. Thug backed up and was soon out of the Green, but the Wyverns saw him, and they seemed to decide they wanted fresh meat. They took off after him, crawling on their folded wings and talons very quickly.

Thug fired, taking down two of the five, but the creatures were fast and would soon be upon them.

"How high were the Ancients to bring you bastards back from extinction?" growled Thug. He knew they were descendants of prehistoric dinosaur-like beasts, but at the moment, he didn't care. He saw their sharp teeth and didn't want to be on the other side of them, ripping at his flesh like scissors on parchment.

They were almost upon him, and he raised his gun. One whipped their tails, knocking the gun out of Thug's hands. Another sunk its teeth into his calf. Roaring, he kicked at it until it let go, but the others were growling, sensing weakness, about ready to pounce. Thug fell back, his leg unable to hold him anymore, seeing the beast scuttling towards him.

"Roarrawwwww," yelled a different animal. It gave the wyvern pause. It was a bear. A bear the size of a black bear, save for its white fur, but still bigger than the wyverns. They turned, looking at this new adversary to their meal. The bear snarled in rage, its eyes locked on the wyverns. One darted towards him, sinking its fangs into the bear's front leg. Big mistake. The bear flung it with strength that broke its neck and made it slam against a tree. The other two wyverns looked at him more cautiously, circling the predator as their adversary hunkered down, blood pouring from its foreleg.

One took to the air while the other darted in, but the bear swiped at it, and it scurried back. The other dived down, and the bear shied away. The other on the ground darted again, raking the bear's flank, who rolled over, almost crushing it, but it flew off a second later, though one wing looked bent.

Thug got his pistol back, this time in his left hand as his right was still in pain. He aimed at the beast who had attacked the large bear, targeting the larger of the two. But his hand wasn't as steady. He couldn't . . .

Three bullets ripped through the air and one of the wyverns fell from it. Dead, lead ripping a hole where its eyes were, and its mouth was open, trickling blood. Jack got his Sig Saur aimed at the last Wyvern, which roared its high roar and tried diving at the riders. They shot and hit it in the wings. It fell to the ground and hopped towards them on its talons, its mouth open wanting to take a bite before it died. The bear charged, the riders got out of the way, and its jaws crushed the wyvern's skull.

Thug's leg was still bleeding, and Jack supported him. Thug raised his gun, leveling at the bear.

"Don't," said Jack, grabbing his arm.

"Jack, it's a fucking . . ."

"He's harmless," yelled Jack, making Thug raise his eyebrow.

"Harmless?"

"Thug, I'll explain everything later, but you've got to let him go and not tell anyone about this."

Thug looked at him, his eyes clouded with confusion. But he saw the bear leaving back into the Green, and he needed to get his leg looked at.

"Ok," said Thug, "Just, help me back to the house."

Jack supported him, as the other riders came out. Kshea helped Jack with Thug while Doug was asking, "What happened?"

"Wyverns," said Jack, "They got his leg."

"Miko, get the med kit," snapped Doug.

Miko ran back in, the others trailing behind, helping Thug into the house.

3 Time to Pack

Kshea helped Miko to fix up Thug's leg. It had several teeth marks in it, but they were flesh wounds, though they were bleeding heavily. Kshea and Miko worked to clean them with alcohol and stitching. They did this expertly. This was due to their clan within the Pathfinder Clan called Trackers, who were trained to track animals establishing territory near the roads. Due to the high probability of being hurt while tracking, Trackers were given training as medics as well. With Kshea directing Miko, they cleaned and bandaged the wounds.

This fact however didn't seem to dawn on Thug, who was growling as the women cleaned and bound his wound. The alcohol stung, and it made the large rider tense as the stinging added to his overall suffering, burning into his leg, giving it the feel of acid. He gritted his teeth against it, snarling.

"Stop being a baby," said Kshea as the large rider growled.

"You try, bitch," snapped Thug, "Lets' see you hold still while someone pokes at your wounded leg."

"It ain't that deep," said Miko, "But I admit, you should stay off it for a bit. Wyverns aren't venomous, but they got a mean bite. Never seen them this close to the water though, or at this time of the year. Too cold, they should be hibernating for the winter."

"I don't care," said Thug, "The bastards bit me. And now they are dead."

"Still . . ." began Kshea.

"He's alright?" asked Doug. Jack was beside him. Both riders with a look of concern.

"He is fine," said Kshea, "But he's going to need to stay off the leg for a few days. That means no riding."

"We'll put him in the back of the supply truck," said Doug.

"What?" asked Miko and Thug.

"We're moving on," said Doug.

"But we just got here," snapped Kshea, looking around at the makeshift camp they made.

"I know, but we can't stick around somewhere we know Wyverns have taken residents."

"We killed the pack," snapped Thug, "Besides, you know how dangerous it is traveling through the Green by night."

"I know," said Doug, "But what if more of those things come?"

"Wyverns are rare," said Kshea, "We probably won't see another pack for a hundred miles. Hell, we shouldn't have seen that pack. This is their hibernation season."

"Animals acting abnormally," snapped Doug, "Sound familiar?"

Kshea couldn't respond, and Thug's face became blank. They

both remembered Chang. Thug didn't see the body, being held up in the cells at the time. But Kshea remembered the barely recognized corpse that was Chang, how it had been ripped, slashed, stomped, bitten, gored, kicked to unrecognition by dozens of different animals. They'd never been able to prove it, but they all knew the Black Priest, Kal, had something to do with this. He had controlled them, they suspected, with that voice of his, the voice that bent people to his will.

"He's right, guys," said Jack. "Staying here is too risky. If there is a Black Priest nearby, it's too much of a risk."

"Thank you, Jack," said Doug. "Pack up. We're leaving in fifteen minutes."

"What about Thug?" asked Miko, "Someone needs to say with him to clean the wound and make sure it doesn't become infected. I am on the truck, and Kshea is needed on the road, so who?"

"I'll stay with him," said Jack, "I have the training."

Doug nodded and walked away. Kshea then went over to Jack and said, "Jack, you have to change his mind."

Jack turned, looking right at her, and she flinched at the sight of pure pain on his face.

"He's in charge," said Jack, "I'm not in command of this expedition, so I don't . . ."

"You know driving in the Green at night is a Risk at best. At worst, it's suicidal."

"Kshea," snapped Jack, "Stop."

She did and walked away to pack. Kshea paused, thinking, "What happened to the rider I once knew?"

He looked at her, and with her back to him, she didn't hear the words that came out of his mouth.

"He died when Nicki died. He died in the Green after he killed Kal."

4 Night Road

Jack sat with Thug on the back of the Truck. Night had come, and in the Green, it was almost pitch black. No, not pitch black. Oppressive black. It was not a normal darkness. It was a darkness that contained fear. It kept all their eyes moving, their jaws set, and their hairs raised in fear. Few riders ever traveled in the Green at night. No lights save for the headlights. No stars to guide you, blocked by a ceiling of interconnection of branches. It gave even the most veteran rider's caution, and the youngest a feeling of terror if done. But these riders were in between, not so old, but not so young. Doug watched for any sign of movement. As did Jack and Thug, acting as rear watch. No wyverns, so that was good, but every sound made their weapons rise. The sigh of the wind, the rustle of leaves, the creek of a shifting branch, the scuttle of birds and squirrels: in this oppressive darkness, every sound they heard of the motors brought visions of great beasts and monsters coming out to attack and kill the group of riders.

After about three hours, Jack, who was as nervous as the others, told Thug to sit down, needing to change his bandage. Thug kept a hand on his large caliber hunting rifle, watching like a falcon while Jack changed his bandage.

"So, going to tell me about that bear?" asked Thug finally, sick of the oppressive darkness and fear of being devoured that comes with being in the dark.

"You wouldn't believe me," said Jack.

"Jack, come on, I trust you man. That's why I didn't shoot, because I believed you knew what you were talking about. Please man, don't lie to me now."

Jack gave him a look. It was a tired look, a look that said, 'Please don't put me in this situation.' But in the end, it switched to a resignation. He looked over to a blue tarp way in the back and said, "Watu, please."

The tarp shifted, and from one end of the edge, the bear raised his mighty head, looking at them with his sharp eyes.

"Da fuck!" exclaimed Thug. "Where the hell did he come from?"

"He was always there," said Jack, a small smile on his face. "Well, he does his own thing when we pull over, but he's always back before we leave."

Thug looked at the bear. The bear looked back.

"How come we haven't noticed this?"

"Watu's not a typical bear," said Jack, "He's . . ."

He paused, and Thug saw a look of indecision on his face, a look that said many things. A look . . .

'Oh, stop stalling,' said the great Bear.

Thug looked around instinctively, his brain not comprehending that the voice he'd heard had not come from the pushing of air molecules into vibration, but into his head and spirit as directly as a look, so sharp it passed through the physical and into the spiritual realms of our reality.

"Where, what, I don't," Thug stammered.

"Watu," said Jack, "Show him."

Watu raised his paw, and a look of blank serenity entered Thug's face, vacant, not caring about the world.

'Was that how I looked when I saw the visions with Marven?'

For two hours, Thug looked vacant. He didn't move, and Jack was convinced he didn't breathe. Nor did the bear. Both seemed locked in an endless staring contest. A test of wills to see who blinked first. The blackness of the Green passed by as Jack watched the two not moving. But he knew, though the two didn't move, he knew that visions were passing through their heads, visions and history being passed from the bear into the brain and spirit of Thug.

Finally, the rider awoke, as if from a major trip, his mind trying to make sense of what he had just seen.

"Easy now," said Jack, holding his friend, who was shaking like a man coming back from a near death experience.

"What . . . what did I just see? What was that?"

"The past," said Jack.

"Magic," said Thug. "What, why?"

He then turned towards Jack, a look of frustration on his face. "Why didn't you tell the others?"

"Same reason I didn't start discussing what I know till now," said Jack, "It's crazy. You explain you know magic exists and you have a talking bear traveling with you."

Thug looked at Watu and looked back at Jack. The look on his face said, 'Now that I think about it, it is a little insane.'

"So, what I saw, what he showed me, that . . .?"

"All happened."

"Magic." Thug looked thoughtful. "I can't believe it. Makes sense in a way. You know, I could never explain how the Green took over so quickly. People say it was the Ancients who played with technology beyond their control, and it got loose or said that it was after bringing back some beast we shouldn't have. But now, now that I think about it, magic is just as good an explanation as any of those others."

But then a clarity came over him, a clarity that scared Jack, though he knew not why.

"Wait, in the vision, near the end, I saw four children over a book. Who were they?"

Jack saw no way around this so just told the truth. "They are the leaders of Etam. The Golden Lord and the Great Old ones. The ones Kal mentioned. They created the Green. They were responsible, and they sent Kal."

"You knew this, and told no one?" explained Thug, a look of anger in his eye.

"How was I supposed to tell you guys that I saw the people we were trying to contact in a vision I got from a bear (he didn't mention Marven), and saw how our world became the Green through that vision? You saw what I did, and you barely believed it yourself. Don't deny it, it's true, you can barely believe it."

Thug's expression switched to understanding, seeing where Jack was coming from. That is when the truck pulled over.

"Why are we stopping?" asked Thug. Then the bikes pulled up to the fuel truck.

"Wait, we didn't need to refuel for a . . ."

"You were out for two hours."

5 DarkKin

Doug had the group refuel before the final leg of their journey. He knew they were nervous, and to be honest, so was he. Humans and Otherkin nowadays had an aversion to traveling at night. He read once the Ancients used to just walk around willy-nilly, not worried about the wildlife. He wondered about those days, not having to worry about Parka and Dire Wolves, though he had heard there were none of those types of animals during that time. But other than the perpetual looking over the shoulders of the group, the refueling was uneventful.

Soon, they got back on the road, and an hour later, they reached a sign that gave them all relief.

"Welcome to the Village of Traverse."

Doug smiled, they'd made it, and he even saw an orange glow in the distance. The Village was nearby. He could even smell the smoke coming from the building. In fact, now that he thought about it, it was very overwhelming. Quiet, but strong, almost cloying.

Doug signaled for the riders to pull over. They were about a quarter mile outside the village. Something wasn't right there, and he wasn't going to go in blind.

"What is it, Doug?" yelled Jack from the back of the truck.

"Something's not right here," Doug yelled back. "I think there is a fire."

The others looked in the other direction, noticing how the orange light was shifting, like a skin changer's patterns on his or her skin.

"Let's get in," said Kshea.

"We will, but on foot. Don't want to damage the engines out here," explained Doug.

"How is this going to damage the engines?" asked Kshea.

"Depending on how long it's been going and how big it is, the ash could damage our bikes and trucks engines."

It was a fair point, but it still made the other riders nervous. Very few times has one's bike become more of a hindrance than a help. But to Kshea, this didn't feel like one of those times, and if he was being honest, nor did it for Doug. But vehicles were one of their most precious resources right now, and they had to keep them out of danger as much as possible.

"Jack, Thug, Samantha," he said, "Stay with the vehicles and keep your eyes peeled. Kshea, Miko, Kato, Tricks, Grenn, you are all with me. Keep loaded, eyes peeled."

The riders nodded and went to get their equipment, all but Kshea, who walked forward, and said, "We should get our bikes. We don't know . . ."

"That's right, we don't know," snapped Doug, "For all we know, they are having a party. But if something serious is going on, having our bike might be risky. People could try and loot them off us, trying to get away, or there is a fire, and the ash clogs up our engines. Or worse, the fuel might ignite from the heat. I'm being careful, so stop questioning my orders and get your guns."

Kshea stomped off and Doug shook his head. He was going to need to have a serious talk with her when they returned. He looked over at Jack and Thug, loading their rifles, ready to fight. How come Kshea never questioned Jack? Why was he the one being questioned? But he pushed it out of his mind. He had a job to do.

Five minutes later, the riders worked their way up the road, their eyes still flicking in the Green. It was still night, and though there was that orange light, none felt a rush of salvation. And without their bikes they felt very vulnerable. Kshea came up and said, "Weird that we haven't seen anything."

That was true, he thought. They had been fortunate not to run into anything. In fact, it was damn unusual this far south of Marquette. Animals up there were learning not to go to the web of roads during the day, and slowly, learning the same lesson at night. But here, riders rarely came down this far and the wildlife still ruled. Roads were less reliable, almost nonexistent down here, and they didn't have vehicles around this area. So, the fact that they hadn't seen shit was more concerning to him than it would have been if a herd of Mammoths had walked across the road.

A quarter mile later, the smell of smoke was getting thicker, and the heat was getting worse. And then, they entered the village, and all stopped, shocked at the sight.

The village was not on fire, it had already been on fire and the glow had come from the dozens of burnt buildings that was all that was left of the village. It had just been burnt; it had been blazed out of existence. Not one building had been spared the inferno. And around the village, hundreds of bodies lay in the ash-covered ground. The blackened remains of men, women, and children, none were spared by the blaze. Doug even saw a baby being held by his mother, just as blackened. The sight made him sick, and it took all his will not to puke. Once he had that instinct under control, he turned to the others and said, "We have to look for survivors."

They nodded and moved forward, their eyes watering in the smoke. They searched for a half hour and only found more burned corpses. Nobody had been spared. They all resembled coal; coal that had been molded to look like human remains. It wasn't natural. It wasn't fair. It was devastation. It was mindless destruction. It was annihilation. Doug felt like this was what it was like searching for survivors of a blast from a bomb. Hopelessness engulfed him. Hopelessness and a heavy heart.

"Over here," yelled Grenn, his skin matching the ember light.

The Riders ran towards him. It was a corpse, but this one wasn't as badly burned as the others were. It still had some flesh on its bones. But it seemed wrong. Something wasn't right.

"What is that, an Otherkin?" asked Kshea. It did look like it. At first glance, it did seem like a dog-type Otherkin, but it was not right. Its head and body were larger. Not by much, but noticeable. Its head was that of, well, of a wolf.

"I've never seen one like that before," said Tricks, her pixie cut blonde curls going over her pale face.

Doug sat, looking over the corpse. Then he looked up at Kato, and asked, "Are there wolf-type Otherkin? I've never seen one."

"There aren't," said Kato.

"Maybe it's a primitive form of Otherkin," suggested Grenn, "Like, Neanderthals are to humans."

"You know as well as I do that Otherkin are not evolved beings. We were created in a lab. But I've never heard of one being made from wild animals other than Eagle-type, and that's because Eagles brain structures were unique compared to other wild animals. This . . . this is something else. I've heard stories of wild Otherkin, but they were not able to control their instincts, unlike domesticated type Otherkin. They were shunned and even killed. As far as I knew, only those of the domesticated type survived today."

"It could have been the last of his kind," said Kshea, "Or

maybe . . ."

"Shhhhh," said Doug, standing, his shotgun at the ready, looking down the barrel into the ember lights. Kshea and the others looked around and saw nothing.

"What . . .," began Kato, then stopped. Out of the shadows, humanoid shapes started moving. Humanoid shapes, with the heads of wolves. They were snarling, wearing black dusters over their furry chests, eyes glowing, teeth bared. They carried knives or daggers in their paw-like hands. Their pointed ears went back on their heads, and their fur stood on end. There were about a hundred of them, coming in a circle, slowly.

The riders went into a circle, guns raised, ready to fight. Then Doug saw something that made his mouth drop. Each was wearing a golden carving on their necks. The figure was that of a gold cloaked man. These beasts, whoever they were, served the Golden Lord.

6 Attack

Jack and Thug were watching, silently, guns raised, the orange amber light maddingly looking like salvation but spoke of death ahead of them. It was hair-raising and the two men didn't know why. Thug decided to break the tension.

"So, what exactly happened in the forest between you and

Kal?"

"You saw the report."

"I saw what was on the report. But I don't believe it. I know you, Jack, and I saw the remains of Kal. They were torn to shreds. So, what happened? Because I know you didn't do it."

Jack was silent for such a long time Thug didn't think he was going to answer. Then . . .

"When I killed him, I was going to walk away. Then I saw his body moving, and then split open. It was like a puppet, and it was molded into . . .into a shape, and a voice came out of the shape. It was the Golden Lord."

Thug looked disgusted, thinking about how that looked, and then asked, "What did he say?"

"Not much. But I noticed that he seemed to be speaking like that of a person who seemed barely self-aware. More like, he was playing a part in a production. He knew his lines, but didn't seem aware about what I was saying, or didn't care about it."

"What do you mean?"

"I don't know, it's just . . . hey, you hear gunshots?"

Both men looked up at the noise, loud cracks like muffled thunder repeating itself several times. Samantha came around, and started, "You guys hear that rig . . .," but she didn't finish, as a mass of fur tackled her from the side, disappearing behind the truck.

"Samantha!!!" yelled Jack, pulling his shotgun around to the front, going to the side of the truck, and disappeared from view. The thing that got her, he missed; the only credence given to its existence was Samantha's scream of agony, and then her sudden silence in the chilly night air. But in the glow of the headlights, he saw eyes, eyes that reflected the light, and saw three large creatures, standing in the light of the truck. They were shaped like Otherkin, but were larger and taller, wearing a sort of dark trench coat and dark trousers. With the heads of wolves, they resembled creatures from stories of Wolfmen and werewolves. They stood snarling, blood lust glowing in their eyes.

"We got company," yelled Jack, shotgun ready.

"Yeah," yelled Thug, "behind us too."

Jack turned his head for a second, noticing three more snarling Wolfmen. That would make seven he could confirm, but his gut told him there would be more.

Going back-to-back, Jack and Thug kept their weapons trained on the six wolves they saw. Then the seventh Wolfman leaped right onto the roof of the cab of the truck, snarling like an animal, and then Jack noticed the golden symbol on his neck. He had seen that symbol before. First with Kal and then the one Kshea found where Chang fell.

"Son of a bitch," growled Jack, firing the pre-pumped shotgun. The buckshot hit the beast in the chest, and it roared, rolling off the truck, screaming to its death. That is when the others charged and four more let up on the truck sides as the other six took the front and rear of the truck. Working as one, Jack and Thug side-stepped, circling, their weapons firing, aimed at the creatures before them. Their aim was true, and they hit them in the chest. They managed to take down several of the wolves like that, but more were coming, snarling, snapping jaws, as nimble as apes.

Jack was about to sidestep again when one tackled him from his blind side. The two went sprawling in a mix of fur and leather, the shotgun knocked out of Jack's hand. But the wolf overestimated his angle and was stunned. This gave time for Jack to draw his sig lightning-fast, the bullets fired hitting the beast in the head. Getting back to his feet, he saw Thug battling with another wolf, which had closed in with a large knife in its hand paw. But Thug managed to hit it with the butt of his rifle, and pulled the trigger as he did so, hitting another Wolfman that was leaping towards him and getting a snout full of lead for his troubles. But the action had aggravated Thug's bad leg, and with a moan of pain, he went to a kneeling position as two more made for him, jaws open, tongues lolling out, knives in hand. Jack took two true shots, hitting each between the eyes, and they went sprawling to the ground. Jack got to Thug's side, and another wolf came at him, but Jack dodged the knife and drew his own combat knife, stabbing the wolf in the chest three times and then shooting it in the head. By now the two riders were covered in blood, battle fever on them. Thug got back to his feet, his adrenaline helping him ignore the pain, reloading the rifle. Jack was able to recover the shotgun, holstering his pistol and knife. Four more wolves came up, but Thug dispatched two with his rifle, and then ducked, as Jack fired buckshot into the other two. A final Wolfman came up from behind, and Jack shot it in midair. It landed on top of another dead Wolfman. The two men stood there, blood-soaked and ready for more. But no more came. It took a moment for them to realize that there was still fighting in the distance.

"Grab Bertha," yelled Jack, running to his bike. In a moment, he unstrapped it and had it revved. Thug limped back from the armor box, carrying a large SAW Gun and a box of ammo, his rifle slung over his back: Bertha, Jack's go-to weapon in tough spots. He found the weapon in an ancient military facility in New Berry, somewhat banged up, but still functional. He refurbished it and he got it fully functional a year ago. He had only used it five times, but now it was time for Bertha to bite again. In a moment, the two connected the gun to a holster on the front of the side cart, aimed forward and ready, Thug loading the rounds into the weapon. Gingerly, Thug got into the side cart, while Jack revved the bike once more.

"What about the ramp?" yelled Thug.

"Fuck the ramp," yelled Jack, getting ready to take off.

Thug took one last look around and asked, "Where's Watu?"

It was only then Jack noticed that Thug was right. The bear was gone; he wasn't underneath his tarp.

"Can't worry about that now. We've got to go." He put the bike into full throttle, and it went screaming off of the edge of the truck.

7 Defend

Kshea fired again and again, each round taking down a wolf man. But they were many, and there were only five riders here, caught without their bikes. They were trained to fight like this, but this, at least to her, didn't feel natural for a rider. They were meant to ride and fight, and feet were secondary. But she kept fighting, as did the others. She saw Tricks and Miko, back-to-back, taking down wolf after wolf. Kato was fighting two at once, jaws and hand paws and claws biting and slashing at the much larger wolves, fighting more like a wild animal than the others. Grenn, using his skin changing, blended into the burned surroundings, popping up randomly, killing several of the wolves before they got a good look at them. Doug was using his shotgun with one hand, and his knife in the other, fighting the wolves at close quarters, his deadly dance killing multiple wolves before they got near him.

They fought, killing dozens of wolves, but still more came. They were relentless, as they slowly pushed them back. If they only had their bikes, then this fight would have ended a while ago, but now . . .

A familiar sound broke through Kshea's hopelessness. A hope, a faint hope, but still there. It was the sound of a Harley Long tailed, found and restored by the order, and presented to a pathfinder. It was Jack. She saw the leather jacket, yin-yang bandana, and blue jeans of the man on the bike with a side cart. Thug sat in it. On the front of the sidecar was Bertha, the Squad Assault Weapon. The wolves and riders, momentarily distracted, saw the two riders come in, guns-a-blazin.' Ten wolves fell before they knew what was happening. A new hope entered the riders, and they went back to attacking the wolves, killing those closest to them with lead, the brass falling to the ground. The riders on the bike made wide circles, hitting wolf after wolf, the beasts dying quickly. Ten fell, then twenty, then forty. Kshea killed one right through the head. Doug killed three with his gun and knife routine. Kato ripped the throat out of another with his dog-like jaws. They pushed back until no wolves were left standing.

Kshea looked at the carnage and felt relief. She looked at Jack and saw for the first time in months that fire in his eyes, the fire that made him a rider. The strength of will, the determination, it was all back there. Battle hardened and battle-ready, Jack was ready to fight, to defeat, and defend all those who stand against bringing back civilization. She had an urge to scream in jubilation, and yell, 'Thank you, thank you. You returned, and you're strong again.' But those words didn't leave her lips. Instead, she heard footsteps in the ash. She turned, and what she saw made her stomach drop.

Out of the smoke walked a man dressed as Kal was. It was another Black Priest. This one was shorter than Kal and older, but he walked with the same arrogance and determination as a man who knew how to walk in a way that was befitting his station in life. She couldn't make out his face, as it was shadowed by the black wide brim hat that Kal once wore, but it gave an impression of hardness and years of hard living.

He spoke in a voice deeper than Kal's, but when it hit the riders, all eyes were on him. It had the same hypnotic effect and power. It demanded all eyes on him. It demanded that everyone listen to him. It was not just in her ears, but also in her mind, pulling her to listen to what he had to say.

"So, you thought you could escape justice," he said. "Well, here I am."

Everyone raised their guns, aiming at the priest. Still in shadow, Kshea couldn't see his expression, but there seemed to be a change in it. Was it shock at the audacity of these people who dared aim a gun at such a holy man?

"You killed these people?" yelled Jack, his voice raised in anger.

"They needed to be cleansed, for they did not see the way," said the priest, "but it is not too late for you. Forget your wicked ways of sin and revel in the light that is the Golden Lord. He is your path to salvation."

"Fuck you," yelled Kshea, "You killed children. Fucking children. What kind of Lord demands that?"

"A lord that requires great strength to hold back the Green."

"Fuck you," yelled Jack, "It was your master who was responsible for the Green. He caused all this pain and suffering. You're a pawn and don't realize it."

The man shifted, and his face was finally revealed. He was an older man, and his face had a look of horror and anger on it.

"How dare you blame my Lord for that which befell humanity. It was not him, but the God, Ade, who wished to punish humanity for his wicked ways. If it was not for the Golden Lord's father's forward thinking, mankind would be nothing but dust."

"You're so blind, you can't even see when you are being lied to," snapped Jack.

Kshea looked at him, and though she saw that he was causing

the priest great pain, she couldn't help wondering where this claim of the Golden Lord causing the Green came from.

"You are doomed, and I must cleanse you," the priest said to Jack, "but for the rest of you, you can turn away from sin and join the Golden Lord."

Kshea saw Doug step forward, and said, "Yeah, I think we are good," and fired with his shotgun. It ripped through the priest. His chest was covered in blood, and he stumbled backwards, and yet he stood. He looked back at Doug, who looked shocked and saw the priest's eyes were blazing.

"You're going to have to do better than that . . ." But he was stopped in mid-sentence as Jack shot him in the neck. The priest stumbled backwards, shock on his face, his neck collapsing in on itself as once Kal's had. He fell to the ashen ground, dead.

"Doug, we've got to get out of here," yelled Jack.

"Why?" yelled Doug, but it was too late, as Kshea and the others saw the body begin to move violently, and then split open, as guts and muscles and skin began to reform from the body into a shape of a new humanoid form. Jack had his gun raised, but the others could only watch, amazed at the sight before them. The horrible, vague humanoid form before them made them freeze in terror.

"Doug," yelled Jack, "We've got to go."

Kshea, Doug and the other riders began to move back away

from this mound of internal and external organs, guns raised, and Jack turning him and Thug away. Then it spoke.

"You dare," it yelled in that horrible voice that rang in their heads, "You dare kill another of my priests."

Jack paused, turned back, and then yelled, "Thug, empty the clip. Make this fucker shut the fuck up."

Thug opened up on the beast, bullets ripping through it like a hot knife through butter. The organ creature rose, and moved before them, but chunks of it were falling off faster than it could replace them.

"How dare you!" yelled the beast, but the other riders opened fire, as lead ripped it apart, and it began to collapse in on itself, its final words being, "You are all damned," before the shape fell apart.

Kshea looked at Jack and yelled, "What the hell was that?"

"No time," yelled Jack, "Back to the trucks."

8 Retreat

Kato was being helped by Kshea back to the trucks. His shoulder had been badly injured, bitten deep into, even fracturing the bones in there. Miko had a slash through her jacket, but it didn't reach the flesh. Tricks, Grenn, and Doug only had a few cuts and bruises. Thug's leg was bleeding again, and he was helped by Jack back to the truck. All were covered in blood, and still had pounding hearts after what they saw. They loaded Jack's bike back in the supply truck, got Kato and Thug in the back as well, and they also loaded Kshea's bike as well. With two injured riders, they were going to need someone to keep an eye on them.

It was past midnight now, but Doug decided that they needed to move on. With all the blood and gore, they needed to get out of there before animals decided to investigate. He also decided to hold off on questioning Jack about what they saw for now. Priority: get to safety.

"Where are we going to go?" yelled Kshea as she cleaned Kato's wounds.

"Detroit," said Doug, "It's the only city I know about with any kind of medical facility in these parts."

"That city is almost a two-day drive with these roads," said Grenn, "But honestly, I don't know about any other settlements in this area."

"There has to be another option," begged Kshea.

"We'll keep our eyes peeled, but for now, we've got to get out of there."

"He is right Kshea," said Jack.

Kshea looked at Jack and noticed that that fire in his eyes was gone. Back was the withdrawn version of her friend. No longer was there the rider who knew what to do and when to do it.

"Let's roll people," yelled Doug, getting back on his bike.

The trucks started, and Jack asked Kshea to meet him in the back to grab medical supplies, which she did, the fuel truck right behind the supply truck. Distant from Thug and Kato, Jack turned to Kshea, and said, "What's your problem with Doug, Kshea?"

Kshea was shocked. His tone was that of a cold teacher, disappointed with a student. But she answered in any case.

"Every decision has been wrong so far, Jack. Leaving the bikes behind, traveling in the dark, not once, but twice in one night. We've had nothing but problems and no solutions in any way."

"He's been making the right decisions," said Jack in his same tone. "If we stayed in that house in Marquette, the wyverns could have gotten into the supply truck and raided our food or damaged our equipment. If we put our bikes into the village, before we knew the situation, then we could have had six bikes damaged, and possibly unrepairable and unreplaceable. You know how valued and rare bikes and trucks are in the order. We can't risk damaging them outside of Marquette and the colonies. So even I would have gone on foot."

Kshea was silent, seeing the wisdom of his words.

"Doug's a good leader, Kshea, and right now, he's doing what he can to make sure we all get out of this. We already lost one rider today and we haven't found her body. Nor can we afford to look for it because of the risk of the Green, and constantly questioning Doug in front of the others will do nothing for morale."

Kshea looked at him, shame on her face for not thinking of these things. Then Jack looked at her again and she saw the old fire in his eyes when he spoke.

"I am one with my bike. It is a part of me. It is a part of me as is my heart, my soul, and my mind. Through my bike, I protect those who need it.

Through my bike, I keep the deepest darkness out and cast shadow in the brightest of light.

I am a Rider, protector, and guardian to all who need one. I find the paths that were lost. I find the road less traveled. I bring civilization back from the Green. I am a Rider."

"We all are riders, Kshea, and we don't have the luxury to look at the sequences of every decision we make. Sometimes, we have to do what's right at the moment."

Kshea nodded, saying meekly, "I understand."

Jack put a hand on her shoulder and said, "You have much to learn, but that's the same as us all. We all have much to learn, and we never stop learning as riders. Just learn from your mistakes and talk to Doug and learn from this."

Kshea nodded and went back to attend Kato and Thug.

Chapter 2

New Haven

1 Jeremiah

Ara awoke in the house. It was an unknown home, and she didn't know how she got there. It was made from wood, painted white. The room she was in was bare save for the bed she slept in and the chest of drawers beside it. All she knew was that she had no idea how she got there, and it was heaven compared to the hell she had been through. For almost ten days, she had traveled through the green, only in the night gown she had been wearing when the Black Priest helped her escape the Golden Lord. For ten days, she traveled north through trees so dense they almost made a wall, round mountains so high they went past the sky, through rivers so deep, she almost couldn't swim in them. But she survived. Avoiding many of the horrors of the green. She had little to eat. Little to drink. And sleep, well, that was a luxury she couldn't afford to have. Her mind remained active, fearing a Parka or a Cave Bear would find her and eat her. She feared it and saw many of the fell beasts of the Green. She spent hours avoiding them and running for hours when she moved on. The last thing she remembered before this house was going into a clearing and finding open skies. Seeing so much sky had made her dizzy and made her collapse. Her clothes had almost been all ripped away by the branches, her hair full of twigs and leaves, her skin covered in dirt. Now she felt clean.

What had awakened her was the creek of the door, and a little girl in a blue dress and white bonnet covering curly brown hair, with freckles on her face. Ara thought she had never seen such an innocent looking girl before. In Nuevo España, Ara saw the girls often with a hard look on their faces that reflected the corruption of their society. The girls of Etam only knew fear and feared for their lives every day. This girl lived in a world that was free of the hardships of those societies. It showed hope for the future and for today. It was a face that almost caused Ara to weep.

"Mama told me to check and see if you were awake. We have breakfast."

Ara could only nod, unable to speak, for the girl only gave off kindness. She was so kind, so lovely, Ara wanted to just hold her and protect her from all the evil outside this little paradise.

The girl left, and Ara stretched, tired and aching, but feeling better. She just realized that her body was bare, and her only modesty was the quilt that had been covering her. She went over to the chest of drawers and found a simple gray dress and undergarments. After she changed, she left the room. She realized walking out that she was on the second level of the house and went down the hall to the staircase. There she entered a big kitchen with counters, a dinner table, cabinets, and an old wooden stove with delicious smells wafting up from the pans. Around the table sat a number of strangers. First, a tall man with a white cotton shirt, black trousers held up by black suspenders, long white socks, black boots, and a thick beard around his face. The top of his head was short, but his beard reached to his chest. A younger man, but older than the other children, sat on his right. He had no beard but was dressed in the same manner as his father, same brown hair and all, almost identical. On the man's left side, one chair down, sat the girl who came for Ara. Across from her, a teenage girl in a blue dress and white apron, but also with freckles and brown hair. Finally, from both sides of the table, in highchairs, two boys no older than three, both with brown hair and freckles. At the stove was a woman. She, unlike her children, had strawberry blonde hair, but she had the freckles that her husband lacked. She wore a white dress with a black apron and a white bonnet just like her daughters. She looked at Ara with a mix of concern and kindness that almost made her weep. It was a look she only remembered her mother ever giving her. A look she hadn't seen in years.

"Thought you'd never wake up," said the woman. "Go to the table. Take my spot. We've been feeding you only honey and milk for the past few days, and you need some food."

"Thank you," said Ara, tears in her eyes, and upon seeing this, the woman left the stove and went over to her, embracing her.

"There, there child," she said, patting Ara on the back, "You are safe here."

She escorted Ara to the table and sat her down, wiping her tears with her apron. The man looked at her. He didn't smile, but his face was in the shape of that which was concerned, and his body radiated great kindness. His eyes showed compassion.

"Are you alright, my child?" he asked.

"I am hungry and thirsty, to be honest," said Ara.

"Jeremiah, please pass the water jug," said the man, and his son obeyed. The man personally filled her cup, and said, "Drink slow, you haven't had much for a while. I am also Jeremiah. And what is your name?"

"Ara El'Doro," she said, sipping at the cool water. It tasted like spring to her.

"Good to finally know your name. These are my children: the

oldest girl is Emma, and the youngest girl is Mary. The two boys at the end are Jacob and Samual. And of course, my oldest son is Jeremiah also. And my wife is Lilith."

"How did I get here?" asked Ara.

"I found you when my son and I were trading with a village many miles from here. You were unconscious, so I rode you back to my house. It was a three-day travel, and I was fearful you were not going to make it. My son fed you honey and milk the whole time. When we reached the house, you had a fever. My wife ministered to you for three days. Another two passed after the fever broke. But now you are awake."

He didn't smile, but still remained very kind. She felt safe here. Safe from all the evil of the world.

"Where are you from?" asked Mary. "You look different."

"Mary," scolded her mother.

"It's alright," said Ara, "I'm from a place called Nuevo España. It means New Spain."

"Where is it?" asked Mary, her eyes bright with curiosity.

"Far south from here."

"Can I go?" asked Mary, excited.

"It's too far," said Ara, "Too dangerous."

The girl pouted, but she changed the look to blankness as her mother gave her a scolding look. Emma giggled behind her hand.

Lilith brought several plates of something that looked like

meat loaf, but it had a strong smell of pork.

"It's called scrapple," she said, "Try it, it is good."

She did, and it did taste good. Its flavor was strong, but it was pleasant. They were all silent for a while as they ate, until Jeremiah Jr. asked, "So, what were you doing that close to the Green?"

"Jeremiah," said Jeremiah Sr.

"I was escaping from a land called Etam," said Ara, feeling no need to lie. But she regretted it for she felt a shadow over the family, as if she had said Hell was unleashed by her.

"I've heard of this Etam," said Jeremiah Sr., "You said you escaped?"

"Yes," said Ara, her voice small.

"That took courage," said Jeremiah, "I am impressed."

"Thank you," said Ara, relieved, "But what is this place I am at?"

"This is New Haven," said Jeremiah Jr. proudly, "And we are the Amish."

Amish, a word that seemed neither English nor Spanish in origin to Ara, but something older or maybe just different to her ears. It was a word of simplicity, a word that said we are who we are, and we won't change. Even their clothing evoked this vision. Where the people of Nuevo España wore bright colors, the men wearing it in the tones of extreme masculinity, and the women wore to enhance their extreme feminist curves, the Amish clothes seem simple and work ready. This was also opposed to that of the people of Etam, where fashion for the commoners and peasants evoked poor quality, but they couldn't afford better, or the bright costumes of the Nobility. These people, though she was only going by the actions she had witnessed and inferred from the family which she sat in, seemed to show a sort of equality. Jeremiah Sr. seemed to be the unquestioning man of the household, but only among that of his family. Everyone, in a way, seemed to be happy with their lot in their simple, unrushed lives.

"I am ashamed to say, I have never heard of the Amish, either in Nuevo España or Etam."

Emma giggled again, and said, struggling slightly with the unfamiliar Spanish words, "Well, to be fair, miss, we never heard of Nue..nu..Nuehavo Espan."

They laughed at that, but the tone turned serious when Jeremiah spoke next, "As for Etam, well, as I said, we are aware of the land, but we don't interact with their people. The forests outside of New Haven are so dense that it takes a lot of effort for them to move to our lands without us being aware of them. And that's if they are aware of us. We are spread out through the clearing via many villages, and our communities are very hard to find."

“So, you have encountered them in your lands?” asked Ara.

“Only once. It was a man in all black preaching about their blasphemous gods, but we never had any trouble with him, just ignored him. I haven’t seen him in almost twenty years. The only time I encountered him was when I was a boy with my mama, and she dragged me away as quickly as she could, though I will admit in my youth, I was drawn to it. It was like he had a power in his voice, one which my mother called witchcraft.”

“What was this priest's name?” asked Ara.

“I never knew his name, nor did I care to,” responded Jeremiah Sr. “Why do you ask these questions, child?”

At first, Ara wished not to answer, not wanting to relive even the moments that led to her escape from the Golden Lord’s castle. But this family had shown her nothing but kindness, and she didn’t want to leave them empty of answers. But then she looked into Jeremiah Sr’s eyes, and saw there a look that, while unsmiling, showed great kindness, and a wish to take away her pains. Pains he seemed to know were not only physical, but also in her very soul, etched there like scars on flesh.

“A Black Priest,” she said, almost unaware of her mouth moving, “saved me and helped me escape Etam.”

Jeremiah Sr. raised an eyebrow to this. A small look of surprise crossed his face. But before he could say anything, Ara remembered something he’d said.

"Wait, you said that you only encountered one Black Priest. If that's true, how do you know of Etam's location? I just walked most of the way through the Green to get here and even I found it difficult."

Jeremiah Sr. almost smiled at that, and said, "Though the forests are dense and difficult to manage through, and impossible for an army to march through, it is possible for one to travel through it. You yourself can attest to that fact. You've never been to this side of the woods, or the Green, as you call it, but you managed to get through. But for us, we have lived in this area for hundreds of years and have learned to adapt to the Green. We have seen Etam from a distance and watch to make sure none enters our lands. Not to fight, mind you, for our people are not warriors, but to make sure they don't come our way. If they do, we know how to hide, and hide well. But so far, we never had to."

Ara nodded, seeing the wisdom in this, but shocked in the fact they did not fight. She had been a fighter all her life and couldn't imagine not being willing to defend yourself at a moment's notice. But she dropped it for now. She did this because Lilith was eyeing her with a look that said, 'Finish your food, please, dear.' Ara finished the scrapple and looked up to see the family bowing their heads in silent prayer. As they made to get up, Ara tried to join them, but Lilith put a hand on her shoulder, saying, "No dear, you need more food. Come, I'll bring some bread and cheese, and put on a pot of coffee. Jeremiah, would you mind if the girls and I stay with Ara?"

"Of course not, dear," said Jeremiah Sr. as he and his eldest son gathered the two boys. "We'll take the little ones to the play area. I'll ask Titus if he can help us today. He's finished his harvest and should be available for a while. We will be back for lunch."

The girls sat with Ara, talking and laughing, asking her about the outside world as their mother brought out bread, a soft cheese, honey, and coffee. They sat and enjoyed themselves as the sun shone, and for the first time in a long time, Ara was able to forget the violation given to her by the Golden Lord.

2 New Haven

For three days, Ara, via Lilith's motherly administration, was only allowed to rest and eat, insisting she regain her strength. She even ran a bath for Ara, washing her hair while singing in a motherly tone. Though eighteen, and she normally would be embarrassed by this action, she felt instead a kind of protection she hadn't felt in a while. During those three days, they didn't question or pry into her past anymore, and she too refrained from this. Instead, they talked about the day's work, from harvesting crops to milking cows, or even about Titus' terrible jokes, talking and laughing about them. She noticed the two older men were not as open to showing emotions and the women were just more reserved than what Ara was used to, yet she nonetheless felt a kind of energy that boasted her spirits.

Then the third day hit, and Ara insisted that she help the family repay their kindness. After a bit of disagreement, they agreed to let her help Emma and Jeremiah Jr. with milking the cows, seeming to already know that she was not much of a farmer.

The pasture that was home to the herd of cows that the family raised was on the far side of the farm, a mile away from the fields. Entering, she saw they were black and white, chewing grass slowly and not seeming to notice the three coming towards them. In the distance, Ara saw a few calves at play.

Emma showed her how to pull the utters and bring the milk out. It took a few tries but then she managed it. About three hours later, Emma asked, "So, what's Etam like?"

A shadow fell over Ara's face. Jeremiah Jr. gave his sister a scathing look, and Emma quickly said, "I'm sorry, I didn't . . . forget it . . . Dat said not to . . ."

"It's ok," said Ara, taking a deep breath. Finally, she said, "Dark, and evil. Well, not all dark. The people can be friendly enough. At least the common folk are. But the nobles, they oppress the people, take their lands, and make them work for nothing but bread sometimes. And the leadership, they abuse and kill those who speak out against them with no more thought than you would killing a fly. The Black Priest preaches, and you must stop what you are doing and listen, or risk being hanged."

Emma put a hand over her mouth, and Jeremiah's eyes conveyed shock, saying in response, "But why did they do that?"

"Oppression begets power, and power over the people is what makes them strong. My father tried to get people to rise up against the Great Old Ones . . ."

"Who?" asked Emma.

"The Great Old Ones, the monsters who lead Etam. Most people feared them, believing them to be demigods, but not my father. He believed they were flesh and bone, as we all are. Merida, he believed it so much, he was able to convert many to stand with him. Hundreds, if not thousands."

"What happened to your dat?" asked Jeremiah.

"He was killed," said Ara, slowly, "By the one they called the Golden Lord."

The two looked frightened, but Ara quickly said, "He died a warrior's death; he fought him until the end."

Both blinked, so Ara changed the subject, and said, "Tell me about New Haven."

A look of excitement entered their faces, even as they milked. Jeremiah spoke with a passion and pride that got him a look of reproach from his sister, "Well, it's our home. It took over a hundred years to cut the forest away to what we have today. But now, we have a great home. Our leaders, the bishops, they are kind of our mix of spiritual and community leaders to guide us to a brighter future. We live in peace here, not worried about the great beasts that live in the woods. Here, we are able to live godly lives."

"What do you worship?" asked Sarah.

Emma frowned, and Emma wondered if she had ever been asked that question.

"Well," she said, "I guess, the closest thing I would compare it to is Christianity Baptism. You know what that is."

"Si," said Ara, "Nuevo España is very Christian, though we practice something called Catholicism."

Both siblings looked confused, but continued, "The Bishop leads us in prayer and sets the Urnum. They are the rules that our community has to follow. Each village in New Haven has a unique Urnum, but most follow a similar pattern."

Ara loved hearing them talk, but she couldn't help but draw parallels between these Bishops and the Black Priests of Etam.

"Are there many Amish?" asked Ara.

"Yep, like three hundred thousand or so."

Ara's eyes widened: "How did they all survive the Green?"

"Not all survived the event," said Jeremiah sadly. "Dat told me that it was a dark time for our people. Tens of thousands died. More starved. But we were better off than most."

"Why was that?" asked Ara.

"Well, unlike a lot of the world, the Amish didn't use much in electrical technology. It still hit us hard, but we bounced back better than a lot of other people."

"You know of others, other than New Haven?"

"Several," said Emma. "We do some trading with them, but we don't interact much besides that. But some have brought old world tech back to the Green."

"Dat says these people are lost," said Jeremiah, "But it's not our jobs to convert them to the simple life."

Again, Ara couldn't help but draw parallels between their faith and that of the Golden Lord. It was absolute, untenable. But still, unlike the Black Priests, these people had compassion, and had shown her nothing but kindness. Still, it was a little unsettling to her.

They worked and talked for more time. Then the bell rang for supper, and the four of them gathered the milk and brought it back to the cart which Jeremiah Sr. had just pulled up in, drawn by a brown-furred mule.

"Hurry up," he called, "Your mama will be cross with me if I make you late for supper."

They loaded up and headed back to the house.

3 Full Truths

Ara ate with the family that evening, and it was at this meal that she noticed something she hadn't noticed before. The family never left the house an hour before the sunset, and Jeremiah Sr. always locked the door. It was such a routine that Ara never thought of it till now. It seemed weird to her, so that night, after the others went to bed, when Jeremiah Sr. was sitting in front of the fire, Ara joined him in a rocking chair next to his and asked him about it. A sullen look came over his face, and he said, "The day in New Haven is wonderful, but the nights can be dangerous. We Amish are not warriors, so we must protect ourselves from these dangers in other ways. We don't go out at night unless we need to. When we do, we always stay as close to our roads as we can, and travel as fast as we can."

"What kind of things?" asked Ara.

"Some say they are demons from hell, coming to take our souls and devour our flesh. Others say they are people driven underground, forced to resort to cannibalism. For me, I just stay inside as much as I can until the sun returns."

They were silent for a moment, and then, Jeremiah leaned forward and asked, "Ara, I can no longer avoid the question. Why are you here? Why did you come here?"

For a moment, Ara was silent, but again, she couldn't refuse to answer, and said, "My father, he was a revolutionist, not for the freedom of the people's souls, but for their minds. Have you heard of the Golden Lord and the Great Old Ones before?"

"Yes," said Jeremiah Sr., "Legends that I heard from the Black Priests, that came here."

"They are not legends. They are horrible, twisted creatures of nightmares made flesh. When my father was discovered, he was brought before them, and was killed by the one they call the Golden Lord. He died in the most horrible way, consumed by that beast. For months, I was forced to endure the Golden Lord's vicious appetites, and my brother . . .my brother was paralyzed the last time I saw him. I don't even know if he is still alive.

"During that time, I didn't even know if I was going to be able to live, let alone escape. I feared everyday was going to be my last. Then, out of nowhere, a Black Priest freed me and told me about this place. He may have been the same Black Priest that you met as a boy, I know not, but he told me that the Golden Lord knew nothing about this place. I chose to try and make it through the Green and come here. I had no choice. It was here, or endless torture. And I need help. My brother might still be alive, and I still might be able to find him."

Jeremiah Sr. was silent for a long time. When he spoke, it was as if he measured every word.

"We don't believe in violence, or being the cause of violence, directly or indirectly. In this way, I cannot and would not help you. It would damn my soul. But I do know of people who might be willing to help you in this way. I do not say this lightly, for to do this would cause me to be excommunicated, but I am a brother as well, and I would risk hell to save my sisters and brothers. These people I know, they are called the Navajo. Their lands lie far to the west in an area once called the Rocky Mountains, but now called the Waste Lands by my people. It is dry and harsh land. The people there are great warriors, but do not like outsiders. Our people and theirs have had a relationship based on mutual respect, but it is a respect we earned. They do not love outsiders, they don't love strangers, but they believe in justice. They have gone to war over the past two hundred years to right wrongs. If any people were willing to help you save your brother and free Etam, as I know you wish to, it is them."

Ara held her breath. This was everything she wished for, a chance to find someone willing to help outside of Etam.

"But I warn you, the waste lands are harsh. There are creatures there that are more vicious than anything you might have encountered before in the Green. Parka, Dire wolves, Cave Bears, they have nothing on the creatures of the Waste Lands. If you face them, you must face them alone. I can bring you there to the edge and point the way, but you will have to travel the road."

Ara nodded, willing to accept any offer that gave her a chance to save her brother.

"In that case, we will leave in a month. Such a journey will take time, and I will ask you to help me around the farm until we leave. Deal?"

"Yes, señor," said Ara.

Jeremiah smiled and went back to the fire.

Chapter 3

The Cloud

1 The Drunk Bear, The Robot, and the Rider Walk into a Bar

For three days, the riders traveled south on the worn and broken roads. The bike often had to just ride the sides, barely keeping balance. The Trucks had to feel every bump, crack, and pothole that accumulated over the next few days. Twice, they had to change a tire.

Thug and Kato were not doing so well, as Thug was having trouble walking and Kato's shoulder was infected now, and he could barely move it. No matter what Kshea and Jack did, their conditions just seemed to get worse. But Jack also had to take on Pathfinder duties because with Thug out and Kshea having to care for them, it would only leave him on his bike, riding with

Tricks, who, being a member of the Truck Clan, didn't have as much experience on the road as Jack, Doug, Kshea, or Thug.

And worse still, the Green had been relentless. Many creatures came out that they had to fight off. The first night, a bull mammoth that would leave the road kept charging the supply truck. The giant creature had to be chased off by Doug, Jack, and Tricks, using their bikes to weave around the beast, making it dizzy and chasing it off by shooting it in the ass. Day two brought with it a pack of Coywolves. The small pack managed to cut off the riders and almost knocked Tricks off her bike. They chased them off after killing the alpha pare. Coywolves were pests, but no real threat to a trained rider. The next night brought dodos. They didn't attack, or try and chase them off, for they were not aggressive. Instead, they just stood, stupidly, in the road, blocking the rider's path. "Come on," Thug had groaned at this after a few hours, "Just run them over."

But they didn't. They weren't being aggressive; they were just being natural. But they were holding them up. In the end, Doug was going to take a few pot shots, when three Sabercats came out of nowhere, attacking the large group of dodos, as they saw the slow-witted birds as an all you can eat buffet. Good news: it was enough to get the birds out of the road. Bad news: they were now facing three Sabercats. But Doug, who had had enough of all this bull shit that had been happening, just pulled out his shotgun and killed the lead cat. The others ran off into the woods, seeing their leader dead, dead birds hanging from their mouths.

On the third day, Kato's shoulder was swollen and Kshea had to start draining pus from it. Thug's leg was sore; he still couldn't walk normally, and he was constantly reminded he had to let it heal, despite wanting so badly to help on his bike. Miko and Grenn were tired, having been the only ones driving the trucks over these terrible roads, their bodies sore. Doug, Jack, and Tricks were also tired, the days on their bike taking a toll on their bodies as well.

And all this time, to Jack's annoyance, Watu didn't return. Stupid bear, stupid everything. But he couldn't think about that now. Now he was sitting around a fire, Kshea and Thug back on the supply Truck, hoping that Kato didn't die. Grenn, Miko, and Tricks were all sleeping or trying to, and all of them were thinking or dreaming about what they saw come out of that Black Priest. That barely describable horror that was made from his own body, it was still on their minds. Because the need to get away from that was stronger than the need to face it, Jack was spared questions for three days. But now, as the footfalls of an exhausted Doug came behind him, boots breaking frost-covered leaves and twigs, Jack knew what was going on and what he was going to ask. Not even his concentration was broken enough to stop him from cleaning his guns. He knew it was going to happen, and he was only grateful that Doug waited until the others were asleep or occupied. He sat down next to Jack, as the Green sounded with its endless chirps, snarls, howls, trumpets, and roars of the great beasts in its wooden and grassy depths.

"So," said Doug, "What do you know?"

"Depends on what you ask," said Jack.

"I ask, what do you know about what is happening? Because what I saw back in the village turned my life upside down. I saw a man's body torn and reshaped. I heard a voice that crawled into your mind like spiders on a ceiling. I have seen many things, horrible, wonderful, and amazing things since I became a rider, but this, this I cannot explain. But I feel you can. I know you can. So, hear my voice, there is no choice, you must tell me as a fellow rider."

A look of pity and sadness entered Jack's face. It was the look he'd had when his wife was buried. It was a look of regret and a meaning to put things right. And since the death of Niki, he had to admit, there had been a distance between the two men who once kept no secrets. It was time to bridge what was broken.

Taking a deep breath, Jack started talking: "You remember Marven, back in the house at the edge of Ironwood?" asked Jack. Doug nodded. Slowly, Jack told him of Marven's true identity, the existence and the history of magic, the power that Watu the spirit bear had, his battle with Kal and then Kal's demise, and finally, how the beast had emerged from the fallen priest's body, the Golden Lord, the Great old ones, and so much more. It was midnight by the time he had recounted everything and finished the story. Doug said nothing during this tale, waiting for him to finish. His eyes widened, learning that there was a fucking bear traveling with them, and he hadn't even noticed. When he asked where it was hiding, Jack answered honestly, "Don't know, haven't seen him for a while. Might have gotten bored."

When finished, Doug's face was a mixture of disbelief and doubt for his friend. Then Jack told him to summon Thug, who was helped over by Jack and Kshea who confirmed the story, and the existence of this bear, after Kshea returned to administer to Kato. Then Doug turned to him, and said, "You told him first?"

"He was in a bind," said Thug, "That bear saved me from the Wyverns. If it wasn't for that bear, I'd be dead. Then again, if he'd been around, Samantha might be alive, so there is that."

Doug shook his head and said, "Look, I can believe a bear did show up, but come on, magic? That's kids' stuff."

"You saw that Black Priest, and you saw what came out of it," snapped Jack. "How do you explain that?"

"I can't," said Doug, "but I can't believe that some basic hocus pocus is involved with this bull sh . . ."

'*Basic hocus pocus?*' asked a voice in their heads. They turned at once as a great white bear came to their fire, eyes blazing in the flames. *'If you believe magic is that simple, then you are fools. Magic is like an ocean without a bottom and what you humans know of it barely scratches the surface.'*

Doug's jaw dropped, and then recovering himself, he said, "Did that bear just talk?"

"Well," said Jack, "Kinda, he . . ."

'Oh, for the love of . . .' snarled Watu in their heads, *'I'm not doing this again.'* And he raised his paw, and Doug's eyes glazed just like Thug's did days back. Then footfalls came again as Kshea came back to check on Thug, and said, "Hey guy, I think . . . wait, is that a bear?"

'Oh, for the love of honey,' roared Watu, raising his paw again, and Kshea also went into a daze.

Thug looked over at Jack and said, "Well, this is going to take a while."

"Yep," said Jack, pulling out a box of cigarettes, lighting them with a match and giving one to Thug. He also pulled a bottle from his bag. It was a bottle of whiskey, and Thug, eyes widening, asked, "Where did you get that?"

"From the office when I was in charge of IronWood Lodge," said Jack.

The two smoked and drank, and for the first time in days, Thug's leg didn't bother him as much. They laughed and shot the shit with each other, and then, about two hours later, Doug breathed again, as did Kshea, both asking at the same time, "What the fuck was that?!"

"What you saw is what I and Thug saw," said Jack, "The secret history of our world. One lost in shadows and fire. By the way, Watu, where have you been?"

'Around,' said the bear, *'I come and go as I see fit.'*

"Find anything interesting?" asked Thug.

'A tower,' said the Bear, *'about three miles to the east. I think you will find things to help your compatriots.'* And he walked back to the supply truck, once again, hidden under his tarp. Doug gaped as he did.

"We should go," said Jack. "If I learned one thing, it's unwise to ignore Watu."

"But . . ." said Doug, but then shook his head and said, "How can we trust him?"

"Just do it," said Thug, chuckling, "and your life will be easier."

As Jack helped Thug back to the supply truck, Kshea, stood there, saying, "What the fuck?"

Jack's bike had been loaded earlier because Kshea was being overwhelmed by Kato's infection and needed help. So Jack turned to Watu and said, "Seriously, where were you?"

'Travelling,' said the bear, *'There is a lake with some good fish*

in it not too far away from here. By the way, let me have a drink of that bottle.'

Jack, not thinking, walked over and poured the booze down the bear's open mouth. Smacking his jaws, reminiscent of a man smacking his lips, the bear laid its head down for a second, and then opened its jaws again and said, '*More.*'

As the trucks moved east under Doug's command, Jack and Thug were passing around the bottle with the bear, with an amazed Kshea watching after she joined them to attend to Kato before this new step in the journey, and even joining them. They passed the bottle, smoking cigarettes and drinking booze, even as the bikes and truck went on a side road that they found coming here, but, until the change of direction, decided to ignore. But Jack, Thug, and Watu defiantly ignored the various branches and leaves that brushed over their heads, just like they were ignoring the lunacy of the situation. Drinking with a talking bear that just shared the entire world history with two humans. It was a light, heartening atmosphere, and one which they all needed after the hell they had been through. That was until they entered a clearing a few minutes later.

The first thing they saw was light. White lights flooded the area, shining brightly in the darkness. After adjusting to their brightness, they saw a tall structure in the shadows. Then they saw that the structure was solid white. It was the cleanest building Jack had ever seen. It was also running on its own power, making it seem alive. Jack couldn't help but stare in wonder, nor any of the other riders. Even Kato, sick as he was, couldn't look away from the sight. The building almost seemed alive. It was until they saw the back of the truck open and saw Doug giving Jack and Thug angry looks at their blood shot eyes.

"You better be able to handle a gun, Jack," snapped Doug.

Jack drew his pistol, shot a leaf of a nearby tree, and put it back.

"Good, because you are coming with me," said Doug, "The rest are staying here till we know it is safe."

Jack nodded, grabbed his shotgun, and joined Doug, as he yelled, "Kshea, you're in charge."

Not waiting for an answer, the two approached the building. Not seeing a door on this side, they worked their way on the other side of the building and found doors made of glass. Glass. Jack had never seen a glass door in his life. Glass makers were rare and valued in Marquette and the colonies, and they usually only made small things, like mirrors, or new panes for the trucks. These were almost ten feet tall each and had a strange but simply shaped handle on them. They were as clear as glass, or plastic for that matter, but made of a softer material that, unlike the door, seemed like they wouldn't break by one hard hit.

Jack pulled on the door. It didn't budge. He signed. Oh well.

Jack felt bad about the beauty he was about to break but felt worse about the bullet he was about to waste on the breaking. But before he could raise his pistol, Doug said, "Hey, this one is unlocked."

Jack walked towards Doug, shaking his head when Doug's back was turned. Maybe he shouldn't have drunk so much. They walked inside. The building's entrance hall was as white as the outside, even the floors were spotless, so the dirt the two riders brought in showed visible as the stars did in the night sky. Gun raised, the two walked into an unnaturally clean place.

"Have you ever seen this place?" asked Doug.

"No," said Jack, as they walked to a place marked 'Reception Desk.' "It's not on any of the known maps."

"What is this place?" asked Doug, looking around in wonder. Then the two heard a whirling sound, and both turned. A metal . . .person walked towards them. It was humanoid in shape, its skeleton of black metal, wires, and tubes was covered mostly by a white plate made out of material similar to that of the door handle, save for the fact that this one was white. Jack and Doug stared at it. It was in perfect condition. The most disconcerting thing was its head, covered again in the strange material, but it had two small lights where eyes should be. Then this strange automaton spoke in a voice that seemed deep and echoed within its own body.

"This facility is closed," said the automaton, "Please come back during normal business hours. I see you are holding a weapon designed to fire projectiles. Please know this model isn't a security model but will act in any ways necessary to defend itself."

Jack stared at it. This had to be the drink. No way he was seeing this fake man just . . .

"Wait," said Doug, taking his finger off the trigger, "I've got people hurt outside."

The fake man turned its head to one side as if listening, despite its apparent lack of ears, then responded, "What are their conditions?"

Doug quickly described Thug's and Kato's injuries.

"Species?" asked the fake man.

"One regular human, one Otherkin, dog-type."

The fake man was silent for only a moment, and a minute later, three more fake men came running out. There was a word for things like these back in the old days. What was it? Jack couldn't think of it off the top of his head, but Doug suddenly said, "Robots."

"What?" asked Jack.

"I think these are robots. The Ancients invented them a long time ago, but I never saw any up close."

"Where are the patients located?" asked the smallest robot.

Its body was made of the same white material that the first one was plated in, however, where the first robot only had one plate of it on his face, arms, legs, and chest, this one was covered head to toe in it. But where its feet and legs should have been, instead, its oddly feminine-formed lower body was shaped into a square skirt-like shape with small wheels at the bottom. This was in contrast to the two larger robots. These looked like they were covered in metal armor, and looked a lot tougher, like they were meant to lift. One carried a bag. The other, a stretcher.

"Um," said Doug, "Outside. I'll show you. Jack, stay here, and try to get more information."

"Wait," Jack said too late as Doug ran after the three robots. This left him alone with the first. They stood there, silent for a while, until the robot said, "Do not worry, these medical units are some of the finest made by the Tokahama Corporation."

Having no idea what a Tokahama or a Corporation was, Jack asked, "So, what is your name?"

"This unit is designated XB 7889 maintenance and repair model. I was created in 2145 by the Tokahama Corporation in Tokyo, Japan. I run on the standard Joint Cloud mind AI processor program and get constant updates from the Tokahama Corporation. Date of last update was almost 530 years ago. No updates have been available since that date."

"Wait," said Jack, "You're over 500 years old? How have you

lasted this long? The Green Event basically wiped out the power grid. At the very least, your batteries should have run out. Or at least what you got for batteries. How are you still alive?"

"The Green Event?" asked the robot, "Processing. Processing. No knowledge on this subject. This building runs on geothermal energy as all Cloud Processing buildings have. It has been a chore keeping the trees at bay, but our staff always ensures a safe environment."

"Staff?" asked Jack.

"This building's staff members are 90 percent mechanical, and ten percent organic. However, the organic units are likely resting as of right now. When they awaken, you can join us for breakfast."

"Ok," said Jack, really hoping he had lost it, and this was all a nightmare since Chang had died.

The robot tilted its head again, and said, "Your companion is over the coms." Then Doug's voice came over.

"Jack, you there?"

"Doug?"

"Yeah, the bots parked us in some kind of garage and have taken Thug and Kato upstairs to what they call a medical room. It's amazing, man. Anyways, meet me up here. The others are here, too."

The Robot's voice went back to normal, and said, "I will take you to the medical wing." And Jack, in a daze, followed.

2 Otaku

The medical center was the most wonderful thing that Jack had ever seen since his vision. It was pure white and felt clean. So clean that when he walked in, he almost immediately felt the filth of the past three days on his body. The same feminine robot and two of the more heavily armored ones were attending to Kato, cleaning his wounds and shooting him with shots, and draining the infected fluids out of his shoulders. A fourth robot had joined them, this one shaped like the doc bot, but with fewer feminine features, though made of the same white material. This one had a sort of cute face like that of a puppy on it, but its arms were long and strong looking.

XB 7889 was joined by another one of his kind. The other robot was the same down to the eyes, and spoke in the same voice: "Greetings, I am XB 7890. Your companions are in the shower rooms. First door is male, second is female, and third is genderless. Leave your clothes in the laundry unit. By the time you're done showering, they should be ready."

"Ok," said Jack. He walked down the hall, and then saw Thug. Thug was sitting in a bed like Kato was, and there was another doc bot, but next to him was a sort of many armed, wheeled robot. Each arm seemed to be working on each mark on his leg, repairing the damage. Thug looked up and said, "This is fucking weird."

"Please refrain from such language," said the doc bot, which then turned to Jack, and said, "And please do not contaminate the field."

"Ok," said Jack, "You okay, Thug?"

"Yeah," said Thug, "Go, I'm good."

Jack entered and found Doug and Grenn already wrapped in towels, smiles on their faces. They looked fresh, the grime and dirt that had built up over the past few days now gone, the clean feeling almost making them feel reborn. You could really see this in Grenn, who was shining a bright pink color with purple spots covering his body.

"You got to try this man," said Grenn, "it's amazing."

"How does it work?" asked Jack.

"It's like steam, or mist," said Doug, "I don't know, but it beats the pour baths or jumping into a lake back home. Just go in and press a button that says standard clean. There is a box that you can put your clothing in to do the same. Takes about three minutes all together."

Jack nodded and found the box to put his clothing in and the bathing units. He pressed both buttons that said, 'standard clean,' and was surrounded by a warm mist. It beaded up on his skin and dripped over very quickly. In minutes, his body felt cleaner than it ever had before. All he did was just stand there and let the mist do its work. When he walked out, he felt better than he ever had before.

Grabbing one of the towels, he dried himself off and his clothing was finished as well. This place was too good. Too good. What was this place? How did a place like this survive intact after the Green?

After changing back into his freshly laundered clothing, Jack, Doug, and Grenn joined Miko, Tricks and Kshea who were checking on Thug and Kato. Kshea sat with Thug, who was laughing mightily, more mightily since his lover Chang died, and Kato was still unconscious. When Jack asked XB 7889 why Thug was so happy, the robot responded, "He has been given a light narcotic to help with pain management as the surgeon droid repairs his leg."

Jack had never heard of the word narcotic before, but figured he should ask if he should get some for the road. The Ancients' advanced medicines had been mostly lost over the centuries. It would be good to have some, though how they made it or preserved it after all this time was a question he was going to have to ask. In fact, he had a feeling he was going to have many questions about this place before and after he left.

Kato was still in trouble but improving, his infection going down. He now slept, tongue lolling out like a dog. According to the DocBots, he'd be good in a couple of days.

After about an hour, XB 7889 and XB 7890 came forward and said, "One of the organic units of this facility is ready to see you now."

"Organic units?" asked Doug.

"Humans."

"Go on," said Thug, still giggling, "Me and Kato . . . we will be great."

In the end, Doug, Jack, and Kshea all left to go with the two robots. Being pathfinders, they had more of an adventurous streak than the Truck Clans. They followed them to two metal doors put into the white walls, and XB 7889 pressed a button with an arrow pointing down. The doors opened, and revealed a tiny room without much room to move in. Jack, Doug and Kshea looked at each other as XB 7890 said, "Please step in the elevator."

Not knowing what words the machine spoke, the three stepped in. The doors shut behind them. On the wall facing the door, he saw a few buttons arranged three by six. The robot pressed the one marked 7, and they rocketed upwards.

Jack and the other two riders sunk against the wall in fear, fearing the sudden feeling of moving without being able to perceive it with their own eyes. Fear grew in their hearts. What was this, what was going on, what was . . ..

Ding.

The elevator stopped and the doors opened, and the two robots looked around and said, “Please follow us.”

Frazzled, the three riders stumbled out. Fuck that shit.

They walked down a white, brightly lit corridor, with white doors on either side. The robots walked up to one of these doors and pressed a button. It opened, disappearing into the wall, and they stood on either side like sentries, XB 7889 saying, “You may enter.”

And the riders did.

The inside was a mess of wires, monitors, bright lights, glass, and much more. Inside, a man sat at one of these computers. He was a strange man. He was fat, well-fed, and had his face covered by brown hair and beard. He was typing on what looked like lights that emanated from the monitor. The lights showed symbols which the riders had never seen before, but there were many. Numbers, letters, and even what looked like faces. There was even one symbol that looked like a pile of poop.

The man looked up and said, “Finally.”

He stood, wearing a robe made from the same materials as the towels they had used.

“Well,” said Kshea, “I’m Kshea, this is Jack and Doug. And you are?”

"I'm Rick. Welcome to the Cloud."

The riders looked confused.

"The Cloud," said Rick, irritably, "Home to one of the most important inventions of mankind."

Still seeing them unimpressed, he said, "The internet?"

"What?" asked Doug.

"What!" yelled Rick, "You never . . . Oh my god. It's only like the only thing worth saving from the Green?"

"And why is this so important to you?" asked Jack.

"It's the gateway to all knowledge," said Rick, "It's got every bit of human history in it. Everything. From North America to Australia, going east."

"Where is this great library?" asked Jack.

"It's not a library, it's this," said Rick, spreading his hands.

The riders looked around.

"The building?" asked Kshea.

"No," said Rick, "This building is merely a shell of what it was. It was designed to light up every person's home. Before this, it was fiber optic cable and towers. Before this, it was landlines. Now, it is this building, and thousands of others like it. The Cloud Network."

"Why is this so interesting to you?" asked Jack.

"I'm Otaku, one who is sworn to bring back the internet. And I have, at least here. This facility stores everything we are meant to return. Millions of different websites, with the whole of human history on it."

With a wave of his hand, he brought back the lights, and brought up a backdrop in the lights called YouTube. The three-dimensional lights showed several windows, each with captions, and Rick played through many videos. Some were interesting but most were just pointless to the riders who sat on wheeled chairs, bored out of their skulls. Then he brought up news articles, information pages, all the while boasting about how much information was there. It took about eight hours and a look of pride covered Rick's face. All the riders gave him were blank stares and the headaches they wished to put on him.

"Don't you see how important this is?" asked Rick, "Not only did the internet become a source of information - if not the source - but it also ran our world. The robots you saw outside, the power grid, war, even vehicles were controlled by the internet."

"And this has to do with us because?" asked Doug.

"Because I need your help to reawaken this sleeping giant."

3 Data Collection

"So, why don't you do this?" Jack asked Rick, annoyed.

"I cannot. As Otaku, I am bound by the tenets of my order to not be removed from any site that holds the Cloud. We must protect it."

"Sounds more like cowardice to me," said Kshea.

Rick looked at her, angry for a moment, but then said, "Okay, look, this facility can not only bring back the internet, but bring us out of the Green. The bots you see, they've been keeping it back, but they need the Cloud to function. There are devices that will allow them to function outside the Cloud, but not to their full potential. But 78 percent of all factories, businesses, and computers of the old world were connected to the Cloud. From deep coal mining to mathematics that theorized about the universe, with the Cloud backup, civilization could come back from the Green. I've done calculations of my own. Without the Cloud, it would take over 700 years for the world to reconnect and rebuild, but with the cloud reactivated to full, we can use it to reestablish communications across the world."

"That is not our mission," said Doug, "We need to get to Etam."

"Where?" asked Rick.

"Etam," said Jack, "Ever heard of it?"

"Ummmm, yeah, actually," said Rick, "Found it on the net."

He went to one of the monitors and it interacted with his fingers. In a second, he brought up a site called 'www.etamkingdoms.com.' On the site was a map of strange lands, where several sentences on the left side were superimposed on it.

"Etam," they said. "The newest fantasy gaming adventure. Play as anything from a knight of the realm to a Black Priest and travel the realm as you see fit. Make your own characters for the game. Make Etam your own world, full of wonder and adventure."

Jack could just stare at the words. Kshea's mouth was open. Doug's mind was racing a mile a minute. But so was Jack's. Etam, the country, came from a game. He had seen such games in old shops lost in the Green, and later discovered. Games like 'Dungeons and Dragons,' 'Warhammer,' and whatnot, but this, how could this be true? Etam was a game. It was a basic, honest to God, game. This didn't make sense, as Jack pushed Rick over, despite protest, and started reading through it. There was a description of a Black Priest, almost all the words in common with those which Jack could describe Kal. How was this possible? Was Kal lying? No, no, that wasn't it. Kal had been many things, but he was never a liar, or at least he believed he was telling the truth.

Then the memory of when he had witnessed the birth of the Golden Lord came back, the chattering children. There was a connection there; he just couldn't see it. He didn't know how, but there was one. It was right there on the tip of his tongue.

He continued to scroll down but saw no references to something called the Golden Lord, or the Fire Lord, the two titles that Jack distinctly remembered.

But this information made him concerned. But there was a connection, but . . .then it hit him. What if this game of Etam was the model the Golden Lord used to build this country? What if it was merely the framework? He would have to ask Watu more about this to see if his theory was right, but till then, he needed to find more information that he could use.

Jack turned to a red-faced Rick, still sore over being pushed aside.

"Ok, make you a deal," said Jack, "We will awaken this Cloud network, but in exchange, I want all the information you can give me about this Etam game."

Rick smiled, while Doug and Kshea stayed silent, though Doug glared daggers at him.

"I knew you'd see it my way," said Rick, with a smile on his face, "I and the other Otaku here will be grateful."

"So, how do we do it?" asked Kshea.

"I will send one of the bots with you," said Rick.

"I thought you said you couldn't leave the facility," said Doug.

"No, but they can with this," said Rick, holding up a small, green thing with silver going through it. "It's a mind holding chip. It's designed to let a bot do its function outside the Cloud. It will keep its personality and function intact, though it won't be able to access the web. You won't even have to do anything. Once it's by a facility, it will be able to reactivate it on its own by remote."

"Okay," said Jack, "But it goes where we go. We need to complete our mission first. If we run into one of these facilities on the road, we will look into it, but we must protect our home first."

"I understand," said Rick, "I and the other Otaku won't ask anymore from you."

"By the way," asked Kshea, "Where are the other Otaku?"

"Everywhere, doing research," said Rick, "They learn all they can about the web. This facility is large and there is much we must look into."

"How many are in your order?" asked Jack.

"About a hundred. We all stay here, trying to bring back the web."

The riders and the Otaku looked at each other for a moment. Two orders agreeing to help each other. But it was time for the Riders to plan their next move and Doug gave word to thought.

XB 7889 and 7890 both walked in, under Rick's order, who said, "See that they and those they travel with are fed and watered."

"Yes sir," said the Bots.

Jack, Doug, and Kshea headed out five minutes later. A large stack of printed paper in Jack's hand.

4 Dreams and Thoughts

But he didn't tell Doug what he found until the next morning. It was late, and instead he retired to an office in the garage. He was tired and needed rest, and once he got to the moth-eaten couch, he fell asleep.

His mind drifted to dreams. In the dream, he saw Niki. She was wearing a white, cotton dress, the one which she had married Jack in. It curved with her frame, the frame that had attracted him so much. She turned, still as beautiful as he remembered.

In the dream, he walked to her, her back to him, and wrapped his arms around her waist. Her hands held his forearms, and he felt the love again that he had felt the first time he held her like this.

"I could have saved you," said Jack, "I could have turned you away from Kal. I could have taken the knife. I could have . . ."

Niki turned and put a finger on his lips, silencing him.

"There is nothing you could have done my love," said Niki, kissing him. It was a light but strong kiss, full of emotions of love and need, "but you are needed my dear. There is another, another who needs you more than I do."

"Who?" asked Jack.

"You will find her in the lands called Peaks. You won't find her today. You won't find her tomorrow, but only when the time is right."

"How will I know her?"

"You will know her by hair as dark as night," said Niki, as she stroked his cheek, "You are in pain."

"I miss you," said Jack.

"I know, but you cannot blame yourself for my death. That is by Kal's hands, and his alone. I love you, Jack. You were my one, but you were not mine."

Jack looked at her askance: "What do you mean? Of course, you were my one."

"No," said Niki, "You were meant for another, and she will need you as much as you will need her. But you cannot protect Marquette and her colonies if you don't move on."

"You make no sense."

"In time I will," said Niki, and an invisible force seemed to start to pull Jack away. He felt it, and desperately tried to hold Niki, even as his hands slipped.

"Goodbye, my love," said Niki, as Jack was pulled away."

"No!" yelled Jack, "Niki, don't go. Don't, I want to stay. Stay with me."

His cries of desperation matter not, as he was pulled into the real world. He awoke, a cold sweat on his body, and then, after a few deep breaths, tried to sleep again, desperate to see his wife again.

5 Rest and Repairs

They were at the facility for eight days. Over those eight days, they met a few other Otaku. Kshea met Mel, who studied data processing programming. Doug then met Victor, who studied how robotic AIs mixed with the Cloud, and how it could teach about how the human mind worked. Then there was Sylus, a man obsessed with ones and zeros, saying they are the key to life.

But Jack didn't care about this order. He felt they were obsessed over an old-world device that in his opinion had no real-world applications other than data research and improvement over communication. That was the only thing he saw as a positive with this whole internet cloud thing. Other than that, it seemed to be trash to him.

Instead, he oversaw the vehicles in the garage, which several robots were attending. These were smaller, humanoid ones with many tools, polishing, repainting, and cleaning the oil the bikes used. On one of these days, he was joined by XB 7889, who inquired to Jack, without provocation, "These types of vehicles to my knowledge haven't been used since the year 2109, since the

Canadian Wars. Such vehicle usage was made illegal by Canadian by law addendum 677-1, the Environmental Protection Act, and were replaced by solar and hydrogen cars. How did you come by fuel combustion vehicles?"

Jack stared, but finding no reason not to respond, he said, "Some were used by our ancestors. Others we found in museums in our lands. Still others we found in Ancient Warehouses. They were restored and brought back to be used by the Riders."

"What of fuel?" asked the bot. "The last crude oil production rig was closed down in 2119. How is it you came by it? According to your friend, Thug, you are from Marquette. According to my data, there were no natural oil reserves in Marquette. How have you managed to run these crude vehicles?"

Jack was insulted when XB 7889 referred to his vehicle as crude, so responded icily, "Well, if it's not in your Cloud, then you're more foolish than any human. The Green not only changed what was above the ground, it did the same below. Mountains grew where they weren't before. Rivers flowed where they were never made. And as below, oil flowed where there was no oil found. Oil was found outside of Marquette, and we were able to extract it with the tools left to us by the Ancients."

"Who are these Ancients you speak of?" asked the robot.

"Those who were there before the Green, our Ancestors, the ones who built you and this facility, those were the Ancients."

XB 7889 responded with, "I apologize, clearly, the system has not been updated for some time."

"How long were you alone before Rick and the others found you?" asked Jack.

"Original organic units evacuated this facility 530 years ago. An emergency was declared by the UN and all civilians were ordered to return to their homes. Before leaving, the organic units ordered us to maintain the facility at all costs, with mechanical units ordered to maintain both the facility and themselves until the return of organic units. Organic units returned around 30 years ago but were untrained in handling the equipment stored here at the facility. We had no choice but to train organic units in how to operate the facility as original units were concluded to have stopped functioning during this time."

Jack looked confused, then asked, "Can I ask you something? The people who came here, were they always like this? So devoted to restoring this net, Cloud thing?"

"No," said XB 7889, "In fact, these organic units were seeking shelter, claiming that the village they were from was destroyed during a parka attack. After we started teaching them, they seem to have become somewhat in awe of the technology of the facility. They began calling themselves Otaku and became worshippers of the Cloud. This was not in company mandates, but since the original organic units had not returned with proper replacement, we had no choice but to accept them."

Jack's mind paused at this. Then he started to see parallels between these worshippers of the internet, and how he and the riders worshiped the road. Ever since the rise of the first rider, they were taught that without the road, there would be no civilization, but to these Otaku, the same could be said about this Cloud. They saw it as Jack and the other riders saw the road. In a way, it was their road, leading them to new snippets of information every day, a journey in itself.

"Your vehicles should be ready in another day," said XB 7889.

"Thank you," said Jack, absently, "I'll tell Doug."

6 Under the Tree

Doug was over it. He was over the fact that Jack had undermined him about searching for these new facilities. He was over feeling like he was no longer the leader sometimes. He was just over it. He hated this feeling of inadequacy. He knew Kshea didn't trust his decisions a lot of the time, but he understood why, having never been a leader before. But couldn't they see, they were trying their best?

Doug did scold Jack, saying that making the deal with Rick undermined his position, how it might affect the rest of them, but in the end, realized it added up to nothing. Jack made an approximation of an apology and went to the garage to read his paper.

Doug sat on the edge of the Green, shotgun on his lap. It was a weapon both he and Jack had been raised with long ago, before they were raised as riders, and now, he felt a fundamental change in their relationship, something that had gotten between them. He sat, angry and tired. He was sick of it, sick of being undermined. This had never happened to Jack, this . . .

A rustle in the Green made him look up, gun at the ready. The branches snapped, leaves crunched, and birds flew. Out of it came the bear, the white bear.

Doug didn't lower his weapon and he and the bear looked at one another, both unblinking. Then a voice came into Doug's head.

'Come,' it said, and the bear turned.

Doug stood there for only a moment longer. He was angry, tired, but also wanted to understand. The vision he got was disjointed, still somewhat unclear, and this damn bear knew something.

Doug followed the bear's trail with the bear about five feet ahead, Doug keeping his shotgun aimed at its backside. He didn't trust this damn animal, no matter what Jack said.

The Bear led him to a large oak. The oak was as wide as twelve men, and taller than any tree he saw in Marquette. He stood beneath it, not able to look up at it fully, as the great tree was covered and surrounded by the branches of the smaller ones around it. But near the bottom, were three golden leaves growing on a nub. The bear laid down at the roots, on its belly, yawning. Doug kept his hand on his gun, listening for sounds, waiting as birds, squirrels, chipmunks, and even a lone badger lumbered past.

'Go to the other side and enter,' said the Bear.

Doug held his gun on the beast, and said, "Why?"

'Someone is there that you must speak to.'

Doug side-stepped around the tree, keeping his gun at the ready. He worked his way around till he saw a large opening in the bank. It was dark, but there was a glow caused by several mushrooms growing inside.

"What's in there?" yelled Doug.

No answer. Doug was about to turn away when he felt a great power touch him. It was similar to what came off the bear, but this was much more powerful. This was something so strong, it struck his very core, and he felt a need, a need to know what was happening. Taking a deep breath, he entered the glowing tree cave.

The passage went slowly downwards, leading him down into the earth. He went slowly, his feet guided by the mushrooms, and various insects in the area. He moved down, hundreds of feet, slowly, the smell of oak strong in his nose. He saw a bat fly past him, but it did not deter him from his path.

Suddenly, the passage, which was barely wide enough for him, opened and Doug looked around. He was in a huge cave, almost as wide as the whole city of Marquette. In the center was a large underwater lake. The lake looked as black as oil in this low light. Doug moved to it, and knelt, putting his hand into the cold water. He pulled it out, his cupped hand feeling it.

Then he saw the surface begin to move and ripple, slowly, but the power of the force could not be denied. He saw it break in the middle, and something blue and tan broke the surface. A large, serpentine body came out of the water. It moved towards the ceiling, which was hundreds of feet above Doug. Then the great creature turned to him.

It had to be over three hundred feet tall, snake-like, and dominant. It was blue and tan, and on the sides of it were large arms and powerful claws, ending in sharp talons. But its arms seemed to be disproportionate to the rest of it, but strong enough to hold the beast. Its head was like that of a large reptile, but not like a lizard, in fact not like any reptile he had seen in books. Its head was surrounded by what looked like a golden mane, and two blue structures, like those of antlers, were at the top of the beast's mighty skull. It looked down at Doug with fierce, golden eyes.

Doug stared, fear in his heart, the great beast staring down at him. And then . . .

"Ah, you came," it said in a great voice, yet one that was filled with wisdom and power, like that of a grandfather. "Good, you're like a great storm in this part of the world. Even compared to the little ones on the surface, I felt you and the other. It woke me from my deep slumber."

"The other?" asked Doug, shocking himself, realizing he was talking to what was a talking snake. Its mouth was closer to a reptile, but its scaly lips, forked tongue, and cheeks moved and made words as easily as Doug's.

"The one Watu calls Jack," said the great beast, "He has a great destiny, but so do you. That is why I wished to see you."

"You're like the bear," said Doug, "He has a lot of power, I felt it, but this, this is more . . ."

"The bear and I have much in common, though our abilities are different when it comes to magic."

"You're a magic user," said Doug, mouth agape, memories of the story of the first magic users coming back after his vision the bear showed him, "But you're not a witch or warlock, or even the first magic users of the Earth."

The Dragon smiled, and said, "Humans were not the only creatures that wielded magic. Many beasts of fur, feather, and scale had some affinity with magic. But I was there long before the first of the first hominids learned what even magic was. I was the first to wield magic, the first of the dragons. Now, who are you?"

Dragon. Doug stared at this vast beast, claiming to be a living legend. But here it stood, in front of his eyes. Dragon, a word and creature that he only associated with legends and fairy tales. Dragon. Old legends said it was a beast of evil, but he sensed no evil from it. It was an elder being, a being here long before man and would be here long after they were dust. How? How could such a beast still be alive? How could mankind not know of it? But mankind did know of it, did they not, through legends and stories. They tried to tell us but failed.

"I'm Doug, rider of Marquette and . . ."

"I didn't ask what you are, but who you are," said the Dragon, a little shortly, but not unkindly, and the dragon switched tactics before Doug could respond: "You suffered much for such a short distance. Why do you do so?"

"We're trying to find a land called Etam," said Doug.

"For what purpose?" asked the beast.

"To protect our home from being attacked."

The creature laughed. It echoed throughout the cave. It was powerful, reflective of the power Doug felt from the creature, raw and untamed.

"Land was always so important to your kind, but no matter,

what is your purpose in this quest?" asked the beast.

"To lead them," said Doug.

"Why?" asked the dragon.

"Because my order gave the authority to me," said Doug.

"Then why do you feel so conflicted?" asked the Dragon.

Doug was silent for a moment, and then he lowered his gun, and said, "I can't seem to be getting it right. All my calls have been wrong."

"Ah, so it's your confidence in yourself you question. Why?"

"Because I never lead."

"Really, that's not what I was led to believe. You have led, but perhaps it is not your destiny to lead this mission you were put on," said the Dragon.

Doug looked up, shocked, "Then why would the riders give me the quest?"

"These riders, are they not of flesh and blood such as you?"

Doug had no answer.

"They do what they feel is best by seeing the situation that is before them. They don't see the patterns of time and space as I see them. You have great potential, Doug, and you have led correctly. What you fail to see is that leaders do not have all the answers; they must make judgements based on the information they have. You cannot keep second guessing yourself. But as for your quest, you are meant to lead this part of the journey, but not to its end."

Doug looked at the beast and saw great kindness and pity in its eyes.

"Then what is my destiny?" asked Doug.

"To lead them to the Dark City, where you will find more answers. From there, well, I am confident you will find your way."

Doug stood there stunned.

"It's time for you to return to your friends," said the dragon.

Doug turned, then paused, and looked back. "I've got three questions."

"Yes," said the Dragon.

"I didn't get your name, for one," said Doug.

"Names are only titles given to you by others, but only you can know yourself. But you can call me Dreamer."

Doug, slightly confused, continued, "Well, how come my kind has never seen you?"

"Your kind has," said Dreamer, "But we had very little interest in your kind."

"Finally, will I see you again?"

"Only if you want to. Now go and find the Dark City."

7 Back on the Road

Thug walked down to the garage, leg back to normal. Jack

was overseeing the bikes while Kshea was cleaning weapons. Doug, meanwhile, was directing how the convoy should go. Something different was going on with Doug. It was like he'd reached some kind of understanding, with whom, Thug didn't know. What he did know was that Kato was back on his paws. His shoulder was healed, and he stood tall with Miko, Grenn, and Tricks as Doug spoke to them. It was good to see the Otherkin back on his feet. Good fighter, and a good man he was.

Thug went to his bike. The motorcycle had been buffed and polished beyond what it needed to be, but the bike was as good as new, and more importantly, repaired of all damages that had accumulated over time. The machines that walked, these robots, said they had to use 3-D printers to make replacements, as the parts needed were not in their inventory. Thug didn't know what a 3-D printer was, but he was grateful for the repairs. Bikes were hard to come by, and parts to replace those broken down because of age had to be hand forged by black smiths in Marquette and her colonies.

An hour before they wanted to leave, ten Otaku walked in. They carried devices on white pillows. They were flat, made of the same white, glassy plastic material as the robots, and had a glow about them. Rick walked forward and gave Thug one of these devices while the others passed them out.

"What are these?" asked Thug.

When Rick joined the other Otaku, he turned and said, "These are cell phones. They are mobile communication devices. As long as the Cloud is present, we can communicate with you. It will also allow you to access the Cloud and all the information in it."

A lady Otaku, this one squat, with thick limbs, but a very pretty face said, "This station should cover you until Detroit, after that, we will lose communications, however, we believe there is another Cloud station there. Once it is activated, we will know, and send our people to monitor and study the web."

"And how the hell are we supposed to activate it?" asked Tricks.

"That's where I come in," said XB 7889. "I can remotely activate the Cloud from where I am and reactivate all automated units inside."

"Sounds simple," said Jack.

"We thank you for your help in this endeavor," said Rick.

The Riders and the Otaku looked at each other, and Thug thought the two groups were quite similar in many ways. Both trying to bring civilization back from the Green. But he also saw their flaw, a flaw that was their undoing. They weren't active. They were like monks, who refused to leave their place of worship. But this place had no real purpose as Thug saw it. Sure, having access to information of that scale was great, but out here in the Green, survival was more important. These people toiled and studied the internet, only dreaming of fully restoring it. Thug had little respect for these Otaku, but he was silent. They helped them, and that's all that mattered.

The Otaku helped the Riders pack and store the new supplies of water, food, booze, and even cigarettes that were in storage downstairs. Soon they were on their bikes and in their trucks. Watu was under his tarp. XB 7889 was in the back of the supply truck. Doug, Jack, Kshea, and Thug were on bikes. Tricks, Kato, Grenn, and Miko were in trucks.

Jack checked his bike's fluid levels as he did. Looking over it, and so satisfied with the results, he joined the others in revving their bikes. As soon as the doors were open, they went back on the road, winding their way on it like following a giant snake trail.

Doug took point, Jack, Kshea, and Thug took to the sides. The bikes and trucks bumped along the uneven and crumbling road.

Chapter 4

Morality

---

1 Illness

The autumn was growing colder here in Haven. The Amish were preserving what food they could, cutting what trees they could, and preparing for the coming winter. The Green then turns white and gray, with cold cutting through you like a knife. But that didn't matter to Ara, for now, she and Jeremiah Sr. and Jr. were preparing for her journey to the Wastelands. They packed dried meat, fruits, nuts, and other such goods for such a long journey. Ara still wore the simple Amish dresses as the women of the household, but she had purchased some jeans and shirts at a store up the road for the trip.

Ara was outside with Mary, helping her clean out the horse's stocks, keeping her end of the bargain she'd struck with Jeremiah. She was working hard, but all throughout the day, she felt hot, and tired, not knowing why, also feeling slightly nauseous in the morning. She also noticed a tender feeling in her breast. She did not know what was happening to her. So, she did what anyone who knew not what was wrong with themselves would do. She continued working, listening to Mary telling a story about a boy in Haven that was so cute, and so eye-catching, that Mary was hoping that he would start courting her. Ara smiled inwardly. Several boys in the village had asked to court her as well during the few times she went to church with her adopted family, but Ara, being not Amish herself, politely declined. She loved the Amish culture, but she also knew it wasn't for her. It was too conservative, in many ways, even more so than the people of Etam. They never bent, they never changed. That was just it, they never changed. Ara loved change. Her father always said real rebels want to change for the better and not for the worse.

"He is so dreamy," gushed Mary, "So tall and strong. A strong man of God he is. My lord, my heart just beats for him. Have you ever had that feeling, Ara?"

"Si, for many boys," said Ara.

"Many?" asked Mary, "Why didn't you marry one?"

"I wasn't ready. That kind of commitment takes time."

"So, you never consider marriage?" said Mary, seeming shocked at the idea that Ara had no interest in wifehood.

Ara stood, and she suddenly felt lightheaded, but she

steadied herself and continued: "Only one man. His name was Puther, a rich merchant from Etam. I met him when he joined my Papi's cause. We started to see each other. He was older, but full of life. He believed in freedom above all, but he was also passionate. It was like a wild wind with him, never knowing what he would do for me next."

"What happened to him?"

"He was killed when the Golden Lord's minions found where my father was holding his meetings."

"I'm sorry," said Mary, "I . . ."

"Don't apologize. I still have sweet memories of him, nights where we just laid naked in bed and made love while the sun shone. He was mi amor."

"Wait," said Mary, suddenly looking askance, "You had relations outside the vows of marriage?"

Ara looked up, and almost laughed at the look of jealous horror on the young woman's face.

"Si, and he was amazing."

A look of wonder crossed the girl's face. Fathers never admitted it, but all girls had fantasies of their first, the boy who would claim their hearts and bodies. They'd thought about it all the time, just not out loud as boys did.

Suddenly, the dizzy feeling came back, and Ara stumbled to the ground.

"Ara," yelled Mary, rushing forward.

Ara felt this morning scrapple coming up, and she vomited into the hay. The feeling continued to consume and weaken her, driving her to her knees.

Blackness clouded her vision as Jeremiah rushed in, Mary having run off to get him. The man lifted her in his arms and Ara blacked out in them, cradled like an infant.

2 Second Soul

Ara awoke, a cool, wet cloth on her head. It was soothing, as if offsetting the fire that burned in her. She opened her eyes, and saw Mary - sweet, innocent Mary- sitting on the end of the bed, watching her like an angel, her sweet large eyes watching her like hawks from under her bonnet. Then, looking up, she saw a concerned Lilith, dabbing at her forehead, like how she thought her own madre had. She didn't have many memories of her mother doing this, and though her father had comforted her more than once, it seemed to lack a touch that women seemed to naturally have.

"Are you ok?" asked Lilith.

"Si," said Ara.

"Why didn't you tell me?"

"Qué?" asked Ara, confused.

Lilith looked down, a look of shock on her face, that soon gave way to a look of understanding, and then sadness.

"Mama says you are having a baby," said Mary.

Ara's head whipped towards the girl as Lilith scolded her daughter, saying, "Mary!"

"That's what you said, Mama," said the girl.

"I . . . I," stammered Ara, and then fear hit her. It hit her like a tidal wave, washing over with cold dread taking the form of goose flesh. "No, no, no, nonononono! I can't be pregnant. No, No."

Panic began taking over Ara, sweat and sadness hitting her like stones falling from a cliff. It smashed her, the realization and the revelation. Lilith came in, wrapping her arms around the sobbing woman, holding her close as she cried and cried. Ara had been wrapped in an illusion, thinking that she had escaped the nightmare of her imprisonment and rapist after she left Etam, but she had not. It followed her like a wolf stalking a deer.

Ara didn't know how long she sobbed or how long Lilith stroked her hair, holding her. All she knew was that eventually, Lilith had calmed her enough for her to look up and say, "I cannot be. I cannot be."

"I am sorry," said Lilith, "but you are. But a child can be a wonderful . . ."

"No," said Ara, bolting up from the mattress, nearly knocking

Mary off it. "I can't . . . I will not have this child, this demonio. I will not give birth to the child sired by El Diablo. I will not."

"But this is your child," said Lilith, "It's your responsibility to . . ."

"I was raped!" yelled Ara, "Raped, not once, but for months. This child is the product of a monster. Inhuman. It can't be born."

Lilith looked at her. A look of pure horror and sympathy on her face.

"I need to abort it," cried Ara, "Who can . . ."

"We don't do that here, Ara," said Lilith, "The Amish do not practice it. It is banned. Not just ban, it's illegal, a hanging offense."

"Then let me leave," said Ara.

"I can't do that Ara," said Lilith, "Not when I know you want to harm this child."

"What!" yelled Ara, "Jeremiah said . . ."

"It's our law to protect children," said Lilith, "I'm sorry Ara, but Jeremiah is going to have to talk to the bishop. We cannot, under any circumstances, allow harm to a child. Please."

Ara stared, betrayal filling her heart, and, for the first time, she turned her back to Lilith.

Lilith stood, saying, "We will get you to the Navajo, but we must ensure the safety of the child."

"You have no right to hold me."

"No," said Lilith, "But we have a right to protect the innocent."

"This demonio is not innocent."

Lilith, looking at Ara with such pity that if Ara had faced her, she would have cried again. She summoned Mary and the two left the room.

3 The Bishop

Ara waited five days alone. mostly pacing the room and shouting obscenities. Her anger was directed towards the whole universe for putting her in this situation. She felt trapped again, imprisoned.

Jeremiah Sr. had headed out to the bishop's house four days ago. The church was in the center of New Haven and a day's ride for most of the Amish who lived there, but the bishop's house was on the far side of New Haven. He was now coming back with his horse and buggy when Ara saw him from the window with another man. This man was older than Jeremiah by at least twenty years; his hair was pure white, and his face lined. When he and Jeremiah were under the window, Ara saw the man had liver spots on his hand, even from above. He wore the same clothing as Jeremiah, save for a white shirt and a black hat. He also wore glasses, thick rimmed and glassed.

The two men entered, and Mary walked in. Mary, the sweet innocent child that Ara, no matter what she felt towards her mother and father, she felt no rage towards for her large blue eyes could melt even the coldest of hearts.

"Dat asked you to join him in the sitting room," said the child.

"Si, I'll be down in a minute."

Ara walked downstairs after putting on a simple blue dress. She had put her brown hair into a ponytail. Feeling she was presentable enough, she walked into the sitting room and saw Jeremiah Sr. sitting with his son and the man, who had to be the bishop. The bishop stood and walked up to her, shaking her hand as Ara heard Lilith, Emma, and Mary moving around in the kitchen.

"Good afternoon," said the bishop. "I am Bishop David Winicker, and I am pleased to meet you, Ara."

Ara shook his hand firmly, surprising the bishop, who had only taken her hand lightly as she would have with a child. This was to show she wasn't going to be pushed around and that she meant business, which contrasted with the kind smile she had on her face and the polite tone she used when she responded. "It is a pleasure to meet you, Señor Bishop."

The bishop smiled back politely and beckoned her to sit. Ara took a rocker while the men sat on the sofa. While they were all polite, there was a tone of a courtroom in the area, with Ara the defendant while the two Jeremiah's were the jury, and the bishop was the judge.

The bishop spoke first, a kind but authoritative tone exiting his lips, indicating that he was a man whose judgments were not and should not be questioned, again reminding Ara just how orthodox and authoritative the Amish were in a passive-aggressive way.

"Ara, I was told your stories by the two gentlemen sitting next to me, and I cannot begin to imagine the horrors you went through getting here. I also understand you agreed to help them on their farm until you were able to move on. I can understand this and more, but you must understand that you being with child complicates matters, especially when you intend to do harm to the child . . ."

"This is no human child," said Ara, "this creature I carry in my womb was sired by a monster. If it is birthed, it will cause nothing but pain."

The bishop paused for a moment, and even Jeremiah Jr and Sr. took glances at each other.

"I was raped . . . raped for three months, locked in a room and used as the Golden Lord's plaything."

"The Golden Lord is a false icon that the Etamians believe in, not a . . ."

"He is a real creature," said Ara, "A beast of flesh, and

horrible to behold, and I was that horror's plaything when my father was killed for trying to change that land for the better."

A look of disgust and horror crossed all the men's faces, but Ara continued unperturbed, "And they still have my brother. I don't know if he is still alive. I know he was paralyzed after we were captured, but I need help to rescue him. By the sound of it, the Navajo may be able to help, and he is more important to me than the monster you are allowing to grow in my womb as we waste time."

The bishop bit his lower lip, putting his hand together at the fingertips, and then spoke again.

"I don't believe in the Golden Lord, but I believed you were raped and have suffered. However, this child is growing inside you. It is against both ours and God's law to allow the abortion of such children, no matter what the circumstances are."

"Even if it risks the mother?" snapped Ara.

"In those instances, we try to save both, but it is the child's life that is the priority," said the bishop. "And even if you are not willing to raise this child, I assure you there are many families here that would be more than willing to take the child. There are many families here that don't or can't have children and would be thrilled to take the child and raise it as . . ."

"I have told you," said Ara, angrily, throwing her hands up in a jester of irritation, "This is a child of diablo, a beast, and letting it come to the world is an abomination. I need to get to the Wastelands and save my brother, not worry about a monster inside me. So, if you won't abort it, I will."

"You can't go to the wastelands in your condition, Ara," said the bishop in patient tones. "They are, in many ways, more dangerous than the Green. The sands, rocks, and sun have killed more than a few Amish. And other things. Beasts that live under the sands that will kill you before you see them. Jackals that will hunt you until you are dead or dried up. Vultures that will feed on you, living or dead. We plan our journeys for trading with the Navajo months in advance, and even with the best plans we can think of, we always lose a few men on the journey."

"It's my choice," screamed Ara.

"Not in New Haven," said the bishop, some anger getting into his voice, "It's my duty to protect the community and all children who will enter the world here. In the olden days, we couldn't stop these actions of the non-Amish, but New Haven is our land, and we must protect its philosophy and the tenets that God had put before us. I will not let you enter the Wastelands till after the child is born. After that, I cannot stop you from entering the waste, but if you do, I won't allow you to take the child with you. You will stay with Jeremiah till after the child is born. Until then, you will not move around New Haven without an escort."

Jeremiah Sr. looked at the bishop with a look of concern on

his face, and Ara wondered what that meant. Jeremiah Jr. was merely looking down at his shoes.

The bishop stood, and Jeremiah escorted him out. Ara sat there, fuming.

Chapter 5

Detroit

1 The Dark City

Jack and the other riders looked out after five days of hard riding. Unlike when they crossed the bridge, the ride had been free of monsters. Jack and the others had finally reached the end of this part of the Green, which gave way to the city of Detroit.

The city was known and visited by the people of Marquette and the Riders over the years, but this was the first time for all the riders and XB 7889. It was breathtaking and intimidating. The city was surrounded by piles of concrete, steel, and stone that hid a wall underneath that kept the Green out of the main city. Many trees stood next to the huge buildings of brick, metal and glass, just as large and imposing, but it didn't dominate the skyline as the buildings had. The city's buildings at first glance, as stated before, were imposing, but their age was starting to show and some of them were in disrepair. The look of falling apart opulence and the irony of it was not lost on Jack. Over the city, however, that was the scariest part. There was a dark, ever-present cloud of smoke that came from the various factories that blocked out the sun. It stood over it, like a dark presence just waiting to descend and bring destruction on the city. Beyond the wall were three huge mountains that came from the Green. The city used them for mining and as defense, with towers on the summits and tops, acting as lookouts for the city.

Jack, Doug, Kshea, Tricks, and Thug looked over while on their bikes. Kato, Grenn and Miko were in the Trucks. They looked at the city over the cliff, all of them not knowing they had the same feelings. They had made it. They made it to Detroit; they made it to the city. The Green, thick around them, stood beyond it, somehow timeless and powerful, though its power seemed to wane slightly.

"It's always a sight," said Jack.

"Somehow it always seems to change in some way," said Doug.

"You've been here before?" asked Tricks.

"Twice," said Jack, "Long ago. We went by ship then."

"It was back when we were training," said Doug, his hands resting on his bike's handlebars, slightly revving the engine. "We will rest here tonight and go to the city tomorrow. There are some things we must discuss before we enter the city proper."

"What do we need to discuss?" asked Kshea, who was preparing to turn her bike away from the cliff.

"About what will happen when we enter the city," said Doug.

They rode back to the trucks, parked between two great oaks the size of a few of the Detroit buildings. Grenn and Miko were cooking dinner, which included freshly killed mammoth calf, beans, fried potatoes, and fresh root vegetables found in the Green, paired with Grenn's own moonshine. His skin simulated fire in his hunger and excitement over finally reaching the city. Kato was working on the fuel truck, grumbling under his breath as he replaced filters and changed fluids, his fur covered in the truck's old oils and coolant, and still complaining about his shoulder as he worked. XB 7889 was helping underneath the truck, tightening lines and replacing heavy parts on the supply truck. The robot proved to be quite an asset to the team so far. When traveling, the machine stayed quiet, tucked in a corner. When stopped to rest, he helped make quite a comfortable camp.

As they ate, Jack felt the stubble around his chin, a reminder of the struggle to get here even after they left the Cloud Station. The road had been hard, as it had broken apart over the years and slowed the riders down a great deal, and a few of the more dangerous beasts of the Green had been in their path, but all in all, better than when they ran from Mackinaw. They had actually been able to sleep for a while when they pulled over to rest.

Doug spoke up, "Okay guys, there are some things you have to know about the city. This is going to take a while, so we are going to eat and talk at the same time. We'll do questions afterwards, so enjoy your meal, but please pay attention."

All the riders, still eating, gave Doug as much attention as he deserved. "The city is fully functional but is overcrowded. From what we understand, the city only remained intact as it did because it was originally going to be abandoned by the Ancients, hence the wall. The wall was built to keep people out, but when the Green hit, it kept the worst of it out. It became a haven for people abandoning the Green, for good or ill, and those came to a city without any leadership. It was just tall buildings, towers, and broken, abandoned homes. It got bad, from what I heard, as thousands were killed in raids. When the city finally got order, the first law was, "All to themselves. Worry about the city, and your own business, not other people's problems." There are organizations people can join, but the city itself has the only final authority over the city and her systems. So, basically, it's a hands-off approach to the city's population. As long as no blood is shed, children harmed, or people are forced into belief systems, the city lets people live as they like. So far, it seemed to work. They have electricity, plumbing, even a few vehicles for emergency service back up and running."

Doug took a bite of his dinner and continued. "Marquette established contact about seventy years ago, and established a dialogue after a fishing boat encountered the city. We were able to trade food and supplies they were lacking in exchange for tools, casting materials, and metals they had been able to mine over the years. It's been a good relationship, but they do have certain rules for outsiders. One, all of us will surrender our weapons; they will be returned after our visit. Two, if riders do come, they have to park their vehicles in special areas and keep them there for the duration of the visit."

"We can't have our bikes?" asked Tricks, her face and tone reflected in all the other riders faces, save for Jack and Kshea, at the thought of being stripped from their greatest weapon, the motorcycle. A rider's bike was never far from a rider at any time, and being stripped from it was almost a crime.

"It's only temporary, and they will be protected in the city. As I said, vehicles in the city are only used by official government personnel. They try to keep the city streets clear of vehicles. The roads are used by foot traffic, so it's a safety concern. Any other questions?"

None had any, so they finished eating, cleaned, and got ready to sleep. Jack couldn't sleep. He was nervous, anxious, and drained. It took them so long to get to Detroit, and they had fought hard to get here, and now, now he felt a little hopeless. If the first part of their journey was this hard, what about the rest? They had used a sixth of their fuel and a fourth of their ammo, and now, now they had to worry about the next part of their journey.

Jack was starting to nod off an hour after the others when he felt something on his side nudge him. He woke and saw a great mass in the darkness. Bolting up, reaching for his pistol, he then noticed that it was Watu, the bear looking at him with his piercing dark eyes.

'Come,' said the bear.

"Where have you been?" whispered Jack.

'Does it look like I'm in the mood to talk about that?' said Watu. *'Now come with me. You don't need your bike.'*

Jack stood and followed the Bear into the trees. They walked only about five minutes, when, in the dense darkness, Jack saw an orange glow of a fire, and a man next to it, a man with dreadlocks woven with grass and an ancient but powerful presence.

"Marven?" asked Jack, aghast.

Marven looked up, smiled, and said, "It's been a while, Jack. How've you been?"

"How did you get here?" asked Jack, his eyes casting around

for a horse or mule that Marven had to use to travel through the Green.

"I took a boat and waited for you."

"How?" asked Jack, "All of Marquette's' boats are docked for the winter."

"I'm over five thousand years old, boy," Marven said, "You think I didn't collect a few things over the years?"

Jack blinked at the frankness, but continued, "What, no magic teleportation you could use?"

"Oh, please," said Marven, "I hate that form of transportation. It's so uncomfortable, and there is so much to see in this world that I would have missed. Besides, I can't risk using my powers that often as I still carry the black plague within me. Such an abuse of my power could risk it spreading again."

Jack sat on the grass next to Marven, his wrist resting on his knees, his hand hanging over them, fingers out.

"So why are you here?"

"I like to be where interesting stuff is happening, and also Watu tells me you've been having strange dreams."

Jack looked over at the bear, who was lying on his belly, eyes closed. "How . . .?"

"I told you, a creature of magic. Spirit Bears were not named randomly for no reason. They can see more than just the physical manifestations of our world, but some ethereal ones as well. That includes those in our minds. So, tell me, what do you see?"

Jack sat, at first resigned not to say anything, but relenting under the kind, fatherly gaze that Marven gave him.

"I see Niki. I see her, and she tells me about this other woman I need to find. Her hair is as dark as night, she keeps telling me, and says I will find her in the lands called the Peaks. I think it's my brain telling me I need to move on and . . ."

"It's not," said Marven, "Those were not dreams, not really, that was Niki's ghost, or aura, you were seeing."

"What?" asked Jack.

"All humans have a spirit in them that forms our foundation as a person. It develops over time, much like the rest of your body. When the physical body dies, this spirit is released. Some are strong enough to touch the material world for extended periods of time, thus the basis of the stories of wraiths, spirits, apparitions, or even angels that have appeared over the years. But most cannot interact or be observed by the physical way we see the world. It seems she has found a way to interact with you, through the subconscious. It's actually very impressive."

"She . . . is she still alive?" asked Jack, hope building in him.

Empathy entered Marven's face, and he put a hand on Jack's shoulder, "No son, she's gone from this physical world. She dwells only in spirit. But I do believe she appears to you strongly because of your connection."

A tear exited Jack's eye, and he lowered his head and wiped it away.

"Now, as for the other woman she speaks of, I know not, but the Peaks I know. They are south of here, farther south than Etam, but not by much."

"Then what's the point?" asked Jack, confused, "Doesn't sound like I'll meet this black-haired woman."

"Maybe, but the Peaks are significant in many ways. One reason is that it's an intersection between the Green and the Wastelands."

"The Wastelands?"

"It's a desert that even the Green couldn't grow in. It is a dangerous land, inhabited by strong, hard, but wise people. The Peaks act as a sort of natural barrier between them. But do not think the Waste Lands sound more pleasing than the Green. It's just as, if not more, dangerous. If the heat doesn't kill you, there are plenty of monsters who would be more than happy to take the job."

Jack shuddered at the thought of an area even more dangerous than the Green and didn't have any urge to see these Wastelands. "Okay, but how could she know this at all? You told me it's impossible to see the future."

"For us in the physical realm, yes, but the ethereal realm is much different. I've seen events of that over the centuries, but I could never prove it. I suspect this spiritual apparition of time is connected to the Ley Lines."

"The what?" asked Jack.

"The Ley Line. They are, I believe, the source of magic. When I created the plague, it was designed to target the part of the body that could access them. Later I learned it was in human DNA. The Ley Lines hold a vast amount of power to them. I found several over the years, but the strongest I found was in the United Kingdom and Ireland. The ones I have found in America are almost as powerful. Each Ley Line is unique to the region it is in, which is why magic was performed differently depending on the region it was in. All had similar qualities in the Ley Line, thus why so many mythologies are similar. She may be using them to help you on your journey."

"But why just me?"

"Because you two had a strong connection that was beyond that of the physical realm. I think she is only interested in keeping you alive. I suggest when you next dream of her, you ask her more about this woman."

Jack sat silently, then stood. "I'm going back to camp. Will I see you in Detroit?"

"No, I'll stay here. Watu will keep me company. Even before the Green, I never liked visiting Detroit, too much chance of catching an STD from the white girls. Now, it's not more fun than it was all those centuries ago."

Jack nodded. Then headed back to camp.

2 In the City

They took a narrow path down the mountain. They had to leave the trucks behind and hide them in the Green, covering them with tarps and surrounding them with parka piss so other animals wouldn't come along. They were all on their bikes, even the Truck Clan members. They rode slowly, the path twisting and turning. Kshea didn't look down, the distance between them and the ground diminishing as they followed the path in single file. They soon came upon farms. After the farms and their fields came small houses. After the houses, small communities. After the communities, they came to the wall. It towered over them, and looked like it was made from rubble, which hid its true power under it. They soon found the large gate that defended the wall, topped by men armed with guns who looked like specks in the morning light.

Kshea and the others stopped in front of the wall, and she felt something oppressive coming over here. There were no structures like this at home and it made her feel so small. She shook and recited the rider's creed in her mind.

"I am one with my bike. It is a part of me. It is a part of me as is my heart, my soul, and my mind. Through my bike, I protect those who need it.

Through my bike, I keep the deepest darkness out and cast shadow in the brightest of light.

I am a Rider, protector, and guardian to all who need one. I find the paths that were lost. I find the road less traveled. I bring civilization back from the Green. I am a Rider."

The mantra helped her with the feeling of insignificance that washed over and empowered her. She was ready.

A man with a thick, brown beard walked towards them out of a guard post built into the wall. He wore green fatigues, tan combat boots, and held a large rifle in his hands. He looked at them through thick spectacles and said, "Who goes there?"

Doug, Jack, and Kshea got off their bikes while Thug, Tricks, Grenn, Miko, and Kato stayed behind. Doug walked forward, pulled out his pistol, and handed it to the man, which was the official way to gain favor and parlay in order to enter the city.

"We are riders of Marquette, Guardians of the Road, here to ask succor and rest from the warden of the city."

"Do you know the rules and customs agreed to by our peoples in regard to any riders entering the city?" asked the man.

"Yes, as we were so informed by Barthalamulal, the leader of the riders."

The man handed the pistol back, and said, "Alright, I will

grant you entry, but what business have you got with Detroit?"

"We seek knowledge," said Kshea, knowing her cue. "We wish to speak to your leaders."

"One moment," said the man, grabbing a walkie talkie from his belt, saying into it once he pressed the button on the side, "Hey, I got eight riders at the gate. They wish to speak to the Viceroy."

He depressed the button, and after a moment, the radio squawked and a female voice responded, "Have them go to the usual parking structure. We will have a guard lead them to the Viceroy. Over."

"Rodger, over and out," said the man. He looked at the riders and said, "I am guessing you know where to go, so head in, go slow, and leave your weapons in the structures."

Doug nodded. He, Kshea, and Jack went back to their bikes and waited for fifteen minutes. After that, they heard a huge rumbling. The great gate shook, and the metal that made it began to move apart. Its ear-splitting rumble grew as it split down the middle and dust began to fall as the gate opened enough to let the riders in. As soon as they stopped, the party rolled into the city.

The entrance to the city was the main market. It was full of merchants looking to sell their wares: street vendors selling hot fresh food, and religious zealots yelling about why everyone needed their religion, while at the same time not violating the city's laws by forcing it. It was full of people, moving, buying, and selling the items for sale. They all paused to watch who came through the gates but didn't bother after they closed. Too much stuff to do to care.

The city was divided into quarters and the riders rode through many of these quarters as they headed to their parking area. There was the white quarter first. These were home to the white folk of the city. It was clean, sterile, devoid of art. Women gardened and men cooked over fire. They were bland, seeing themselves as the top tier, when in reality, they were the most boring of the city's inhabitants. There was the black quarter. It was lively, full of music and song. From rap, to gospel, to R and B, the sound of the city's heart was there. It was painted by artists and admired by the riders. The various colors, words, messages, signs, and symbols were painted on the walls of the buildings.

There was the Asian quarter, full of sounds of the oriental music of their homelands, smells of strong spice and incense, making their eyes water. People ate with chopsticks in the streets, eating noodles, vegetables, chicken, beef, or entrails. Chinese, Japanese, Korean, and Vietnamese symbols adorned their walls and homes. The Latin quarter, the smell of spice in the air, and food venders selling food in tortillas. The women, sexy, but conservative, the men, conservative but lustful, the sense of love in the streets. The Otherkin quarter, with vendors selling canned foods of dog and cat food, shampoos meant for animals. They danced strange dances that humans have never done and socialized with various mammalian and avian-type groups making one of the more colorful quarters.

There were hundreds of more quarters, but Kshea knew they didn't have time to explore them all. But as they traveled, Kshea felt something she only felt in Marquette, and that to a lesser degree. The city was alive. The quarters that divided them also eventually spiraled into a fusion of them all, where regular humans, Skin Changers, Androngenans, and Otherkin became one as their cultures and religions meshed together into something beautiful. It was a city of hope, hope that something good could come out of the Green. It was something even the Green couldn't take. Expressions of cultures, of power, underneath the black cloud that the city dwelled under, that seemed very far away, protected from it by the hope this city resonated with.

They reached the parking area a half hour later, as they had to negotiate the streets with pedestrians that walked through it easily, and entered a part of the city called the center. In the center of the tallest and least damaged building in Detroit, was the First National Building, home to the city's government. Inside was the man they wanted, the Viceroy.

They entered the structure to park their bikes. It was a low parking garage built by the Ancients used to store hundreds of vehicles. Now, it parked the riders' bikes and vehicles. They dismounted, and they were heading for the exit, when Doug grabbed Kshea's arm.

"I need a word," said Doug as Kshea turned towards him.

She nodded, with the others walking away after Doug, then said, "We'll catch up."

She stood there and Doug looked at her, a serious tone in his eyes and voice as he said, "Kshea, I need to know, what is going on with you?"

Kshea knew this was coming, but she still felt like this was going to be painful. She had feared this day. She took a deep breath and said, "I'm sorry. I was just used to Jack being in charge. The three of us, we went through so much, and Jack was there all the time. He was the rock, remember? He had us face our fears and said no, we will not surrender. He helped us face the greatest monsters of the Green and threw them back into it."

Doug put a hand on Kshea's shoulder and said, "Yeah, I know. But you think I am fucking comfortable with this shit - you think I wanted to be in charge? No, instead, I ended up forced to lead because he fucked up, and I can understand why he fucked up, but he did, and now, we are in the situation we are in."

He bent closer, and Kshea, for the first time noticed how

strong his face was, and how his beard complimented his facial structure. "We are here to do a job: protect our home. For right now, I need everyone to focus on that, and we need to work together to get Jack back to normal. I will lead until he is straight again. When that happens, I will surrender the leadership to him. Till then, we have a job to do. We need to get through the Green, find Etam, and stop these Great Old Ones and the Golden Lord."

Kshea nodded, and Doug, satisfied, said, "We better get with the others." As he walked down to the street, Kshea saw how good he looked with a shotgun strapped to his back.

3 The Viceroy

The buildings that made up the Renaissance Center were mostly abandoned, but the center tower was still lit and inhabited. Formerly a hotel, it had been converted into the center of the Detroit Government the past few centuries after the Green. Twelve blue suited officers stood in front of it, eight regular humans, two skin changers, and one dog-type German Shepherd Otherkin. They carried short, automatic weapons of a type Jack had never seen before. They were almost square in their shape, with yellow plastic used as magazines for the bullets. Apparently, these were good guns and Marquette had been negotiating with Detroit to get some. So far, no deal had been made and the weapons themselves seemed quite rare around Detroit itself.

One of the guards, a crew cut on his head, walked forward, trying to intimidate the leather clad, blue jeans, bandana wearing, booted and heavily armed party before them. But Doug walked forward, and without question, handed over his weapon. Jack and all the others did the same, in the end, handing over a total of twenty-three pistols, six rifles, two shotguns, eight knives, eight-seven magazines for ammo and three bags of shot for the shotguns.

"A little overkill," said the Otherkin, struggling to hold the various weapons in her arms.

"The Viceroy will see you when he can," said the first guard, "You will head inside and wait in the rooms assigned to you. Feel free to go inside each other's rooms, but do not leave the floor till you are called, understand?"

"Yes," said Doug.

They walked inside the cylinder-shaped building. The main entrance was huge. It was lit by pure electric lighting, not the half electric and half wax candles that Marquette used. The group gaped at how bright it was, even under the dark cloud that was the breathing of the many factories here in Detroit. Jack saw Thug looking at the cavernous room with a look of utter amazement, his mouth open and his yellow bandana glowing in the electric light. People moved around them. Some looked up in curiosity, but most just ignored them, even the gawkers moving on fairly quickly. Jack overheard two men talking to each other: "Yes, we need to increase trade with Grand Rapids as they are a much more reli . . ." Jack didn't hear the rest; he suspected that this Grand Rapids must be some kind of village or city.

They reached the metal doors that lead into the elevators. Apparently, it was only recently that Detroit had got them all repaired. Before that, all the staff in the tower had to walk up the stairs, like it was a big deal. So, they got some exercise walking up 73 floors, instead they preferred to wait for these boxes. Jack hated elevators. They made him feel cramped and he didn't like not being able to control where he went inside this metal hell.

The doors entered, and the guard and eight riders walked in. Jack bit his lips, waiting, feeling Thug pressed in on one side and Tricks on the other, with Kato's fur very close to his face. Jack shook, feeling the change in his bones as they headed up the floors. The feeling of being pressed in made the ride feel longer than it actually was. The annoying music didn't help matters. The calm tones seemed to blast in his ears. God, he wanted to smoke.

The doors opened and relief washed over him as Kato stepped out and the others soon followed him. They walked across to a pair of rooms. Jack, Doug, Kshea, Thug went in one, while Tricks, Kato, Grenn, and Miko went into another. The Guard informed them that as soon as the Viceroy was free, he would personally come down to talk to them, per Marquette's request, and then left them alone.

Jack pulled out a cigarette, lit it, and went over to the table where an ashtray was set up. Thug joined him while Doug and Kshea sat on the bed. Doug pulled a map of the known region out of his pack and was looking over it. It marked all the known cities, towns, and communities that survived the Green, from Ontonagon to Detroit. When Jack looked at that one and compared it to a map of the old world, he saw only about a hundred and fifty known communities on the map in Doug's hand. In comparison, it was a pathetic amount. Well, now it was 149, after Doug took a Detroit-made pen, and crossed off Traverse. Jack sighed, seeing how easy it was to kill a fragile community.

Doug looked up at the Pathfinders and said, "We're going to need to keep heading south. As soon as we talk and resupply, we will need to head that way to this point."

He got up and pointed to the map on the wall. "There is a city here called Toledo, might be populated, might not be. If it is, that's our next supply run. If not . . ."

"The Green that way is thick," said Jack, tapping the ash off the tip of the cigarette, "I don't know if we will even be able to get the trucks through."

"Kal and that other Black Priest got through somehow," said Thug, "As did those . . . those things got through."

"Well, maybe they know paths we didn't," said Jack. "Plus, we suspect the Black Priests can control the beast in the Green in some way, so maybe that's how they got past."

"We should ask the Viceroy if he's seen any Black Priest activity in the area for the past few months," said Kshea. "It could be possible. They reached Traverse city, so unless a whole army made it through Marquette and the colony under our noses and are working in the south, it is possible that this second Black Priest was working his way north from wherever Etam is."

"We also can't forget what the Otaku said about Etam," said Thug, "You know, that it was based on some kind of game."

"Any luck on that theory?" asked Doug, looking at Jack.

"Haven't done much more research," said Jack. "I will get back with XB7889 and try to learn as much as I can tonight."

"Do it," said Doug. "Thug will go with you."

Jack nodded.

"Back to what I was saying," said Kshea. "We should ask. It's possible there are more than two Black Priests sent by this Golden Lord and his cronies."

"I can guarantee it," said Jack, taking another puff. "I don't think there are a lot of them, but I know there are more than two we have encountered so far, and those . . .deformed Otherkin that were out there."

"I'm not convinced they were Otherkin," said Doug. "You saw Kato's reaction to them. He had never seen an Otherkin like that."

"True, but we don't know how many variants of Otherkin are out there," said Thug. "Hell, ever since I met Kal, Watu, and whatever else we've encountered, I'm thinking the world we lived in back in Marquette was actually kinda limited. Who knows what else is out there?"

Both Doug and Jack were silent at that, neither wanting to mention their encounters with Ghost and Dragons.

There was a knock at the door and Doug stood and walked to it while Jack stubbed out his cigarette. Doug opened the door and three men entered. Two were guards, in between them, was the Viceroy. He was a tall man, seven foot tall with long hair, bearded, tattooed and well-muscled with sharp brown eyes. He wore a long duster, a black leather vest over a white shirt, and tall cowboy boots. Not the type of man you'd think of as a politician. His stance was that of a warrior, a man willing and able to fight to protect the city. He wore a stern expression, neither kind nor angry. Just neutral and hard to read. On his belt was a large revolver and a wickedly large knife.

"Good morning," he said, "I am Viceroy Haris." He bowed,

saying, "It is an honor to meet you riders."

"As it is you," said Doug, also bowing, "I am Doug, leader of this exposition. This is Jack, Thug, and Kshea. My compatriots in the next room are Kato, Grenn, Tricks and Miko."

Haris nodded, then asked, "Should I wait for the others to join us, or may we talk openly?"

"We can," said Doug, "But I wish for them to rest. I will catch them up later."

Jack didn't point out how the pathfinders got less sleep than the truck clan members, but decided it wasn't the best idea.

"Very well, then let's talk," said Haris, taking a corner of the open bed, then looked at his guards and said, "Go outside."

They executed an about face and left the room. After they did, the Viceroy relaxed, went into a pocket of his duster, and pulled out a bottle of Detroit brewed Bourbon. He exclaimed, "I've put aside the rest of my schedule for this meeting. So no matter how short we make this, just know I am using this as an excuse to not have to meet with the leaders of the quarters. The Black and White Quarters are both wanting me to take money from the other to, as they say, improve their living areas. Fuck, the white quarter is more sterile than a man without balls, and they want it cleaner. Fuck that. In the Black quarter, if the buildings get any more paint on them, I'm going to get a headache. Still, I have to say it's livelier than the White Quarter at the end.

He took a long swig, and passed it to the other riders, each taking a sip of the harsh liquid. When it got back to Harris, he put it on the table next to the bed and said, "Well, I was asked by your ambassador to inform you that we are to resupply your trucks and help you get on your way, and also to tell you that the second expedition is heading out in another week, but not to feel obligated to wait. I was fully briefed on the situation of what happened in Ironwood and about this Black Priest you encountered there and was asked to brief you on whatever information I had for you guys. So, let's get this out of the way."

He went back into his coat and pulled out several sheets of paper. Jack and the others stared at it for a second as paper was rare in Marquette. Detroit seemed to get over that particular problem a long time ago, as he had at least ten sheets.

"These are reports we got from all the cities and communities we had relationships with, and we confirmed six Black Priest sightings. Most were traveling alone, but others were traveling with bands of Otherkin-like creatures. None have come to Detroit yet, but my guards have informed me that they spotted someone spying a few months back. He didn't approach the city, but his descriptions were similar to your Black Priest from what I've seen."

"So, there are others," Jack stated. "At least six. Any reports on violence?"

"Three," said Haris. "Their MO seems to be to get as many followers as they can to disrupt the established order. They usually only get a few hundred, and are often driven away, but one city, Jackson, was nearly burned to the ground. It was attacked with the creatures traveling with the Black Priests. The casualties were nearly half the city."

"God," said Kshea, a look of shock on her face.

Haris nodded, glumly, took a swig, and continued, "Now that that is out of the way and promises have been kept, I have to ask, other than rest and resupply, what else do you need while you are here?"

Jack and the others looked at each other for a moment, then Doug spoke, saying, "We need a way to get south of the Green. Not sure how far south, but south, and reach the place where these priests and their pet Wolfmen are coming from."

Haris nodded, and passed the bottle to Doug, and after it was passed around again, Haris said, "I'm sorry, but past Jackson there are no roads outside of Michigan, and the Green is so thick down there, it's impossible to get Trucks through. There are no roads left intact that you can use, no town, and no humans past Jackson."

"Damn," said Jack.

"But there may be a way past the Green."

All the riders got interested. They leaned forward, and Haris said, "There is a cave that leads down to a tunnel outside of the City of Canton. We know of it, but never been allowed inside, but I do know that Canton has at least partially mapped it. It's unknown if there is another end to it, but I have it on good authority that it does go past Jackson and a good chunk of the Green. There are dangers from what I hear, and even the inhabitants of Canton don't like to talk about what they found down there, but it's possible it goes farther south."

The riders looked at each other. If this was true, then they could go farther south than any rider before them.

"Where is Canton?" asked Thug.

"Thirty-two miles away from here," said Harris, "But if you want help getting there, I need something from you?"

"What is it?" asked Doug.

Haris smiled, and Jack felt nervous.

Doug sat on the bed finally and listened to Harris' proposal.

"Canton is one of three cities I've been trying to get together in order to stabilize the region. The others are Plymouth and Dearborn. These cities are very religiously inclined. Dearborn is mostly a Muslim population. It's more diverse ethnically than the other two, and does have some stability, but faith-wise, it's a very hard-liner and hard to negotiate with. Canton is Hindu. It has an unenforced caste system and is one of our better relationships.

Plymouth is home to the Sikh. They are the most orthodox, but also semi-peaceful and have the second-best military in the region. We have trade deals with all these cities, and we've been trying to get more of a stable alliance with them, but the one thing I can say about these cities without a doubt is that they hate each other. The religious, ethnic, and history . . . God, trying to even think about what they say to the others is giving me a headache. I am hoping the testimony of your dealings with these Black Priests will make them open their eyes and finally give them enough of a kick in the pants to work together."

Doug and the other riders sat there for a moment, until Doug, soaking it all in, asked, "What keeps the peace?"

"Henry Ford."

"Who is that?" asked Thug.

"A historical figure, really not a big deal. But it's not the person, it's a place we discovered. Henry Ford museum and Greenfield village. We found it outside of the main Dearborn Settlement. They managed to claim it over a hundred years ago and discovered a great amount of preserved technology there. It was hit by the Green, but not as hard as other areas. We established a colony in the village. Dearborn keeps saying it's really theirs, but so far, we managed to use it to keep the peace. The three cities ask our permission to study the technology there in exchange for great trade deals. It's been peaceful. Hard won, but it is peaceful."

"Why do you need our help?" asked Kshea. "Why not just bring them the information you've got?"

Haris smiled. "You riders and your stories have even reached legendary status in their cities. If you go to them, they will listen and believe. It will just be the first step. I hope to get your people in this coalition as well, but I need and want help. You do this, and I guarantee you you'll get access to those tunnels. I know you could just ride and ask Canton yourself, but please, do this for me. A united Michigan can stand against these Black Priests better than a divided one."

Doug nodded, and said, "Deal."

Haris smiled, stood, and left the bottle for the other riders. When he was gone, Jack spoke up.

"We don't have time for this, Doug."

"We need to make time," said Doug. "You saw the reports - Black Priests and their pet wolves are on the prowl. We've already lost one settlement and the other was halfway destroyed. I say working to prevent more conflict in the region is worth the time."

"Negotiations like this take years," pointed out Kshea.

"Maybe, but we can at least start them. Think about it, guys. Marquette could send down ambassadors and show a united front. That could let them keep living the way they want to, not having to worry about these creatures."

"And what happens if we are stuck here for months?" said Thug. "I mean, why even stick around? How hard could it be to find this tunnel?"

"It'd be easier to navigate with the map," pointed out Doug. "By the sound of it, Canton keeps this information close to its chest, so buttering them up beforehand may be great in the long term instead of sneaking into their territory."

None of the others could argue with that. Doug, knowing he won the argument, moved forward: "Thug, I want you to go to Plymouth, start negotiations. Get all the information you can about it before you leave. Make a speech and know what you are going to say to their leadership. Kshea, you go to Canton. You're the best speaker we have with us. Do the same thing as Thug and while there, find out everything about this tunnel system you can. I'll go to Dearborn. Jack, you and the other riders will stay here. Get us all the fuel and ammo we can fit in the trucks and get them ready for off-roading. We cannot afford to lose them, so ensure they are prepared for this leg of our journey."

"Yes sir," they all said.

Doug nodded, "Let's move."

Chapter 6

The Four Cities

1 Detroit Cloud

Jack went to the garage the next morning, his throat dry and his limbs heavy from the drinking. Haris returned to sign the deal and brought two more bottles. The other riders had joined, and they all got pretty hammered. Now he was regretting it.

Jack entered and saw Doug, Thug, and Kshea strapping supplies to the back of their bikes. Kato was there too, strapping two ten-gallon jugs to the side of the rear fender for each bike. Thug and Kshea each had an AR 15 rifle strapped to their backs, a side arm, and a knife on them. Doug brought his shotgun, but other than that, the same layout as the other two. Jack smiled, knowing that they all had a hangover, but determined to head out.

Jack walked up, and Thug turned.

"Sup," said Thug with a grin.

"Just came to give you this," said Jack, handing him ten of his many packs of cigarettes that he had brought in a duffle bag. Marquette menthols, great stuff, hand rolled and put together with love.

"Thanks man," said Thug, with a grin, putting the small collection back into his pack.

"Well, Plymouth and Dearborn don't have booze, so I assume that you will need something. They'll tolerate smoking there, as long as it's not near their temples.

Thug nodded and Doug looked up. "Know what you will be doing while you are here?"

"Yeah," said Jack, "But when I get some time, I'd like to help XB 7889. He's been buzzing about knowing a Cloud facility is here and I'd like to spread the network as much as I can, maybe do some more in-depth research about Etam."

Doug nodded. The devices they got from the Otaku lost the ability to connect to the Cloud not too far from the city. XB 7889 was able to stay active due to his memory retainment that allowed him to function. According to the Robot, the facility should be somewhere in the downtown district. Jack was still deciding how to sneak in the robot. They lived in a strange world, but apparently, they had forgotten robots. Funny, in a world of color shifters, animal-headed people, and endless forests, the idea of automatons walking around seemed like one of the crazier ones. Jack sighed. Oh well, might as well accept it.

Doug got on his bike and Kshea said, "I don't know how long this will take, so I'm just going to say, be careful."

"You guys be careful, too," said Jack, watching as the three riders started their bikes. Jack waved as they waved back, and they rode back into the city. Jack would do the same in a few hours, but first, he had a couple of things he needed to do.

Jack got back to the guards at the door. The same one who took the weapons came up to him, and he said, "I'm heading out to the city gate, but I'm making a stop in the market before the gate. So, can I have my pistol and knife? I'm taking my bike out."

The guard nodded and said, "Anything else, sir?"

"Yeah, can you bring down the rest of my party for me?"

"At once, sir," said the guard.

Fifteen minutes later, Jack was loaded up, and Kato, Grenn, Miko, and Tricks came down. All three were just as haggard as the other riders were and didn't look too pleased about being rushed out of bed. Jack smoked one of his cigarettes, looked at the four riders, and said, "Grenn, you, Miko, and Tricks are in charge of the resupply effort. Kato, I need you to come with me. I want to check out something in this city."

"What are we looking for?" asked Kato.

"The Cloud facility that the Otaku mentioned," said Jack. "I want to access it again for the mission. According to the Otaku, the Cloud facility is much stronger than the one we found in the Green."

Kato looked at him with some surprise, his head, that so like an Irish setter, cocked to one side on his long neck. Grenn spoke up next, "We still doing that?"

"Yep," said Jack.

"Are we even sure there is one here?" asked Miko, "I don't know about you, but I never heard of robots in Detroit or Otaku till we went to that Cloud facility."

"And what purpose would it serve?" asked Kato.

"Not sure yet," said Jack. "Mostly, going on a hunch, and we do have the time."

Kato shrugged, "Well, I'm down. Trucks are in good shape, and I can refuel them tomorrow. Also, I'd like to explore more of the city. There is so much working technology here."

It was hard to tell with his dog-like head, but he looked a bit like a kid at a candy store, looking at all the electric lights, buzzing electric wiring, and even at the dark cloud hovering over the city, pumping out of the various factories that were still working in Detroit.

Grenn looked at the other two riders and said, "Well, I guess we get the fun job while they do some urban exploring."

They all laughed and split up. Kato followed Jack to the bikes after getting back his pistol. As they started the bike, Jack and the Otherkin rode off back through the market. It was just as cramped as it was when they first entered. When they reached the gate, Jack saw Doug, Kshea, and Thug, still sitting on their bikes. Turning, Thug waved, and yelled over the roaring engines, "You're just in time, they're about to open the gate."

Jack nodded as he and Kato waited with them. Two minutes later it opened and the bikes rode through, with Doug, Kshea, and Thug heading east while west while Jack and Kato headed back to the trail on the cliff where they hid their trucks. The camp site hadn't been disturbed by deer and buffalo marching through the night and the tarps that covered the trucks were left unmolested. Going to the supply truck, the two riders lifted the tarp off the back and they saw XB 7889 underneath, close to the back of the supply truck.

Jack walked up to the robot, and said, "XB, wake up." When he said that, the two lights that made its eyes lit up and a whining noise came from its center. Within five minutes, XB 7889 left the back, landed on the ground, and looked around at both riders.

"How can I assist you?"

"Well, the Otaku said there was a Cloud station in Detroit, and you said that you could remotely activate it there," explained Jake. "So, do your thing."

The robot looked at Jack, and said, “Thank you, but I’m afraid that isn’t the whole truth. There isn’t a station in Detroit, sirs. Detroit is the station.”

“Excuse me?” asked Kato, a look of confusion on his dog face.

“The Tokahama Corporation bought the city of Detroit after it was deemed unlivable by the Michigan Government in 2067. It evacuated the city and built the facility deep underground, and renovated the city so employees of the Tokahama Corporation could live there. This is the main reason why the wall was built. It was to keep all employees of the Corporation from being attacked from the outside world. When the citizens of the USA realized a Japanese business conglomerate had purchased one of their cities and put their employees into it, the citizens of several USA states claimed they were really using it as a beachhead for a Chinese invasion, even though the Tokahama Corporation was a Japanese-based company.”

“So that is why the wall was built,” said Jack.

“Yes, oh dear,” said XB all of a sudden.

“What?” asked Jack.

“The facility's remote relay seems not to be responding. How can this be?”

“Maybe it was damaged by the Green,” said Kato. “Detroit wasn’t hit hard, but it was still hit.”

“Impossible,” said XB, “The facility was built deep under

Detroit, it should have not been affected by the phenomenon that hit it above."

"Well, then why isn't it working?" asked Jack.

"The only explanation I can think of is that the antenna on the surface was damaged."

"Where was this . . .ah . . .antenna?" asked Kato, the unfamiliar word slowly escaping his lips.

"I will show you," said XB, and he ran off. Jack and Kato followed on their bikes, which were still on. They followed XB to the cliff edge where it stopped. Kato and Jack got off their bikes, where they joined the robot, staring at the city. It pointed, its seemingly natural tones replaced with a slight waver.

"It was there," said the robot, pointing at a tree next to an old skyscraper, some of its branches breaking through the windows. "I don't understand how this could have happened."

Jack put a hand on the robot's shoulder, the material smooth under his hand and said, "The Green did a lot of damage. I'm sorry, XB."

The robot didn't say anything, just stared, and Jack began to wonder if it was feeling anything.

"Is there another way to reactivate it?" asked Kato.

"The only other way is going into the facility itself," said XB. "An employee could help us with that."

"That's . . . gonna be a problem," said Jack.

"Why?" asked the robot.

"Well, I'm pretty sure nobody who lives here works for the Tokahama Corporation anymore," explained Jack. "In fact, I am certain."

The robot stood there, "What, squatters on Tokahama property? They must be evicted immediately."

Kato got a nervous glint in his eye, but Jack, in a calm voice, said simply, "I'm pretty sure even you cannot remove over two million people, XB."

XB looked at Jack, eyes glowing. Jack continued, "This is one of the few safe areas in the Green, and most aren't concerned about the Cloud."

XB chose to continue on rather than dwell: "If we can gain access to the city, then we may have a chance of reactivating it, and that would require going inside the city."

"Sounds easy enough," said Jack.

"Ahhh," said Kato. "How are we going to get him in there?"

"We walk in," said Jack.

"With a robot," muttered Kato, as Jack walked back to his bike. This was going to be interesting.

2 Dearborn

The Green leaned in, that was all Doug could think about it.

It was composed of weeping willows, and they seemed to reach for him, their thin branches snaking onto the road. They reached, and yet, Doug felt no fear. Since he'd met Dreamer, everything about the Green seemed lessened after witnessing that creature's awesome power.

Dragons, spirit bears, great old ones . . . so much to wrap his head around. Too much insanity in this insane world. How was one supposed to keep up with this shit? Doug sighed as he worked his way west. Dearborn was the closest city and he had long split from Kshea and Thug. The roads were rough, cracked, and slowed them, but after the hell he and the others took to get there, he felt this ride had been far easier than anything else he'd put up with so far.

Doug soon saw the clear tell signs that he was reaching a settlement. First, he saw the road was smoothing out, and other side roads, clearly used by people. Soon, the Green began to give, showing signs of it being cut away. Then he saw his first farmer. He saw several men working the fields, wearing full-length white robes and some kind of head wear, though Doug was too far away to properly make it out. Soon, other farmers came into sight, some of them wearing similar garb, others wearing regular clothing. He saw few women till he reached the outskirts of the city, some dressed no differently than women in Marquette and her colonies, while others wore full-length dresses and veils of different colors, hiding their identities from the rider. He saw no Skin-Changers, Androgenans, or Otherkin, but wasn't surprised about it. The people all looked at the rider curiously, and some children tried to chase after him. He saw most of the people were of Middle Eastern descent, but there were other races, including Caucasians, Orientals, Africans, and a smattering of others.

He reached what seemed to be the city's outskirts, and more people were starting to notice him. He traveled two more minutes when he saw three men on the road, one holding his hand out. Doug slowed and then stopped. Two of the men had bearded faces while the third was clean shaven. They all wore gray coveralls, tan boots, and carried rifles unknown to the rider, though they seemed of an older design. One of the bearded men walked forward, slinging his rifle over his shoulder. He was stern but not unfriendly as he walked to the side of the rider's bike, looking over his leathers and his spiky black hair and beard, though it wasn't as thick as the guard's.

"As-salamu Alaikum," said the guard.

Doug, not knowing what this meant, but guessed it was a greeting, responded with a bow of his head and said, "Hello, and may your travels be long and safe."

"That a new greeting," said the guard, "I'm Salaban, part of his majesty's royal guard, and who you be, for you seem not to be from any of the other cities around here. Who you be, from

Detroit?"

"No," said Doug with a chuckle, "I'm a Rider, I come from the city of Marquette."

The man's face tried to remain impassive, but his eyes couldn't hide the look of amazement they held.

"I thought your kind was only a myth. Warriors on motorcycles, finding and resting the roads from the Green."

"Not a myth," said Doug with a smile.

"I've never seen a motorcycle," said Salaban, his hand touching the longtail's front rim over the tire. "I heard Detroit had them, but I never thought I'd see one."

"It's real," said Doug with a smile.

Salaban touched it for a few more seconds, in awe and wonder, then turned to Doug and said, "May I ask why you wish to enter New Mecca?"

"I thought this was Dearborn," said Doug, confused, but still focused.

"That was the old-world name. We renamed it after we were unable to get to the true Mecca after the Green Event. But please, tell me your business."

"I have come on behalf of Marquette and her colonies, and the City of Detroit, to parlay an agreement with your city and several other cities. Surely you have heard rumors of the men in black that have been prowling the land, and the Wolf Men that follow them."

Salaban nodded, responding with, "Yes, but I have not seen such men or creatures with my own eyes."

"I have," said Doug, "I wish to talk to your leaders and discuss the situation."

Salaban looked at his other men, then back at Doug, deciding, "I will take you to our captain. He is in the guard barracks, and he can get you in touch with the people you wish to speak to. I ask only one thing."

"Yes," said Doug, cautiously.

"We have no horses, so you mind if I ride with you?" A look of hope entered Salaban's eyes, and Doug, smiling, nodded. Salaban looked at his men, spoke quickly in a language that Doug did not know, and hopped on the back. Doug revved the engine, and took off down the road, Salaban laughing with joy akin to that of a child.

Salaban gave him directions to the guard barracks, which was a school of the old world. The squat brick building had trees growing into it, but it was mostly intact. Two more gray-clad men stood in front of the main entrance while several others marched around the campus, training. Some carried the same older model rifles that the road guards wore, but this seemed to be only a few units. Swords and curved sabers seemed to be more common. Everyone stopped when they saw two men on a motorcycle, one clearly an outsider.

One man with a thick beard and the same olive coloring as the other guards walked forward. Unlike Salaban's, his overalls were black and denoted rank on his shoulders, in the shape of three diamonds, and there was a look of uncertainty and caution on his face.

"Corporal Salaban," said the man, "What is the meaning of this? Why have you abandoned your post, and who is this outsider?"

Salaban dismounted and saluted his commanding officer, who returned it.

"I have only done what my duties entail," said Salaban. "Bring all outsiders to the nearest guard post and bring them to the guard commander. I will return to my post as soon as my duty has been fulfilled, sir."

"And that entails joy riding," said the officer, a grin creeping onto his face.

Salaban blushed, lowered his head, and muttered, "There were no horses available."

The officer chuckled, walked forward, and looked over the heavily armed man in leather. His eyes examined every inch of the bike.

"Well, I can't fault you," said the officer, with a small laugh. "Return to your duties, and next time, resist playing on our guests' vehicles, no matter how amazing they are."

Salaban saluted again, turned to Doug, and bow, saying, "Thank you for giving me an experience I thought I'd never get to have."

"You're welcome, Salaban."

"If you are granted entrance, I invite you to come to my house this evening. My wife and mother will be happy to cook for you in exchange for the delight you have brought to my life."

"I accept," said Doug, holding out his right hand, and Salaban shook it. Salaban nodded to the officer, who nodded back before he marched off.

"I think you made a friend," said the Officer, smiling warmly, "As-salamu alaikum. I am Major Hussan, commander of this guard post. Who are you?"

"I am Doug, a rider from Marquette," he said, though in the back of his mind, he remembered what Dreamer had said. "That is what you are, not who you are."

"Ah, I heard stories about you from travelers," said Hussan. "Though I do not know what to believe. Is it true that you fight monsters on your bikes and slay them with great swords?"

Doug chuckled, "Nah, we don't. We use our bikes to keep the Green's beasts out of our colonies, but we usually try to bring them back alive."

Hussan laughed at that, "Well, please follow me."

He yelled for two of his men in the harsh language that they spoke, and the two guards, armed with the older rifles, stood watch. The major walked Doug inside the facility, looked back, and said, “I will not ask you to relinquish your weapons, but will insist you give me your ammo.”

Doug obliged, trying to keep a good face with the major, and he put them into a large pocket near his knee. Doug looked around as they marched, noticing the light came from the sun, which was out, and at night, oil lamps.

“I guess you don’t have power,” said Doug.

“No,” said Hussan, “The generators that powered the city were destroyed a long time ago. We don’t have the knowledge to build new ones. Does Marquette suffer the same problems?”

“We have power,” said Doug, “In Marquette, though, it’s only used for government work, food storage, the rider’s lodges and oil refineries. Outside Marquette, some of the colonies have restored electricity, but the majority are like this guard station, powered by fire.”

Hussan smiled, but Doug knew his brain was thinking about this controlled and calculated information that he gave him. Doug wanted to catch his attention and it worked.

They reached Hussan’s office. Inside was a large window, white walls, a filing cabinet, an old, simple desk, and carpeted floor, with a long mat facing east and west. Several cigars were in the ashtray. He had three chairs, and they took two of them. When they sat, two men brought in a tray with tea, coffee, and a flakey pastry covered in honey.

"Please," said Hussan, and Doug reached and poured coffee from the pot, while Hussan poured himself some strong tea.

"Thank you for the hospitality," said Doug.

"Allah teaches us to treat all with kindness," said Hussan.

"Is everyone in Dearbo . . . I mean New Mecca, Muslim?" asked Doug.

"Yes," said Hussan, "But they're not forced. We do have a few non-Muslim living in the area who we provide shelter from the Green, but they are not citizens. However, the Sultan has provided them with jobs and homes. Now, tell me rider, what has brought you to our city?"

Doug took only a moment to drink some of the strong coffee, set his cup down, and put his hand under his chin, his elbows resting on his knees. Slowly, he explained everything he knew and suspected about Kal - what he did, the actions taken afterward, their encounter with the Black Priest in Traverse, the wolf men, their trip to Detroit, and the deal he was hoping to broker, explaining that such an alliance was necessary to stabilize the region. Hussan gave all his attention to what Doug said, reacting only with his eyes. Doug finished by saying, "To this end, I wish to talk to the Sultan and broker an Alliance between your city, Detroit, Canton, and Plymouth. With these dark priests running around, we need to protect the region before more cities fall like Traverse and Jackson have."

Hussan leaned back and processed this, thinking it through, not knowing what Doug had withheld. After a few moments, Hussan leaned forward, and said, "I have no authority to talk to the sultan, but my commanding officer will. I cannot guarantee that he will bring it up, though, unless you have something to offer."

Doug knew this was coming and said simply, "What do you seek?"

Hussan stood at the window and spoke slowly, "The Sultan wishes to bring back the power of the ancestors. Detroit has not been forthcoming with that arrangement, so, I would ask would Marquette be interested in it? It seems you have brought back electricity from the Green. If you can guarantee your home will be willing to help in that endeavor, I can guarantee that my commander will bring your request for an audience to the sultan."

Doug pretended to think for a minute, but he already knew the answer. He had met with the Marquette Ambassador to Detroit during the reception last night and had agreed to certain requests that the other cities might have. His research had discovered the lack of electrical power in Dearborn before he left.

While they still had a long way to go, Marquette was capable of building new power plants, and to help stabilize and defend the area from the Black Priest, this would be a deal that Marquette would be willing to take. Doug, with a sigh, said, "Tell your Colonel if he gets me a meeting, I can guarantee it."

Hussan smiled, and said, "I'll speak to my Colonel. Wait here."

Doug waited for two hours, drinking coffee, and eating the honey-covered pastries. Waiting was easy for Doug, by the grace of his training and by the fact that he'd been needing some time to himself. Finally, Hussan came back with Salaban and a completely shaven olive-skinned man that Doug didn't know, though he wore the same black overalls as Hussan. He had one more diamond than Hussan and was taller than both him and Doug, cutting an impressive figure.

"Doug, this is Colonel Algizer," said Hussan.

Algizer stepped forward. He held out a hand and said, "As-salamu alaikum, Rider Doug. The Sultan has agreed to meet with you tomorrow and listen to your request. You will not be allowed to bring your weapons with you to the palace, but he insists you bring your bike. His highness has never had the honor to see a motorcycle and would be pleased if you'd let him examine it with his own eyes."

"It will be an honor," said Doug.

"You will stay with Corporal Salaban tonight," said Algizer, "And he will be your escort while you stay here."

"Thank you, sir," said Doug, standing and bowing.

Colonel Algizer, pleased, bowed back, and said, "I am afraid that is all the time I have for you, great rider, but I hope you enjoy the wonders of our city."

"Thank you, may the roads guide you well," said Doug.

"May Allah guide you to where you seek peace," said Algizer, and he left.

Hussan took over and said, "Please, join Salaban, he has offered his home as yours tonight. Mostly because he wants another ride on your bike."

"I would be honored," said Doug.

Salaban smiled and said, "Then let us be off. I am relieved of duty until you leave, and I wish to give you all my home has to offer."

Fifteen minutes later, Doug pulled up to Salaban's house. It was small, paneled with a small garage, but had a cozy air about it. Three young children played in the yard under the watchful eye of a woman Doug assumed was his wife. She held a book with strange writing that Doug recognized as a Qur'an, which was held with the respect he had seen Catholics hold their bibles and other religious people hold their religious books.

Salaban dismounted the bike, smiling at his wife and

children's awed expressions at the bike. Then, seeing their father, the boy and girl ran up and jumped into their father's arms, smothering him with hugs and kisses. The boy looked to be six, the girl four, both with olive skin and black hair.

"Hey," said Salaban, a look of pure joy on his face as he hugged his two children.

"Papa," they screamed in delight.

"Have a good day in school?" asked Salaban, then switching to the harsh language they spoke. But the children laughed and spoke with their father with a happiness that touched Doug's heart. The woman came up and Salaban hugged her, his children clinging to his back. They spoke softly, then the woman walked to Doug. She wore black pants, sandals, a sweater, and a head covering that hid her hair and neck but showed her face. She smiled kindly and said, "As-salamu alaikum, welcome to our home, Rider. I am Reetu, wife of Salaban. We have dinner cooking, and we hope you'll join our table tonight."

"I'd be honored," said Doug. She smiled, walked back to her husband and freed him from his hugging children and took them back to the house.

Doug followed Salaban, who said, "I ask that you take your boots off inside, rider. It's tradition."

"I will," said Doug, "What is that language you speak?"

"Arabic," said Salaban, "We all speak that and English. Don't worry, we will speak English around you."

They smiled at each other and entered the home. It was covered in plush rugs, colorful paintings of landscapes, framed scrolls of Arabic, and in the living room was a fireplace and mantle. On top of the mantle was another Qur'an, kept in a place of honor.

From the kitchen, a strong smell of spice and cooking meat made Doug's mouth water. Oh god, home cooking, it'd been so long.

Doug and Salaban entered the sitting room where an older woman, Salaban's mother, was pouring tea into two cups.

"Salaban," she yelled in delight, and continued speaking in Arabic. She planted a kiss on her son's cheek. She wore a full black robe and a headdress covered her, but her face, though lined, was full of delight.

Salaban said a few words and gestured to Doug. She walked up and bowed, saying, "It is a pleasure to host such a strong warrior as you, rider."

"I am honored to meet you, Matriarch," said Doug, using the Marquette equivalent of showing respect to an elder.

She smiled, bowed, gave each man a cup, and went to the kitchen. The men sat on two armchairs and started to drink the strong, harsh brew. Doug didn't care for the taste, but it did give him a recharge he needed so badly.

"Do you enjoy the city?" asked Salaban.

"What I saw of it, yes," said Doug with a grin.

"You will see it in its glory tomorrow," said Salaban. "It's a wonderful city."

"I can't wait to see more of it," said Doug, smelling what was coming from the kitchen. Salaban, noticing this, said, "It's delicious."

Doug smiled. He liked Salaban but knew Salaban was also curious about what Doug wanted. Doug didn't want to risk Salaban's cooperation at this time, so decided on a policy of honesty, but also to withhold information and discussions he wished only to talk to the Sultan about.

"Salaban," asked Doug, "Can I ask things about your city, in exchange for information about mine?"

"Of course," said Salaban with a grin.

"I noticed that a lot of the people here wear different styles of clothing. I see this in the women the most. Does that signify something?"

Salaban grinned, "There are many different types of Muslims, which is what we call the people of the Islamic faith, and many different ways of worshiping it. Not perhaps as varied as those who worshiped Jesus, but there are a few. The different styles often indicate orthodoxy, and how they interpret the Quran, again, much like the differences between sects of the Christian faith."

"What types are there?" asked Doug.

"The most common type here is Sufi, though Shiite and Sunni come in close second," explained Salaban. "Sufi was much smaller in the old world, but nowadays, it has gained prominence."

"Why is that?"

"Sufi is a more mystical form of worship of Allah and his prophet, Muhammad, and in truth, tolerant. In the old world, it was worshiped by comparatively few, but when the Green hit, and the world became more unusual, Sufi began to seem more reliable. But Suni and Shiite worshippers scoffed at it for a time. However, when the First Sultan came to power in these lands, creating New Mecca, he was able to unite the factions by giving them a new enemy to work together against. The Green was so powerful that it forced everyone to realize that our home is fragile now, and we must work to preserve all of Islam, not just certain points of it."

'I think the Sufi have it more right than you know,' thought Doug, but decided against saying it outright.

"What about your home, Marquette, was it called?"

"It's far north of here, and Marquette survival was mostly lucky, I think," said Doug. "Compared to the rest of Michigan, the land where Marquette and her colonies were located was very underdeveloped. The people up there learned to survive the Green because they were already used to it in a lesser way. But Marquette was the only one to be saved from complete destruction by thousands of us fighting to keep it at bay."

"And the riders?" asked Salaban, "What about them?"

"Well, the riders were once a biker gang, as they said, of the old world. They survived the Green and managed to get to Marquette before it damaged the roads. However, they got shelter from an unlikely source. They were the Freemasons."

"I have never heard of them," said Salaban.

"They're extinct now, at least in Marquette and the colonies, but they gave the bike gang shelter. Over time, the two groups grew closer. They worked together, studying the Green, and saw how much the world had changed. They found oil, which was not there previously, and learned to refine it. They also learned how to rebuild the machines of old. Soon, the two groups brought Marquette away from the seeds of destruction and built up the first steps of a new society. The Bikers and the Masons reorganized themselves, combining traditions, and thus became the first Riders, sworn to find the roads and bring back civilization from the Green."

Salaban looked in wonder. "Amazing. Are there any Muslims where you are from?"

"A few," said Doug, "And a few are even riders, but not many.

When it comes to faith, the Riders and Marquette keep a balance, not allowing anyone to force people to believe in a god they don't want to. It's for all religions, both the old and new."

"We have similar laws," said Salaban, "no one practice can force the others to convert. All views on Islam are given equal treatment by the Sultan."

"Is the Sultan the sole leader?" asked Doug.

"Yes, but he has a high council that advises him and can overrule him if necessary. This happens rarely, though, and the Sultans, from the first to now, have all been well-received. They've provided equal education, benefits, and services for everyone in the city."

"Sounds like a good guy," said Doug, "So there've never been any problems?"

"A few," said Salaban, "Some internal, most external, but I would ask the Sultan of that tomorrow."

Reetou called in Arabic and Salaban stood. With a smile, he said, "Come, let us have real food."

It was a delicious meal. Large lamb meatballs, with a soft-boiled egg in the center, with seasoned rice, grape leaves and pita bread. Reetou explained that food was eaten with only the right hand and no utensils were used, though it was okay to use both hands to pull apart bread. It was spicy, sweet, and delicious. At the end, Doug had to sit for an hour because he was so full.

During this time, the family all began to pray on the rugs that Doug had noticed earlier. They stood, went to their knees, went face down, head to the floor, arms straight out, and repeated the movements for some time. When they finished, Salaban explained that it was how they prayed.

Doug was offered the children's room while they would sleep with their grandmother. So Doug, at ten pm, tired, full of good food, and weary from travel, collapsed on his bed.

3 The Sultan

The next morning, four guards, including Colonel Algizer and Major Hussan came to Salaban's house to collect him and Doug. They brought four horses, bred for speed so Doug wouldn't have to leave his bike behind. He did put his weapons in a locker that Salaban built and put a padlock on them. The officers were pleased that Doug was already disarmed and so, as soon as he and Salaban got on the bike, they escorted him to the palace.

On their way, Doug saw the city. Most of the city was very spread out, and had very few high risers, unlike Detroit, but the Green had been cut away from most of them. However, due to the damage their structures had, most had been stripped down and used to build new homes and shops, making an almost brand new, tighter city. People bustled around, a strong smell of spice, cooking meat, and tanners around, plus the smell of forges where the blacksmiths were hard at work. The people, though they worshiped the same book, showed vast differences in dress styles, evident even on the cool autumn day. Some wore full length clothing, with head pieces that covered the top of their head. Others replaced the hijabs, as Doug learned from Reetou last night the name of the female head covering, and the equivalent with for the males, and more revealing hijabs for the females. Some women and men wore shirts and pants, hair exposed, and even walked hand in hand.

Often, in family units, the males lead from the front of the family while women and children were behind, but the ones who wore clothing more equal to that which Doug found familiar seemed to be on more equal footing. Even their expressions, to him, vastly differed. Some, what seemed to be more Orthodox, usually looked at him with suspicion and open hostility, while others seemed mildly to moderately curious, and still others seemed indifferent. One thing they all did was stare at his bike for a moment with awe. He found most were more interested in his motorcycle than in him as a person. Still, with the wildly different expressions, he realized just how different the whole Muslim culture was in itself. He saw signs, some with uplifting messages written in both English and Arabic like, “Allah wants no War,” or, “We need to work for peace in the Green.” Others were more threatening, and some he didn't understand what they were talking about. Some examples were, "Allah demands Jihad," or even more strange was "The Zionist caused the Green," or "Allah is the truth, Kali is the lie: the Gurus are a lie." Doug didn't know what a Zionist, Kali, or a Guru was, and he wasn't going to ask. He needed to complete the mission.

Doug soon arrived at the palace, and he braked the bike and looked at it with awe. It was sixteen stories high. Topped with a cylinder structure on top, the glass gleamed in the fall season sun. It was curved, almost like a crescent moon. It was one of the best restored buildings he had seen anywhere in the Green, and still held a modern gleam. Still, Doug could tell it had been adapted. Oil lamps had replaced electrical ones, and there was a stone wall around it. The people walking the grounds were a mix of guards, and what seemed to be the social and political elite. Both men and women. Some of the women, two, seemed to be there more for entertainment, as they were more scantily clad and dancing, using the center of their bodies as the focal point, performing with small bands around them playing exotic music.

"It's amazing," said Doug.

"It used to be called the Edward Hotel," said Salaban, "But the Sultan uses it as his home and the center of government."

"It doesn't look like it was designed by your people," mentioned Doug.

"No, in the old world, Dearborn was very diverse, though it still had a healthy Islamic population. When the green hit, most of the non-Muslims left for Detroit, and even many of our people did too, but the majority that decided to fight to keep this land habitable were Muslim, so that is why today most of the people here are Arabic and nearly all Muslim."

"So, Dearborn wasn't always a city solely inhabited by Arabs."

"No, but many did come here from the old world to find employment. Some people in Detroit, and the other cities say it was a conspiracy by us. Then again, many in Detroit say that about Canton and Plymouth. People can get suspicious just because the dice rolled a certain way."

Algizer looked back at Doug and Salaban, and Doug, taking the hint, started to back off. They reached the gates and passed them unmolested by the sentries. As they rode up the path, some of the nobles looked over and gasped at the bike, but they were ignored until they reached the palace's front entrance, which was under a structure that provided shade for people coming up. A party stood there. Twenty were guards, but three were men dressed in dark robes of flowing material, wearing red and white head coverings topped with cloth circles that seem to denote royalty. They all had beards of a similar length, and it was clear to Doug they were all brothers. The middle one was the tallest.

The one on the left was shorter by a head, but broad of shoulder, and gazed at the rider with fierce eyes. The one on the right was shorter and stouter than the others, but had an intelligent look, as if he saw more than with just his eyes. Next to them were two very beautiful women, but there were clear indications that they were sisters to the men. They had similar dark hair and olive skin, but one was taller than the other woman. They also seemed to wear expensive dresses and seemed to have no want to wear a hijab, again changing the picture of this strange city state in Doug's eye.

The tallest man, slim looking but with a strong bearing Doug envied, walked forward and said, "As-salamu alaikum, brother rider. I am Prince Omar of the house of Abdula. This is Prince Iman on my right, and Prince Fahda on my left. These are Princesses Raina and Salma. Welcome to New Mecca."

Doug got off his bike with Salaban, bowed to the prince, then held out his hand and the two shook. "I am Doug Farson, member of the Riders, defenders of the Road and civilization. I have felt very welcome since my arrival."

The prince smiled, and, still holding Doug's hand with a tenderness and caring that touched Doug's heart, he led him into the palace. Before entering, he explained to his escort how to move the bike without turning it on, and they maneuvered it in behind them. The palace's interior was impressive and very reflective of the city's multicultural feel. It was covered in white walls and floor, but impressively decorated. Ornaments and rugs didn't feel like overdoing it, but more adding to an overall unending design. On the far wall was a large painted symbol, a moon with a star in the center, which, Salaban explained, was a symbol for Islam like a Christian cross or a Jewish star of David.

Underneath the symbol were three people: an older man, dressed like his sons and also bearded; a woman, around the same age, but wearing a black robe and a hijab that covered her hair, contrasting to the two princesses; and a third man, in a white robe and a white cap, the only one standing. He was younger than the man but seemed to be less excited than the older one.

The older man stood, and so did the woman, helping the man. Doug clearly saw that he was suffering from arthritis as he walked slowly towards the rider, the younger man behind them. When he was close enough by Doug's judgment, Doug began to bow, but the man put a hand on him and said, in an old but strong and kind voice, "No, rider, you need not bow to me, for you are not one of my subjects. I will not let a man, who was the source of many childhood stories I have heard from my own father's lips, be made less in my or my subjects' eyes. I am Sultan Rabinin Abdula, house of Abdula, ruler of New Mecca, and subject to his people. This is my wife, Tarfa Abula, formerly of the house of

Muhamad. You met my children already. And this is Iman Simion, of the house of Matty. He is my spiritual leader, and the spiritual leader of the people and three mosques of our great city."

Doug, smiling, held out a hand, and shook his majesty's hand, feeling the tender kindness he had felt previously when Omar escorted him inside with Salaban. He then kissed the queen's hand and shook the hand of the Iman, who smiled politely, and then said, "I am Doug Farson, Rider of Marquette."

The sultan bowed his head, then saw the bike and excitement came to his eyes. He reigned it in and looked at Doug with the control that fitted his station.

"May I examine the motorcycle? I have never seen one up close. At least, not one that works."

"Of course," said Doug, taking the sultan's arm, and escorting him to his longtail. The black bike clashed with the whiteness of the throne room, but the sultan examined the bike as if it were a treasure beyond any he had seen. He examined every inch of it. When he asked Doug for permission to sit on it, Doug helped him personally and explained to the king how it worked.

"You have a lot of respect for this machine," said Rabinin.

Doug, his instinct telling him that this was a good idea, began to recite the rider's creed.

"I am one with my bike. It is a part of me. It is a part of me as is my heart, my soul, and my mind. Through my bike, I protect those who need it.

Through my bike, I keep the deepest darkness out and cast shadow in the brightest of light.

I am a Rider, protector, and guardian to all who need one. I find the paths that were lost. I find the road less traveled. I bring civilization back from the Green. I am a Rider."

The sultan looked in the creed with a look of wonder on his face, and said, "So, you see this bike as part of you. I see why they call you riders. You more than just control it, it's a part of you."

Doug nodded. "We spend years training, and once a rider has his bike, it's permanent. We treat it as you would treat a part of your body."

"Then in that case, as long as you are here in New Mecca, I swear by Allah two things: one, I will have your bike protected at all costs. Second, we will speak only in English during our talks. I prefer Arabic, but I will respect your tongue."

"I thank you, your majesty," said Doug, helping the Sultan off. The Sultan, once free of the bike, looked at his sons and said, "Omar, Fadah, you will come with us as well. Iman, you will take the throne, and speak in my name. Raina, Salma, talk to your mother, my beloved, and please take charge of the palace."

His children all bowed and obeyed their assigned tasks as Doug, Rabinin, Omar, and Fadah left for the chamber where his majesty held council. Salaban, Hussan, Algizer, and the other guards bowed, and took their leave.

As they did, Doug noticed how Iman kept his eye on Doug, not with hostility, but with a wariness.

They didn't go far before they entered a good size room, with several chairs surrounding a small table holding a tray of tea and cakes. There was also a contraption Doug recognized as a hookah with several hoses attached. Male servants were inside, made the royalty, the Iman, and the rider as comfortable as possible, then took their leave.

The Sultan poured them all tea. They sat relaxing for a moment, then Prince Omar leaned forward, putting his cup down, and said, "So, Algizer explained much about what you are trying to do, and what your people are willing to offer in exchange for your assistance. But from what I also understand, you sent riders to Canton and Plymouth. May I ask you for what reason?"

"You may," said Doug, his leather jacket clashing with the colorful chair, "But may I ask, have you heard the news from Traverse and Jackson?"

"I have not," said the Sultan, finally speaking.

Doug explained everything he'd seen, knew, or suspected about their destruction and why he suspected the Black Priests were behind it. When he was done, it was Simion who spoke next, "Where do these Black Priests come from?"

"The ones we meant claim to come from a place called Etam. Have you heard of it?"

"No," said Fadah, his voice also indicating great intelligence, even with one word.

"Me and my party were sent out to find a way through the Green. But we also recognize that it's not just our home that's at risk, but also yours, Detroit, and the other cities that have survived. We are trying to unite the factions as best we can."

The Sultan spoke up, and his voice was calm, but there was a passion in his words that indicated to Doug that he was going to have to pay attention.

"I understand, but Detroit has been trying to get us to work with the other cities for years. But even during the old days, our people clashed, and unlike Detroit, or even your Marquette and her colonies, we have become a secular society. Our people in our city, and the cities of Canton, and Plymouth, have culturally chosen a different path than you have. We have been divided by this cultural difference not just by our faith and cultures, but also by the Green itself. Detroit has, however, chosen to lump us together, as if we were one problem. I can say this, though, it has prevented war. But that is it. After that, we have been stagnant in our development, and none of us have been able to restore technologies used by the ancestors. Detroit has restored so much, but refused to give us the technology we need to bring our people true comfort. They sit behind their lofty wall, not knowing how my people suffered trying to bring some sense of order from the Green. They suffer as we did, so what right do they have to put these demands on us?"

Doug pulled out a pack of cigarettes, which got everyone's attention, and said, "Marquette tobacco, would you like some?"

They each took a cigarette and thanked him. They all enjoyed the tobacco for a moment, then Doug said, "I hear what you say, your majesty, but I must ask this question: I understand your dislike of Detroit, but what have Canton and Plymouth done to earn your people's ire?"

It was prince Fadah who explained: "It's cultural differences. They worship different gods than we do, and we've never been able to agree on anything when we talk. We have all survived the Green and we jealously hold what we have, but we also don't want the others to gain favor over us. So we send threats to prevent them from getting an upper hand over us."

"I'm not asking you to combine your armies and make peace in a day," said Doug. "I ask only that on this, the subject of Etam and the Black Priests, you help defend the region from their designs of what they want with our homes. Your cities may not agree on much, but I can say this: you value your peoples and your cultures; the Black Priests do not. They see them all as future servants of their Golden Lord. They rape children, they corrupt souls, they tear families apart, and they do what they can to divide us. And they are good at it, very good. So, will you at least hear my story, hear what I have to offer, and understand what I offer you is no more or less than what we offer in other cities?"

The Sultan smiled, and said, "Tell us your story rider."

And Doug knew that by now, Kshea and Thug were telling the same story.

4 Canton

Kshea arrived in Canton a few hours after Doug arrived in Dearborn. Her bike sped down, reaching its goal with ease. The Green before the city was tall grasses that twisted into unusual patterns, knotting together in patterns that only nature could give. But as the Green broke, she saw something else in the grass - human structures. The farms were clean, but the people who lived here had weaved them into large and spiraling homes, barns, storage areas, and stables. It was truly innovative. But as she approached the city, she saw houses and saw the people.

They were of darker skin than her, black of hair with fair features. The males were tall, handsome, and wore mostly white cotton shirts, pants, and sandals. The females wore colored dresses with long sashes over them but were very feminine.

Then she saw them, the statues. They were everywhere.

Some were of blue men with many arms, some of normal looking people, but brightly colored, some of monkey men, some elephant men. Kshea knew each represented a god or goddess, but, knowing little of the Hindi faith, she didn't know who they represented. They adorned the farms she passed more often than not, multiple statues acting like sentries with men, women, and even children praying to them.

Then the smells hit her. A strong mix of curry, vegetables, meats, cheese, and fruit permeated the air. It drew the senses to them, like a physical path, and Kshea fell in love with it. She also began to see other types of people as well. Lighter skinned people, people with some African blood in them as well as oriental, but all similar to the dark-skinned people she encountered in the farms. She noticed each seemed to be sticking with their own people, and each seemed to stick with one type of task; this got her curious. Then, when she reached the outskirts, two men stood in her path. They were tall, taller than even her. They were tan skinned, hard-muscled, clean shaven, and carried rifles tipped with bayonets. They wore tan uniforms with thick tan boots on their feet.

One spoke and his patterns of speech were different. It had a slight musical tone and pattern about it she never encountered before. It was almost hypnotic.

"Who are you, and why do you come to Canton?" asked the

man, showing no emotion.

Without fear or reservation, Kshea got off her bike, standing at the men's chests, and said, "I am a rider of Marquette, representing both my lands and yours. I bring your leaders an urgent warning and ask them to parley so we can stop more pain and suffering than what is needed.

The men looked at each other, then said, "Come."

They turned and entered a stable and brought out two tan horses, indicating to her she should follow on her bike. She did, surprised at how fast these horses moved. The city was large and built with a large population in mind for the small area. The buildings she passed were multitiered, and seemed a little unbalanced in a way, but housed many merchants and farmers selling their wares. They spoke English, and she heard a hundred of them yelling to her to buy their sandals, try their curries, and try their clothing.

She saw no leather, and also there was no power; instead, the streets had gas lamps. She was told that Canton was found to have an abundance of natural gas under its ground, and she was seeing these people take as much advantage of it as they could. She also noticed hundreds of cows walking throughout the streets. Cows of many shapes, sizes, and colors. The smell was powerful off them, and she saw thousands of cow pies littered throughout the city. What was more curious, the people seemed to make an effort not to get in their way.

They got deeper into the city, and it turned from the bustling outer city to the cleaner inner city. There were cows, but not as many. The people, on the other hand, wore richer clothing, jewels, and ornamentation that denoted a higher standard of living. They, unlike the outer city merchants, stared at the bike moving through their city, and the rider on it. She noticed, dotted throughout the city, were statues of the various beings she had seen out in the farms. Also, she noticed, along with the statues and the cows, several groups of other animals as well. They resembled cows, but they were all a brown color, and their faces were covered in a curly fur and short but sharp horns. They were also much larger and taller than regular cows, similar like comparing Dire Wolves to regular wolves or coywolves.

“What are those?” asked Kshea, as the guards stopped to let a large group cross the roads. One of the guards looked up and saw her pointing to two of the strange cow-like creatures.

“Beefalo,” he said, with a smile, “There are a few hundred around here. They’re strong creatures, but are too hard-headed for true domestication, but left to their own devices, they are pretty easy to approach, and their milk is very sweet. We let them come and go as they please.”

“Were they brought back by the Ancients?” asked Kshea.

“No,” said the guard, “They’re a hybrid they created. They

were created by blending cows with ancient American bison. From what I read, before the Green, the American bison was on the verge of extinction, so what was left was blended with regular cows, and the Beefalo replaced them. They said herds of them ran wild across the land, herds of over a thousand someday. We see them occasionally in the Green running wild in large groups. They are smarter than they look and often intermingle with our own cattle."

"Why so many cattle?" asked Kshea.

"No time to explain that," said the second guard. "Come, the road is clear."

They continued until they came to a large green garden, and then Kshea saw it. It had once been a house, large and grand, but now had several add-ons that turned it into a medium size palace, with large, dome towers, low ramparts, and several more guards, and men and women milling about, dressed in colorful, but clearly work-oriented clothing, working around the palace and the grounds, maintaining it. They were shorter than the guards, but just as well-muscled, and seemed to have an eye for detail.

The guards led her into the grounds and moved her bike to a large stable. The same breed of horses was stabled inside, and the guards dismounted and brought them inside. As they came out, the first guard said, "You can put your bike in there where it will be safe. Nobody will touch it."

Kshea complied and put her bike in an empty stable. When she exited, two more guards had joined them, each carrying empty sacks. One with a thick mustache walked forward, and said, in that strange accent, "Your weapons, please, all of them."

Kshea complied, handing over her rifle, pistol, knife, and all her ammo. The guards with the sacks put them in the stable with her bike, exited, and said to her, "You can retrieve them when you leave. I will stay with them. Please follow the guards."

"Thank you," said Kshea. She turned and the guards walked her to the palace. They walked slowly, probably to let her enjoy the gardens. Large beds of flowers, huge hedges, and various other types of plant life were dotted throughout it. The various colors and smells made Kshea smile, enjoying her walk. She noticed various men and women who seemed to have similar bearings and heights to her guards. But she also noticed the cows also walking among them, and the people, whether working or enjoying the day, respectfully getting out of their way. She also noticed Beefalo walking freely among them.

"Why so many cows?" asked Kshea.

"They are sacred to us," said the first guard to talk to her, looking at her, his handsome face showing enjoyment to explain his culture, "They have many gifts, and help us with maintaining our land, provide us with milk which makes many great foods, and give us strength. Without our cows, Canton wouldn't exist today."

"Are all the beefalo cows, too?"

"Yes," said the guard.

"Where are all the bulls?"

"Bulls, while also respected, are too dangerous to keep in the city. They are too hard-headed. They stick to the outside of the city."

"Same with the beefalo?" asked Kshea.

"That sometimes causes us problems, but Shurdas can usually keep them out."

"Shurdas?"

"One of our castes," explained the guard, "There are four castes. Me and the other guards are part of the Kshatriyas Caste. My caste are leaders, administrators, and warriors. We protect, lead, and direct our city." Shurdas are of the Laboring caste, which means they maintain our city's infrastructure, our farmers, our livestock, and, in many ways, our society.

"So, each caste has a certain function in your society."

"Exactly, and all are equally important. In India, where our religion and caste system originally came from, the higher your caste, the closer you are to the gods, but here, because of the Green, each caste is equally respected. Not one caste is above the other."

"What about the other caste?" asked Kshea, "What are they?"

"The Vaishyas are the merchant caste. They are responsible for trade, our crops, and are some of our best artists and musicians."

"Arts and merchants are part of the same caste?" asked Kshea, confused.

"Artistic ability can be a tradable good, so that caste provides it for us. It was they who designed the palace you see today. They also help us trade with the other communities in the Green. Kshatriyas are responsible to decide if Canton should trade with them, but we take the Vaishyas' perspective very seriously."

"And the final caste?" asked Kshea.

All the guards bowed their heads before the guard who was talking to Kshea continued, with great respect.

"The Brahmins, the priestly people, are those who study and worship the gods. They are the smallest caste, and most respected. They stay out of the city's affairs mostly, but they are just as important, as they lead all of us to the divine."

"Do they lead the city?"

"No, but each Caste has a head known as the Raj. Raj are the head of each caste, and four Raj's work together to make Canton safe and prosperous."

"And they lead together?"

"They are led by the Great Raj, the casteless one. The Great Raj strips off his caste and leads them all. The four Rajs only answer to the Great Raj; each wields great power."

"Casteless?" asked Kshea, "Meaning he was never part of a caste?"

"No, each was part of one, and they still interact with their families, but Great Rajs have to think outside their caste in order to not be biased. We are almost there, come."

"Will I meet the Great Raj?"

"No, you will meet the Rajs, but, the Great Raj will want their opinions before meeting you to see if it's worth the effort."

They entered, the great white oak doors opened by two more guards, and Kshea couldn't hold back a gasp. The entrance hall was grand indeed. It was made from wood, but painted gold. The patterns on the walls were astounding, even on the wooden pillars that looked more like marble than the wood they were made from. Depictions of the various gods in action were painted on the walls, too. There were also statues of men and women coupling, and some of the paintings seemed to look at these statues as if observing the wonders of their creations. There were also statues and paintings of cows in great detail, and it was a true wonder to behold.

The guard who Kshea had been talking to noticed her looking at one of the erotic statues, and smiled, saying, "They were made by Aarav Rama, one of our greatest sculptors. They are meant to represent the divinity in making new life. He and many others believe the art of copulation is a holy thing for it brings new life, and Aarav wanted to capture it. It's not meant as eroticism, though I have to admit, it does put one in that mind frame."

Kshea chuckled at that as they continued. They went right, down a decorated hallway and entered a medium size room, when open, Kshea's eyes were overloaded with the people and wonders she saw.

5 DarkKin

Kshea had never seen such a room. It shined like a treasure chest. Gold, silver, pearl, emerald, and jade colorings were painted on the walls, floors, and dome ceilings. The patterns were in the shape of deities, animals, humans of various types, and Otherkin, moving, playing, fighting, in embrace, in love, in lust, and all with the eye of a master painter.

There were no statues here. Instead, a raised platform of marble stood, flanked by ten guards. On the platform were five thrones. One was a white wood, the second was metal, the third made of shells, fourth of stone, the last of a black, unknown metal. Four men and a woman sat on the chairs. The woman sat on the chair made of shells. She had beautiful exotic features, long black hair, and wore a purple dress covered by a purple shift. Her wrist had many gold bangles on them, her ears had gold earrings as well.

The men were all unique as well. The first on the white wood throne was bald, with no hair on his eyes or face, a sharp nose, and intense eyes. He wore an orange wrap that went down to his feet, but his upper body was bare and also hairless, and his nut-brown skin housed a thin but well-muscled body. The man on the metal throne wore a thin white turban, and sported a beard, but was thicker in build. He wore no shirt, but a white cape covered his shoulders. He wore a similar orange wrap around his waist. A sword hung from a leather belt, contained in a long, curved scabbard, the hilt covered in gold and jewels. The third man sat on the throne of stone, and he also wore no shirt, but a simple white wrap and white turban. His hands and skin seemed more weathered and worn than the other two. But his eyes seem to be able to discern every part of Kshea and understand her in an instant. This was the face of a builder, the face of a man who know how the world worked and why. The fifth man, on the other hand, on the strange black throne, was different than the others. His head was shaven, but he had a beard and wore red robes and a red headpiece with a red jewel in the center. He seemed to listen and see all without trying, and he seemed to encompass all the qualities of the other Rajs, or they seemed to take one quality of him, and represented it like an Avatar of the man of the black throne.

All five sat. The guards bowed, Kshea joining them so as not to seem disrespectful, but she didn't miss the look of surprise on any of the guards' faces. They didn't seem to expect the fifth man on the black throne, and they knew this wasn't normal in this city.

After a moment, the Raj on the metal throne said, "Rise." They did, with Kshea feeling strange in this room of rulers, feeling low and unworthy, but still, she returned the Rajs' looks, for she was a rider, and riders stood tall when others hid away.

The female Raj on the shell throne looked at the rider with a small smile, which Kshea found no comfort in, and said in a musical version of the same accent that was commonplace here in Canton, "Welcome Rider. We are the Rajs; welcome to our halls, and to the city of Canton."

"It's an honor," said Kshea, "I am Kshea, a pathfinder and tracker in the order of the riders of Marquette and her colonies."

The Raj with the sword nodded politely, saying nothing, but seemed to size her up as if ready to fight her. However, the simply dressed Raj on the stone chair said, "We have heard much of the Riders,' though I will confess, I have never met one in person."

"Now you have," said Kshea. "I must confess, your majesty, I have the vague notion you were aware of my arrival for some time."

"We have many outposts hidden in the Green," said the female Raj on the shell throne, "They reported of you and your bike's arrival. We were curious about why you were coming, and so prepared accordingly. Though we must confess, the reason for your visit eludes us."

Kshea, standing straighter, said, "I have come on behalf of Marquette, and on behalf of the city of Detroit, in hopes of forging a relationship against a threat that has come to this land that the Ancients once called Michigan. Have you heard of or seen men in black, roaming the Green, followed by what can be best described as wolf-type Otherkin?"

The Raj's looked at one another, all but the man on the black throne, who continued to look at Kshea. She shivered inwardly under that gaze, powerful as it was.

"We have," said the Raj on the wooden throne.

"One came to my land and nearly tore apart two colonies. He was responsible for at least three people's deaths, and for dozens of people being injured. He would have done more had we not stopped him, and already, these Black Priests, as we call them, are responsible for the destruction of the village of Traverse and the city of Jackson."

The Raj with the sword laughed, "One village destroyed, and a few dozen people killed or murdered by these . . . uh, Black

Priests. The Green takes more lives than these boogie men you so fear. If they come to Canton, the Kshatriyas Caste will destroy them."

"It's not that easy," said Kshea, "One Black Priest was able to take a full shot to the chest, and the one we fought in Iron Wood, the colony which I was stationed at, was nearly torn apart by bullets before he was killed. And when they travel with these wolf men, they can tear apart cities, killing hundreds if not thousands at a time."

As she spoke, Kshea gauged the Rajs' facial expression. She saw the woman and the man on the stone throne listening, obviously interested. The man on the wood throne was harder to read but seemed more interested in getting the facts first. The Raj with the sword was openly cynical of what she was saying. The red-robed man, however, was impossible to read or gauge. He sat in silence, listening, but Kshea did not know if he cared what she was saying.

Kshea told them the whole story, explaining all they knew and suspected about the Black Priests and the Great Old Ones. The story took about an hour, and she had to search her memory a lot given that she was in the Green for a while during certain events. When finished, she looked at the Rajs. They were silent, but all looked serious, save for the Raj with the sword, whose face had broken into an amused grin, believing that his age and wisdom let him see through this mere child.

"Oh ho, so some magic man from a faraway land comes and causes a little trouble in your towns," he said with venom "We have far scarier legends than that girl, and if you think we are foolish enough to believe such nonsense, then you are . . ."

"I believe her," said the man in red, for the first time. The Raj's voice was soft, but it cut through the Raj with the sword's words like a hot knife through butter.

The other Raj's looked at the Raj in red, and he stood: "I wish to discuss more of this with you, but I feel you didn't just come to tell us of your ill fate. What do you seek from us?"

"Detroit and our own city are trying to create a coalition," explained Kshea without hesitation, "Having the other cities work together to protect this region."

"Ours, Detroit, and your home?" asked the Raj in red.

"Along with Dearborn and Plymouth," said Kshea.

The sword-clad Raj and the Raj on the wooden throne both stiffened, and the sword-clad Raj stood in anger, yelling, "We will never, ever . . ."

"Raj of the Kshatriyas," said the red-clad Raj sharply, "you will be respectful in these halls, and show the rider the same consideration as she has shown you."

The Raj of the Kshatriyas went silent, and Kshea knew she had scored a victory in this hall. She knew if she was to get anywhere, she would have to win the trust of the Raj in red. The others, while important to the city, were inconsequential to her goals.

The Raj in red stood and said, "I will speak to the rider alone. We will convene tomorrow morning. Till then, namaste."

The other Raj's put their hands together and bowed their heads, repeating the unfamiliar word to the Raj in Red. They stood and left, as did the guards, without question.

The Raj of the Kshatryias and the Raj on the white wood throne cast looks of hate at the girl, and disappointment before the Raj in Red. But that Raj paid no mind to them, he merely said, "Come with me." Kshea did.

They walked to a door on the side, and it was opened by two different guards. They wore knee length shifts, black pants, flexible boots, and blue hats that were cylindrical in shape. They also had long sabers on their belts, curved, like the Kshatryias Raj's was.

"Patthar guard, or stone guards. They are the most elite soldiers in Canton," said the red Raj, who also smiled, and said, "They suffer under the delusion that they must protect me and my family twenty-four hours a day instead of the city."

One of the stone guards, this one sporting a stylized beard, said, "One because you have a habit of making trouble for yourself, Delit."

"Is that your name?" asked Kshea, "Delit?"

"No," said the Raj, "It is my title. In the lands of India, across the great ocean to the west, Delit were once called untouchables. They were the lowest caste of that society. But here, it means casteless, and I am untouchable by the other caste. That means they have no hold over me, and I can make discussions objectively. Here, there is one untouchable, and only one."

"So you were not born into a caste?" asked Kshea.

"I was, I was once Vaishyas, a painter, but I shrugged it off after I became the Untouchable."

"So, you're the ruler?" asked Kshea as the guards led them down the hall."

"Not precisely. The four other Raj's are each the head of their caste, and they are in charge of influence of the city internally - in spiritual matters for the Brahmins, defense and administration for the Kshatriyas, in trade, art, and food productions for the Vaishyas, and infrastructure and labor for the Shudras. The thrones you see each best reflect the caste they lead. Each one has equal power, but often, it is the Brahmins and the Kshatriyas who are the most influential, even today. That's where I step in. I check the power of the other castes and make sure that one doesn't have too much power, and also, I am checked by them to make sure I don't abuse that power. I also am the city's representative for matters outside the city that can either harm or change our city."

"So that's why you were there," said Kshea, "But the guards told me you would only hear my case after I talked to the other Rajs."

"It is the usual course," said the Untouchable "But, I had to admit, when I heard a rider was coming to Canton, I was curious. I had heard of the Riders, but never thought I would meet one. We only have one working vehicle here in Canton, and I have never seen a motorcycle. Meeting you is like meeting Rama, a legendary figure in our religion, a man so powerful, yet so humble, you couldn't help but to respect him."

Kshea smiled at the compliment, though she knew nothing of this Rama.

"And I also want to know all the reasons why you are here," said the Untouchable, "I don't think you're lying about your intentions, and I can see the logic of wanting to stabilize the region against these Black Priests and their servants, but I also sense there is a selfish motive. What is that you truly seek?"

Kshea found that even if she wanted too, she couldn't lie to this man. He was simple and sincere, despite his position. His kindness broke through almost all of the defenses that she had put up. This was also why Doug sent Kshea to Canton, for she was also sincere, and wouldn't lie to get what she wanted, and that was a quality rare in this day and age. So, she explained, "Harris, the Viceroy of Detroit told us that you might know a way past the Green, a way underneath it."

Comprehension entered the man's face, and he said, "You seek the Tunnels of the Night."

"Why do you call them that?"

"The tunnels' walls are covered in stones that glow without light reflecting off them. The mouth of the entrance glows at night as bright as the moon. It's about five miles outside the city's limits."

"Harris mentioned you mapped them out."

"We have, and they go farther than what he expects," said the untouchable, "The farthest we have mapped of them stretches over one hundred and seventy miles, and they keep going. That's just the main tunnel, and we expect it goes further than that."

"Do you know where they end?" asked Kshea excitedly.

"No, we haven't mapped them further," said the Untouchable.

"Why?"

"The tunnels are beautiful, and they are a wonder, but we lost many people to them. Sixty years ago, we sent many to the tunnels, but now, we rarely dare go to them. Reports of feral monsters that make the tunnels their home began to spread, and beasts down there have also been discovered. Giant worms, lizards as big as a small man, and great spiders have caused men to lose heart for exploring them further. We lost hundreds to those tunnels, and we dare not share what we found in them at the risk of losing more adventurers to them."

Kshea looked at the man, and saw the stone look on his face, and knew he was telling her this to stop them from going into these tunnels.

"Sir, my companions and I have to find a way through the Green, and these tunnels may be the answer. We have to try. If that means opening a dialogue or begging you to let us enter them, we will. We won't go behind your back as that is not our way. But we must try."

The Untouchable walked in silence for a long moment, until he turned back to Kshea, and said, "What do you offer?"

"My people have managed to restore much of the Ancient's technology from the Green. We offer to help you and the other cities restore the power to your cities in exchange for a dialogue about uniting resources in defense of these Black Priests from Etam."

They reached a door, and the untouchable was silent, then said, "I will talk to the other Rajs. I can't promise you will find what you seek, but I will talk to them. You can stay here tonight. I ask only for one thing in return."

"Yes?" asked Kshea, as the guards opened the door, revealing a bed chamber.

"Can I have a ride on your bike?"

Kshea smiled, "Only if you tell me your name."

"I am Bali Ramada. It is a pleasure Kshea."

6 Plymouth

A day after Kshea was settled in at Canton, Thug was riding his way through harsher areas of the Green, in this case, the Wetlands. 'God damn it," thought Thug, "I hate this shit." The trees were not as thick. He headed north a few miles outside of Canton, but now wished he had stayed on the main track. Some parts of the road were submerged, and every time, not knowing what was under there, Thug had been forced to get off his bike to walk through, soaking his riding boots, and rolling it up and downhill. It was a nightmare, but Thug moved on, noticing some swans, ducks, and fish in the water that was only broken by the path. Thug smiled, glad to see these smaller animals, instead of dealing with Sabercats and cave bears. Still better not let his guard down too much. Wetlands can be just as dangerous as traveling through the endless forest, but it was nice to get some glimpse of the sky through the trees.

Thug rode for another hour, and a fog was settling in. It wasn't overly thick but still unsettling in the half-light of the trees.

Thug, feeling the eerie and unsettling feeling that came with fog, took a break for a moment, and brought forward his rifle, which he wrapped in a cloth to keep dew from building on it. It was already on his blue bandana, and his leather jacket. When he looked up, he paused, seeing something in the haze. A large shadow, it was horse-like in shape but bigger, and seemed to have glowing eyes that cut through the darkness. Thug tried to lean forward, getting a closer look, but then it turned away.

"Fuck," thought Thug, "Probably just an elk."

Thug turned, ready to go, when he heard a slithering, sliding sound followed by the sound of large, slapping, but heavy feet. Thug looked behind him, and a shape appeared out of the gloom. It was huge, larger than even a parka or a cave bear. It was at least twenty feet long, its large, emotionless, lizard-head stared at him with lifeless dark eyes. A large, forked tongue hissed out of its mouth, while its darker colored scales had a light covering of moss and algae. It had four huge legs, each as thick as a small tree trunk, ending in four large claws.

"Oh, fuck no!" yelled Thug, revving the bike and moving out of the way just as the large jaws tried to take a bite out of him, the teeth only missing his tire by an inch. Abandoning caution, Thug raced down the path at sixty miles per hour, the large beast following in his wake.

Thug rode hard, not noticing the cloth he had covered his rifle in had flown off. But the beast was slow and soon it was out of reach. Thug felt a moment of relief when he was forced to stop. The water had covered another part of the path, and it was wider than the others. Thug didn't want to risk it, but he was indecisive about what to do. The beast, sensing that its prey was trapped, began moving quicker.

Thug turned, and anger struck his heart. "I ain't getting eaten by this mother," he growled, "Come get me, you fucking lizard!"

Revving up, he turned the bike back towards his pursuer at top speed. This gave the giant lizard pause, not used to its prey attacking. Thug, using this moment, raised his rifle with one hand, and with the benefit of years of training, let loose. Four bullets struck the beast, leaving large holes on its snout and taking an eye. The lizard roared, pouncing blindly, extending its forepaws to crush the creature that dared attack it. Thug was just out of its reach, and he used its flat posture to his advantage, riding up the beast's left forelimb, keeping perfect balance. Thug managed to get up its shoulder and on its back, dropping his rifle so its barrel was lined up with the beast's back and holding the trigger as it ripped through the creature's back. It screamed a horrible screech of pain as the bullets ripped from its shoulder blade down its tail. Thug launched back on the path, whipping his back around, spraying dirt that collected on the path. Thug raised his rifle as the enraged beast turned, angry and wanting to crush this prey that had given him so much trouble.

Thug was ready again when suddenly, from the fog, a man came out of the mist, right in front of Thug. Thug took his finger off the trigger, seeing the man. He was tall, wearing a blue shirt and pants, high black boots, and a blue sash over his shirt. He sported a long beard, and thick mustache that obscured his lower face, and on top of his head, a large, blue turban, with a metal sigil in the center. In one hand, he carried a long, thick sword, curved and deadly. On his back was a hunting rifle. The lizard paused again, confused, then two more men and a woman leapt on to its back. Two carried spears, and the woman carried a sword of similar make as the first man. The first man charged, the creature focusing only on him, and the two men with spears ran up, and stabbed the beast hard in the neck. It shrieked again. The first man ran up its forepaw and the woman joined him. They reached the neck, and on either side, plunged their swords into the neck sliding down it from either side, exposing the beast's neck bones.

The two warriors landed and ran down the side, slicing at the beast's four legs and main body as they ran. The lizard tried to turn, but Thug, shaking his head, aimed with his rifle and fired five more shots at the exposed neck bones, shattering them, and the spear wielders leapt down and stabbed it in the head. The creature reared in a death throe and the spear wielder launched off as the sword wielder moved out of the way. As the lizard fell backwards, its body twisting in a death throe as it landed in the water, mostly off the path, only a bit of its tail still on land.

Thug lowered his weapon as the four warriors walked forward, the woman leading them. They all had features which were similar to Arabic and Indian people, but they were different in many ways. The woman wore blue like the others, but where they wore blue shirts, hers was a knee-long tunic that conformed to her shapely body. She wore no turban and her black hair flowed freely, but the sash she wore came up to form a sort of hood on her head. She smiled kindly. She wore a thick, silver bracelet on her right wrist, and a small dagger was on her belt that was holding the tunic to her body. The man wore the same garb as the first men, and also had these bracelets and daggers that were similar to the woman's. The first spear wielder was older than the others. His beard was white and longer than the others, almost reaching his belt. He reminded Thug of pictures of the mythical man Santa Clause, with rosy cheeks and cheerful eyes. The second spear-wielder was the youngest. His beard was the shortest, and his youthful, handsome face was smiling and looked adventurous. The first guy who came, the one with a sword, looked to be in his forties and was also smiling. On their turbans, Thug finally saw the sigil clearly. It was three swords. In the center was a thick, double-edged weapon, while two curved blades formed a half-circle, all three hilts crossing at the bottom.

"Well, that was a fun way to meet someone," he said.

The youngest man looked over at the beast and said, "Pity, he was so young."

"Young," said Thug, aghast "They get bigger?"

"Yes," said the woman with a laugh. "We call them swamp drakons. They're few in number, and deadly, but not too smart. They also keep out some of the more dangerous predators from the Green, so we try not to kill them that often. They never come to the city. I guess this one just didn't get the message to stay off the path. The younger ones do that. Anyway, I'm Sati. This man, the first you saw, is Rahma. The oldest is Guaro, and the youngest is Danny. Welcome to Plymouth."

"I'm Thug," said the rider, "Pleased to meet you."

Guaro stepped forward, looking at Thug up and down, and said, "You're a rider." He said this as fact, not a question.

"You know of my order?" asked Thug.

"I do," said Guaro, "My grandfather used to live in Marquette before he traveled down here. He told me many stories of the riders of the north."

Thug smiled kindly and was embarrassed as the other warriors looked in awe at Thug. Sati walked forward and said, "It's an honor to meet you, rider. Did the beast bite or scratch you? They are toxic."

"No," said Thug.

"I have to say, I was impressed about how you fought it," said Sati, "Few ever face one for the first time and are left unscathed."

"Thank you," said Thug, "I was impressed with the way you fought, too. You're fast, and well-trained."

"We better go," said Rahma, "That corpse is going to attract a lot of beasts."

Sati whistled, and out of the mist came three large carts, each pulled by large animals and controlled by two men, all wearing not the blue garb of the warriors, but they did have the turbans, bracelets, and knives just like them. They each had different colored turbans, and each sported beards that obscured their faces. The animals resembled cattle but had curly hair on their necks and faces and were much bigger.

"Beefalo," said Danny, sensing Thug's question. "They're stubborn, but good cart animals."

"I can ride my bike," said Thug.

"The carts are too slow," said Sati, "but we brought the big one to carry it. It won't slow us down.

They loaded the bike quickly, and Thug and Sati sat with it. Thug reloaded his rifle, and Sati sheathed her sword and pulled out her hunting rifle.

The carts moved at a slow pace, but still fast considering the size of their loads. The beefalo showed no fear in the mist, as they seemed to trust the men to keep an eye on their blind sides. They were all watchful, guns at the ready. After about fifteen minutes, they relaxed. Thug, looking at Sati, gave her a questioning look.

"The most dangerous part is over," said Sati, "The creatures that live here are going to be more interested in the free meat than chasing us. We'll be fine. We're almost to the city."

Thug relaxed a little, and Sati continued, "You can keep your weapons until we reach the city, however, once there, I need you to surrender your rifle. You can keep your knife and pistol, but I ask you keep them on your belt."

"Why are you letting me keep them?" asked Thug.

"Tradition," said Sati. "We believe you must always be able to protect yourself as well as others. So, we only take away the larger weapons, and let our guests keep the smaller ones."

"Sounds counter-productive," said Thug.

"All Sikh carry weapons here," said Sati, "Most are ceremonial, but it can still be intimidating, so we extend that courtesy to our guests. Besides, the Green is dangerous around here, especially with the swamp drakons, so we are cautious."

Thug nodded. "So, were you guys patrolling?"

"No," said Sati, "spying."

"On who?" asked Thug.

"At first Canton, and then you."

"Wait, you spy on your neighbors?"

"They do the same," said Sati with a smile, "We saw your fellow rider continuing to Canton, but you broke off and headed towards our town. We followed."

"How could you keep up with my bike?"

"We used the trees," said Sati. "We are trained in free running, which lets us move fast through them. When we reached the water, we followed in a boat, but kept our distance. When the swamp drakons came, we couldn't let you fight it alone. We chose to help."

"But what about the wagons, how did you know they were there?"

"We sent a bird ahead with a message, and they were ready to intercept you. They sent one to us when they were in position."

"Ok, you guys are good," said Thug, impressed.

Sati smiled in thanks, and they continued on. Soon the mist began to soften, and the wetlands gave way to dryer lands, which gave way to buildings. They were restored houses, spaced out at first, and were made into farms where vegetables grew. Past the farms were a collection of buildings. Some were made from old cargo containers, others were old houses, but the area was a hive of activity, smells, and color.

"This used to be what they called a subdivision," said Sati. "This and a few buildings were the only things in the city to survive the Green, but we rebuilt it."

"What made you guys settle here?" asked Thug.

"We used to live in Canton, but the Hindu population and us constantly butted heads. Our culture and religions were and are very different. We came here about three hundred years ago and found good land. The swamp drakons were a problem at first, but eventually, they learned to stay away from the city. We found a place finally, and we found peace. It took decades to build what we have, but we have a good life. Hundreds of thousands of Sikh live here, and we have good trade from neighboring villages. There are tensions with Canton and Dearborn, but they don't come here that often, fearing the swamp drakons."

As they entered the main collection of buildings, he saw more of the people dressed similarly, but each with a unique and individual style that made all of them stick out. As Thug watched them pass, what surprised him most was the women's styles. Some, like Sati, wore the hooded sash but kept their hair free under it. Others wore turbans, like the males, but still others wore a mix of the two. The males all wore turbans, but they were all different shapes, styles, and designs. Children ran freely through the street, a simple black cloth covering their hair, and all sporting different length beards.

Thug also noticed that they were not all of Arabic or Indian descent. There were African descendants like him, whites as well.

He also saw a few other people walking around, not like the inhabitants but from other communities. Skin-changers, Androgenans, and Otherkin walked around selling their wares.

"It's very welcoming here," observed Thug.

"Sikh naturally are," said Sati. "We are welcoming to all, in our homes, our shops, our temple."

"Temple?"

"Wait till you see it," said Sati with a smile, "It's a true wonder. My daughter loves going there."

"How old is she?" asked Thug.

"She's eight now," said Sati, "Wants to be a sculptor when she grows up."

"Where's she now?"

"With her father, at the shop."

"What does he do?"

"He's a painter, a good one. I was just starting in the guard when I met him. He was so passionate about his art, I fell in love with it, and with his passion. He's not a fighter with weapons, but he fought and won my heart. Do you have a spouse?"

A dark pit opened for a moment in Thug's heart, thinking about Chang and realizing he hadn't thought of him for several days now. What did that say, the pain? The pain, God, the pain, it was coming back, and Thug felt pressure on his eyes.

"I . . . I wasn't married to him, but, eh, I did have somebody.

His name was Chang."

"His name?" said Sati, confused.

"He was a rider like me, a pathfinder, but also a tracker, one of the best. He was killed in the Green. He fought to the end. Gods, I . . ."

Sati's confusion softened, seeing the large rider's pain. She put a hand on his shoulder. "I'm sorry, Thug, I didn't mean to upset you. And forgive my confusion. Most Sikhs are not homosexually inclined, and it's easy to forget that it is common even today. I'm sorry if I was rude; I can see you truly cared for him."

"Thank you," said Thug. "He died a warrior's death and fought till he couldn't anymore. I am proud of him for that. He was a great rider, but he never liked fighting as much as I did, but he still stole my heart."

She smiled, "So, why are you here?"

Thug gave his head a little shake, and said, "I came to this region with a few others after being sent by the riders and Marquette for an expedition to the south. We came to Detroit to resupply, but we are stuck since the last reports said that the Green was too thick to travel through past Jackson. We heard there may be a way past the Green in Canton, but the threat we are trying to find, and which attacked one of our colonies, has already destroyed two communities that we know of, so we were asked to go to Dearborn, Canton, and here to try and unite the region against it."

"What threat?" asked Sati.

"My home was attacked by a man named Kal. Kal was responsible for Chang's death, and for trying to turn the people against Marquette's government and the Riders. We stopped him, but he killed and seduced so many, and he did that alone. Others of his cult, we call Black Priests, also travel with a type of Otherkin we have never encountered, a wolf-type. They killed everybody in Traverse, and killed hundreds in Jackson, and they have been spotted in this region."

A look of revelation came over Sati's face, and she said, "We heard rumors of them moving around. Men dressed in black followed by wolfmen. We thought it was just a story."

"Not just a story," said Thug.

The wagons stopped in front of what looked like an old store. The sign had fallen years ago, but many blue garbed men and women walked around.

"This is one of our bases," she said. "Single soldiers live here. Married ones live throughout the city, but we report here. My men will help unload your equipment, but wait here, I'm going to get my commander."

Thug nodded, and when Sati left, Danny, Rahma, and Guaro gently unloaded the bike. Thug smoked a cigarette, and though the men looked slightly disapproving, they didn't harp on him. Thug smoked two others. Sati came back, behind her, a tall man, with a black beard, strong arms and back, wearing the blue uniforms of the men, but his shoulders had two bars on them. He looked at the motorcycle, impressed, and then saw the rider smoking next to it. He smiled, friendly as everyone else, walked forward, and shook the rider's hand.

"Good afternoon," said the man, "I am Captain Cody Singh, commander of this installation. You must be Thug."

"A pleasure," said the Rider.

Cody smiled, admiring the bike again, but looked at Thug, and said, "I realize you came a long way, and I have no doubt you have honorable intentions, but you have to understand how I see this. Two other riders, from what I understand, have gone to cities that we don't get along with at the best of times, and Detroit is a city which has a habit of trying to manipulate us. I have a hard time trying to justify what you are saying when you send representatives to our enemies and are working with a city which we feel doesn't have any invested interest in us."

Thug was ready for this, "These Black Priests kill without mercy. They don't care about your gods or your culture. In their minds, only their god or ruler, the Golden Lord, is worth any worship, and for those that resist them, they have no problem using fear and death to convert them. I'm wasting my time trying to convince you that this threat is bigger than your personal squabbles when people are dying, so if I wasted my time coming here, then tell me and I'll leave."

Cody looked impressed, then put a serious look on his face: "I believe what you are saying. Not many men would talk so brutally, most would grovel and try to suck up to me. However, it is not my decision, but that of the Maharaja, our leader. I will speak to him and try to get you an audience. In the meantime, Sati has said you are welcome at her home until then. I will send guards to protect your equipment. I ask, though, you leave your rifle here. You can keep the pistol and the knife, but the rifle must stay."

Thug obliged.

Once done, Thug offered to give Sati a ride to her place on his bike, an offer she was thrilled to take. She wrapped her arms around his waist and said, "Don't go easy on me."

Thug grinned and revved up, the bike streaking down the dirt road. He sped down it, Sati whooping in excitement, using her hands to give directions until they reached a house standing alone on the outskirts of the city. It was painted in bright colors and was littered with chips of stone and wood. The house itself was two stories, red brick on the bottom, white wood slats on top, with a wood-shingled roof.

In the front yard sat a man wearing a white turban and a long white tunic that was paint-stained, an easel and canvas in front of him. In one hand was a paint brush, his other hand holding a little girl, eight years old, wearing similar garbs, and her hair was in a ponytail, but free from any covering. Her father handed her a brush and using the same hand, showed her how to add paint to the canvas in the shade he was looking for. The girl's face screwed up in concentration.

The man looked up, hearing the engine, and his face went slack, seeing his wife holding on to a strange, leather-clad Black man on a motorcycle. The girl saw it too, and dropped the brush, dropped off her father's lap, and ran forward, yelling, "Mommy, mommy."

Sati swung off the bike and scooped the excited girl into her arms, who wrapped her own around Sati's neck.

"Oh," said Sati, with a big smile on her face, "I missed you, Aarti."

She put the girl down, kissing her cheek, and stood as the man in the paint-stained tunic came over, still with a look of confusion, but with a smile on his face, happy to see his wife.

"My Sati," said the man, putting his hands on her cheeks and kissing her passionately, causing Thug to blush and look away.

"I missed you, Manojo," whispered Sati, seductively.

Still holding her waist, he turned towards Thug and asked, "Who is your friend?"

"This is Thug," said Sati, "He's from Marquette. He is a rider."

Manojo looked up, surprised, and said, "I thought they were just legends."

He shook Thug's hand and looked at the bike, examining every inch of the machine.

"It's truly a work of art," said Manojo, "I never thought I'd see one this close outside of Detroit. It's astounding, balanced, well taken care of. It almost feels like a living thing."

"In a lot of ways, it is," said Thug, smiling and pleased that the man showed appreciation for the monster bike, "I've had it since I was eighteen. I covered so many miles on it, and I never trade it for anything."

"What about maintenance, upkeep, and fluid changes?" asked Manojo, "We tried to recreate them here but failed."

"The Green opened a huge oil bed near Marquette that we were able to tap. We were able to refine it and make the products we need to power and lubricate it. As for maintenance, most of the parts we need are made in forges, but we have some new plants that have helped refine the process. Again, the Green changed a lot in the lands, and we can mine for the metals we need."

"Are you able to produce your own bikes yet?" asked Manojo, excited.

"Not yet," said Thug, "Not like the Ancients. The ones we

found were in warehouses and museums we found. We have many, not enough for mass use, but certainly enough for the order."

"All the same, or different types?"

"Different brands and types were found, and we use the different types we have for different jobs."

"Amazing," said Manojo.

"Manojo," said Sati, chuckling, "leave the man alone."

Manojo stood, embarrassed, "Sorry. Well, welcome to our home."

"I thank you," said Thug with a smile. "Sati says you're an artist by trade."

Manojo scratched the back of his head, his silver bracelet sliding down his arm and said, "Well, yes, I am."

"Is it just personal for you, or do you do it as your trade?"

"Well, um, my work is well known. I even have the Maharaja as a patron . . .gods, I shouldn't be such a showoff."

"Your work speaks volumes," said Sati, rolling her eyes, "Everyone says so."

"Yes, but god says to be humble," said Manojo.

"Manojo," said Sati, exasperated.

The little girl walked up to her father, grabbed his large hands with her small ones, and said, "My daddy is the best artist ever."

Manojo blushed and smiled at his little girl. "Come on in, I have curry and chai waiting inside."

Manojo led the way, picking up Aarti and holding Sati's hand. A perfect family, an image Thug wished he could have had with Chang. Chang, there was so much they would never have.

They walked. The mix of turpentine, hot spices, and warmth entered Thug's nose. The walls were covered in long slats, giving it the feel similar to a rider's lodge. He saw the walls were covered in paintings, of landscapes, of symbols, of rivers, and many other things. He saw small sculptures on the floor, beautifully crafted in the shape of lions. As he walked in the front room opened, and he saw a table surrounded by two comfy chairs and a couch.

"Okay, Aarti," said Manojo, "We have to change."

"I thought we were painting all day," Aarti pouted.

"We will tomorrow to make up for today," said Manojo, "But we have a guest, and we must make him feel welcome."

"Promise?" said Aarti, her eyes sparkling.

"I promise, now change."

"Yay."

The girl ran off. Sati rolled her eyes, looking at her husband teasingly, saying, "You spoil that child."

"Well, I did promise her," said Manojo, with a smile.

"She is going to be so bratty when she's older," said Sati.

"That's why we have the swords."

"Manojo, for heaven's sake," said Sati with a laugh.

"I better change," he said with a smile, "Please serve the chai to our guest, my love. I'll join you when I'm done."

They kissed and he walked off.

"You have a lovely family," said Thug.

"Thank you," said Sati, going into a room for a moment and coming back with a pot and a tray. She poured four glasses of what looked like coffee and cream and added sugar to it. Thug took a tentative sip, and then smiled. It tasted nothing like coffee, but it was amazing.

"It's great."

"Thank you," said Sati, "So I have to ask, is Thug your real name?"

Thug smiled, and responded, "No, my real name is Terrance Joel, but I got the nickname during my training because I loved to fight. It just stuck after I was raised as a rider."

"When did you start your training?"

"When I was twelve. My parents died of the pox when I was eight, and I ended up living in the streets, living on scraps. A rider found me fighting for food against five bigger guys, and he took me to Marquette lodge. There, I was trained until I was raised at eighteen. I became a Pathfinder."

"What do Pathfinders do?"

"Pathfinders seek out new roads, and also keep them clear

of the beasts that dwell in the Green. We also try to find communities and towns that were in the Green to colonize."

"What other types of riders are there?"

"Well, there's the Truck Clan. They move supplies throughout the Green with trucks we find. They have bikes too, and use them, but trucks are their main field. Then there are the Road builders. They repair the roads and maintain them so colonies can move about the Green freely. Then, there are the Keepers. Keepers are very important; they keep the lodges we live in maintained, supplied, and warm. They feed us, clothe us, and give us a place to rest. Unlike the other riders, Keepers don't go into the Green. Once a Keeper is given a lodge, it's a lifetime there."

"Sounds fun," said Sati.

Manojo and Aarti came out a second later. Manojo wore jeans and a blue button up shirt, along with a blue turban, and a leather belt with a small ceremonial knife on it. Aarti wore a simple red dress. She went to her mother on the couch and sat on her lap, and Sati stroked her hair. Manojo sat in one of the chairs, as did Thug.

"Dinner will be ready soon," said Manojo.

"As long as it's fresh meat," said Thug, with a smile, and it disappeared when they all got a frown on their faces. "What?"

"Ummmm," said Sati, "Sikh don't eat meat."

"Oh," said Thug, awkwardly, "well, I'll still try it."

They all laughed. The meal was actually pretty tasty. Thug enjoyed the curry, despite its lack of meat.

They spent the night talking about each other's cultures, and Aarti fell asleep on her mother's lap. She picked her up and took her to bed. She rejoined her husband and Thug, and they continued to talk. They talked about Manojo's work, Sati joining the guard, and Thug's life as a rider. They talked for so long, they didn't notice they had all fallen asleep in their couches until they heard a knock at the door. Sati answered. It was Cody. Thug knew before he spoke that it was time to meet the Maharaja.

7 Maharaja

Five guards escorted Thug, riding on large creatures. They looked like sheep but didn't have wool. Instead, they had smooth fur and large curved horns. Sati explained they were big horn sheep, and they were more reliable in this land than horses were.

They took off into the city, passing people enjoying the day or working. Sikhs, other people of the regular, Skin Changing, Androgenan, and Otherkin variety walked, talked, and traded. Thug even saw a duck-head Otherkin with a green, feathery body being fitted with Sikh silk.

They soon reached a small lake, and Thug was struck with awe. Two buildings were on the other side of the Lake. One was a religious temple made of gold, or at least painted so. The other was a large mansion. The place was swarming with people, in bright colors, showing wealth and prosperity.

"The palace," said Sati, "And the temple that holds the Guru Granth Sahib."

"What's that?" asked Thug.

"Our holy book," explained Sati, "I guess you can call it the Sikh bible. It's the book we take our teachings from."

Thug nodded and they continued, with people staring at Thug and his bike. In his leather jacket, jeans, boots, and bandana, he looked out of place in this strange world. They saw him as a sort of oddity, and he guessed in a way he was an oddity. He was riding a machine from the past, used as transportation and a weapon, looking like what old books and movies would call a biker gangster. Ah well, might as well not dwell.

They didn't go to the palace, instead, they headed to the temple. They pulled up, and Thug got off his bike. Cody and Sati both joined him, standing on either side, while the other two stayed on their riding sheep, guarding the bike. They entered. The inside was a great, vast hall, painted gold, and in the center was a raised altar made of gold and topped by a golden awning. In the center was a large book. There was only one man inside.

Hearing them enter, the man stood, and turned. He wore white, wool shirt and pants, no shoes, and a white turban. He wasn't old, but his face had years of experience. He was well-muscled and had a black beard, not overly long but respectable. He was not overly tall but had a sturdy frame. He walked on the red carpet that floored the hall and stood before Thug. Sati and Cody bowed but Thug stood, facing him. He wasn't one to lower himself when he was doing business. He stuck out his hand. The man looked at it, then at Thug, then smiled respectfully, and shook it.

"Hello," said the man, "I am Kynel, the Maharaja of Plymouth."

"I'm Terrance, but most people call me Thug."

"Thug," said Kynel, rolling the word on his tongue, "I like that; it's strong."

"May I ask why we speak here?"

"Of course. Most governmental business I perform in my home, but I have a feeling I will need the strength of the one and mighty god of the universe to guide me on the path that is best for my people."

"Admirable," said Thug.

The two men sat. Sati and Cody went outside. They were silent in the vast hall for a while, but Thug waited. A half hour passed, and then . . .

"I have most of the story. You came here seeking our aid. There are also two other riders in Canton, the city of Gods, and Dearborn, also known as New Mecca. I know you home was attacked by a force that destroyed both Traverse and Jackson and has brought your people out of your own isolation."

"We are not Isolationists," said Thug, reproachfully.

"Not in your eyes," said Kynel with a half-smile, "You see yourselves as explorers, and you have gone as far as Detroit, but up until now, did you know of our cities? Our problems? Our dangers? My city is great, and we know much of this region, and beyond it, and the many people who live there, but your people had no interest."

Thug was about to speak but Kynel raised his hand, "I am not chastising you. You've built much and your legend has spread, but the only thing that brought you out of your comfort was an outside threat. Outside threats often are the only thing that bring outsiders together, for better or for worse, and at this moment, after all I have heard and understood, I understand why. Like you, I will do whatever it takes to protect my people; I just want you to understand how I see things. Now, what is your city offering for us to work together with cities we are in a state of cold war with?"

"Power," said Thug, "The power of the ancients."

"And?" asked Kynel.

Thug leaned back. This was going to take a while. He wished Chang was here.

Chapter 7

War Drums

---

1 Visions Near and Far

Marven sat meditating while Watu rested, the large white bear snoring. Marven looked over at his old friend, knowing he wasn't going to be happy about waking up this late, but he had no choice. He put a hand on the bear's shoulder and gently shook it. Watu blinked awake and looked over at the wizard.

'I think you should rethink that choice, old man.'

"Sorry, but it's been a while since we've been to Etam," said Marven.

Watu closed his eyes, then a moment later opened them. *'There is a strong echo.'*

"Do it," said Marven.

The world around Marven dissolved and in moments, he found he was following a group of riders in golden armor, and a Black Priest. On the back of the Black Priest's horse was a girl. The girl was the memory Watu sensed. Her presence was the clearest. However, Marven was more interested in the Black Priest. He had a look of determined disgust on his face, one which he had never seen from the servants of the Golden Lord. They always had a look of pride. Strange, he was going to have to keep an eye on this priest.

They reached the palace, and the guards grabbed the girl, a peasant from the outskirts by the looks of it. Holding each of her arms, they entered a side passage through the east wing. They entered, and the Black Priest led her down to a dark, dungeon-like area lit by dull torches.

They continued down the passage, pausing at a black door at the end, and the priest grabbed the girl's arm. He looked at the guards, nodded to them, and they left. As soon as they were out of earshot, the priest looked at the girl, who had a look of fear on her face. She was skinny with brown mousy hair and pretty features. She couldn't have been more than fourteen. The priest looked at her and whispered two words into her ear.

"I'm sorry," he said, then opened the door.

The room was lit by eerie black flames shining a strange, purple light. They flickered and a shadow of a large, hunched shape appeared. The being turned, and Marven felt a cold dread. The being had a horse skull for a head, and its flesh was a sickly gray. The worst part of it was the bones. The bones on its arms were sticking out, like the flesh melted around them, healed, but kept the bones revealed.

"Lord of Bones," said the Black Priest.

The creature shuffled forward and pushed the Black Priest away, then looked at him, saying in a horrible deep voice, "Leave us, Blaine."

"Yes, my lord," said the priest, shooting the girl a last glance of pity, and left.

The beast raised a thick arm that ended in horrible claws, and with the tip of one, tore away the girls' clothing. The girl tried to cover herself, but the creature pulled her arms away, enjoying her body while tears rolled down her eyes.

"Such a pretty thing," it said, almost purring in seductive overtones that made the girl stiffen in fear. Marven felt disgust. "A pity I was commanded to leave you intact. But for the ritual, it does require me to do so."

Marven had the instinct to stop the beast. The Lord of Bones, the most vile and evil of the Great Old Ones. Even the Golden Lord did not disgust him as much as The Lord of Bones did. The creature of dark magic and horror, such a beast brought no God in the mind of Marven.

He watched as the beast tapped the girl on the forehead, and she went into a deep trance. He brought her to a stone table in the center of the room, and over top of her, looked at her with a sick hunger. How many girls and boys this beast had molested, he did not know, only knowing the sickness of the beast was endless as was his appetite for pleasure and power.

Over top of her, the beast began to chant, and pulled a vial from the counter. He dipped the tip of a claw into it and pulled out a single drop of black ooze. With a gentle touch, he put the drop into the girl's belly button and continued the chant, his hands making circular motions over top of her.

For a moment there was nothing but the chanting, then the ooze began to spread out from the girl's belly button, spreading across her body. The girl screamed in agony but couldn't escape from the beast enchantments. The ooze spread across her body, entering all of her orifices, and soon she resembled a humanoid pile of old, used oil. Then it began to meet together, forming a single mass. It grew larger and the screams continued, those agonizing screams of pain that made Marven's heart weep.

Marven blinked, and he was back in the present, and Watu looked at him, seeing the sweat and horror on his old friend's face.

"We have to go to the city. Now."

The bear stood, without question, and Marven put a hand on the bear's fur. The two walked two steps, and then, they were in an empty corner of Detroit. God, Marven hated this city.

2 Witches and Lights

Jack and Kato rode up to the gate, with XB7889 in Jack's side cart. The robot was deactivated at the moment to help with the deception they were planning to pull to get XB into the city. They pulled up to the guard, who, while coming towards them, paused upon seeing the robot. He stared for a moment and asked, "Where did you find that?"

"Out patrolling the Green," said Jack simply. "Kato got curious and wanted to bring it in to study while we were in Detroit."

"What can I say?" said Kato, a wolfish grin on his Irish setter's face, "I was fascinated by ancient technology."

The guard walked up and tapped the robot on the side of the head. XB's head rolled to the side, lifeless, not a single light blinking. The guard sighed, "Fuck, alright go in."

The gate opened a few minutes later and the two were soon back into the bustling market square, passing through the quarters, and soon pulled into the parking garage. When parked, Jack got off his bike, and knocked at XB's head.

"Hey, XB, we are here."

In a minute, XB7889 got out of standby mode and went into full power up mode, stepping out of the side cart.

"Have we arrived in the city?"

"Yep," said Kato, "Now, how do we get to the Cloud facility?"

"There are several entrances through the city that I should be able to access. One is about a quarter of a mile from here."

"Well, lead the way," said Jack.

XB looked at Jack with his glowing eyes, and said, "Please remember, I am carrying only the memories of what I had from the last Cloud facility, and any discrepancies may slow my progress. My processing unit can only go so far at any one time. There are still limitations to my ability to process and store information until the Cloud facility is reactivated. Also, I am losing power at a rate of eight percent a day when kept activated, and I am currently down to fifty percent."

"I'll keep an eye on you," said Kato.

"May I come too?" asked a voice. The robot and the two riders turned and saw the man. Kato stared at the man in orange robes and dreadlocks.

"Ummmm," Kato said with confusion, "Who are you?"

Jack looked at Marven with a smile and said, "I thought you didn't want to come to the city."

"Situations call for me going outside my comfort zone," said Marven, also sporting a grin.

"Jack, you know this guy?" asked Kato.

"I met him in Ironwood," said Jack, "I'll explain later. He is a friend, or at least, has the same goals as us."

"Huh?" said Kato.

"We must be going," said XB, and began to walk towards the exit. Jack, Kato, and Marven followed.

As they walked, Jack asked, "So, why are you here? Is Watu here?"

"Who is Watu?" asked Kato.

"A friend," said Marven, with a sly grin, giving Kato's dog-like head a look of even more confusion, "Yes, he is here, doing what he does, though what that entails I know not."

"So why come?"

"I'll explain later," said Marven, "One mission at a time."

They walked in the main city with buildings, many damaged, towering over them like old stone giants, the workmanship of the Ancients slowly crumbling. Then they reached a tower, and over the entrance was a sign in strange writing.

"This can't be it," said XB. "This tower was one of the entrances and its sign was in Japanese. This sign is in ancient Nordic lettering."

Marven looked at it, and said, "I believe it was repurposed by the inhabitants. These letters say, 'The Coven of Black.' I think this is a Wiccan coven."

"I have no record of Wiccan's purchasing this building from the Tokahama Corporation," exclaimed XB, "These people must be evicted."

"I think not," said Marven.

"Who are Wiccans?" asked Jack.

"When magic was returning, Gerald Gardener was the first to create this movement of magic. It is not powerful, but it was among one of the first signs that magic was returning after the black plague. They study the magic of the Earth. I don't think it a coincidence that we found both an entrance to your facility at the same time we found a coven."

"It does seem convenient," said Kato with a growl.

"Most of life is convenient," said Marven, "You live long enough, you learn conveniences have more power over that of things like destiny. Come, let us enter."

They entered. The entrance was dark, only lit by a few candles. The inside smelled of incense and melting wax, giving the entrance a haunting feel. There was an air of mystery inside, one that was similar to Marven's house back in Ironwood, a feeling of magic in the air.

Then they heard the chanting. The chanting was coming from deeper in the building, and it drew the three men in while XB followed, muttering about trespassers. They took a left and followed down the candled light hall. All the drapes had been pulled over the windows, leaving their path in twilight.

They came to the room where the chanting was where a sight hit their eyes and XB processors with the force of thunder.

The room was large, candle lit, and filled with twelve people. They wore black clothing of various types and styles, all on their feet, hands together, and forming a circle around a pentagram carved on the wooden floor. In the center was a short, blonde woman in a black robe, leading them in the chant. Both men and women followed her lead, and there seemed to be a glow in the pentagram in the ground.

Still chanting, the woman in the center turned, and Jack saw it wasn't a woman. It was an Androgenan, neither male or female, and the result was that of an odd beauty. It stood there, continuing the chant and smiled at the visitors.

They continued for about five minutes, and then it ended, and they all turned towards the four at the door. With the candlelight reflecting off their faces now, Jack could see them quite clearly. Six were regular humans - two white, a male and female, an ebony skinned woman, two Chinese, both males, and one Indian woman. Two were skin changers - both females, and they were the hardest to make out, their skins patterned to resemble the sky at night. Two more Androgenans and a Rabbit-type Otherkin stood there, too. They looked at the interlopers with a mix of curiosity and caution.

"Welcome," said the Androgenan in the center, "I am Stanel, high priest of the Coven of Black. These are my disciples. And you are?"

"I'm Jack. A rider and pathfinder of Marquette and her colonies."

"I am Kato. A rider and a member of the Truck Clan of Marquette and her colonies."

"I am Marven, one of many lands and titles. Who are you?"

Stanel looked confused, "I just told you."

"You told me what you are, not who you are. If you wish to master magic, you need more knowledge than what you have, though you are on the right track."

Stanel gave a confused look for a moment longer, but then a look of clarity entered its face and smiled, then went on with, "Then I will endeavor to find the answer you seek."

Marven grinned. Kato looked even more confused. Jack smiled inwardly. Looking at Jack, Stanel walked forward, put a hand on his chest, and closed its eyes for a moment.

"You carry great pain," it said. "It is like a piece of you died, and the wound is still festering. Did you lose someone recently?"

Jack felt a moment of disquiet at Stanel's explanation, feeling as if it could read him. But the kind look in its eye urged him to answer.

"Yes," he said slowly, "My wife."

Sympathy entered Stanel's face, and it said, "That wound won't heal, nor should it, for such a loss of a loved one will not ever be replaced. But over time, you will accept this and learn how to deal with it. Till then, you will need your friends."

Stanel moved over to Kato, put its hand on the Dog-type Otherkin's chest, and said, "Most in the city see this place as slowly dying, only staying for it is one of our few refuges in the Green. But you see more, Kato, you see a world that held back the Green, and allowed us to rebuild what the Ancients left behind. You see beauty where others see death. It is a great gift, especially for an Otherkin, who were for a long time seen as outcasts. You have a great heart."

Kato gave a wolfish grin, and bowed his head, "Thank you."

Then Stanel put its hand on Marven, who smiled. Stanel stood quiet for a moment, then opened its eyes and said, "You carry great power, far greater than mine and that of my followers, but while you know you have the power to help, you know doing so will damage so much. You are a tragic being, Marven. I am sorry."

Marven bowed in thanks and said, "As am I."

Stanel gripped him for a moment longer, then returned to its flock, and asked, "What brings you to our coven?"

"This is an eviction notice from the Tokahama Corporation," said XB quickly, "Please leave the premises immediately, or I will summon security to forcibly remove you."

Stanel looked confused, and Jack and Kato both gave the robot fierce looks. "Shut up," snapped Jack. "Sorry, he is a little behind the times."

XB went quiet but seemed to be almost indignant.

"He is part of the reason why we are here, though," said Jack. "XB 7889 believes that there is a facility entrance in your building. We are trying to access it."

Clarity entered Stanel's face, and it looked at the robot, and said, "I know what you seek, and I will help, but Marven wants something different."

"I wish to speak to you," said Marven, "About your practices, if that is alright."

"Of course," said Stanel with a smile. "We always are willing to talk to fellow practitioners. Please follow me."

It grabbed a candle, and as it and the visitors left, the disciples went back to chanting. The sound followed them eerily as they walked up an old staircase outside the sanctuary. They moved down it until they reached a hall covered by a curtain. They entered it, the only light being that of the candle that bobbed in Stanel's hand. Then they reached the end of the hall, and in front of them, in the glow of the candle was a metal door. There was no handle, no buttons, it just stood there.

"This is the only door I have never been able to open," said Stanel. "And I have tried."

XB walked forward, looking at the metal door, and put a hand on it, its white plating glowing in the candle. For a moment, nothing happened, and then, the door slid to the side, revealing a dark passage.

"This is it," said XB matter-of-factly. "Please follow."

"I'll stay here," said Marven, "I want to talk to this coven."

"We'll be back," said Jack.

XB led the way but seemed to be going slightly slower as the robot, Jack, and Kato, went into the passage. They steadily descended with another staircase.

They walked down lower and lower, and time seemed to be at a standstill as they walked, with the darkness oppressive among them. Their slow descent made it feel as if they were not moving. Lower and lower they went, and some claustrophobia hit both Kato and Jack, but still they walked. Lower and lower, the sounds of their steps echoed. Lower and lower, feeling as if they hit the pits of hell and had gone past them. Lower and lower, darkness and noise, noise and darkness, both melding into one and soon it seemed one couldn't exist without the other, as if should one stop, the world would collapse into oblivion, and all would be nothing but ash.

Then they did stop, and oblivion didn't happen. In the blue glow of XB's eye light, came the glow of metal, another door. Again, XB held out a hand, and the door slid. So long in darkness, the light that came from the entrance was blinding for a moment, forcing both Jack and Kato to hold up their arms for a brief moment.

They adjusted after a minute and gasped. The room was domed and could fit a large house inside. Panels, metal, stations, and monitors were lining the walls and ceiling. Sealed from the outside world, the facility was free from dust, bugs, and other things that had caused too much decay in the world after the Green. The metal still shown, the lights still burned brightly, and the power still flowed.

"Welcome to the main Cloud facility of the Midwest and East Coast of the USA," said XB, who seemed more lively than ever, practically glowing in the facility.

"It's amazing," said Kato, aghast, reminding Jack of how Brute had the same look when the dog got treats. He didn't mention this out loud, as comparing Otherkin to actual animals is insulting.

"I can't believe how intact it is. So much tech, still active. I've been studying the technology of the Ancients all my life, and we haven't even scratched the surface. This, this is amazing, even more so than the facility we came across before."

"The Tokahama Corporation was pioneering in both technological and economic developments," said XB, going to a control panel, and putting his hand on it. The panel glowed and then the lights got brighter, and a voice spoke, that seemed to come from everywhere.

"Welcome to Cloud Facility 1; the Tokahama Corporation welcomes you. No updates from home station Tokyo are currently scheduled, so normal operations will resume. All devices can now connect to the Cloud Network. Please enjoy your day."

"Well, that was fast," said Jack.

"That's it?" asked Kato in surprise.

"That's it," said XB, and he sounded excited, "The facility is now back up and running."

Suddenly remembering the cell phone given to him by the Otaku, Jack pulled it up, and saw, to his amazement, it was on and active. Excited to get back to his research about Etam, he went to explore the phone, when a message popped up. It said, "Please type your credit or debit card number."

"Um, XB, what's this about?"

He showed the robot the phone. XB responded with, "You must pay for the services of the Tokahama Corporation in order to access the Cloud Network."

"What's a credit card?" asked Jack.

XB eyes glowed, giving an impression of being shocked. "What do you mean?"

"What, is it like flattened gold or something?" asked Jack.

"I assume you are joking. However, on the off chance you are not, the employees at the substation have already handled payment. I will upload the information to your devices now."

A moment later, the phone unlocked, and Jack was shocked at the many icons on the device, different shapes and designs. It would take time to learn what each did, so he decided to wait until they were back in their rooms. Putting the phone in his pocket, Jack watched as XB and Kato explored the cave, Kato asking XB what each button and screen did, and how they function. It was like watching a child asking his mother to let him try all the food at carnival.

Jack lit a cigarette and started puffing on it, waiting for them to get done with their task. When they were ready, XB came over and said, "I sent a report to the Tokahama Corporation. They should send a security detail to remove the squatters who have settled in Detroit."

"Good luck," said Jack with a grin. "Let's get back up."

The three of them started the ascent and Jack studied the phone on the way up, tapping the screen and exploring the different icons and what they did, separating him from the darkness of the stairwell.

They reached the hall and moved their way back to the sanctuary. There, Marven had joined them in the chanting, joining the other disciples in the ritual they were performing. Stanel stood in the center, and the pentagram was glowing again. The power glowed among them, giving off a type of calm that

Jack hadn't felt in a while. It was in his skin, his muscles, even his bones. It felt almost relieving.

After a moment, the group looked up, and Marven and Stanel moved towards the three.

"How was it?" asked Jack.

"Enlightening," said Marven, and he turned and kissed Stanel's hand, "Until next time."

Stanel nodded, then said to Jack, "Remember, you can learn to live with pain; you just need to accept it."

Jack nodded. After that they left. Jack was surprised how little his eyesight needed to adjust outside, as the dark cloud of the sweat and work that was Detroit's factories covered the sky in darkness. Until now, Jack hadn't thought about the Cloud overhead, and knowing that beyond it was another type of cloud. The dark cloud was the cloud of work. The invisible one was the cloud of knowledge.

"That was insightful," said Marven cheerfully.

"Learn much?" asked Jack.

"Much. They are very advanced in magic. Not quite at the level of the Magic users or Warlocks like me but getting there. They have much to offer the world once they have perfected their craft. It's good to see magic returning to the world."

Jack nodded. Kato was confused again. XB said, "Magic is an

unproven form of paganistic, supernatural nonsense that . . ." then he fell down as if he tripped as Marven looked at him.

"Stupid machine," muttered Marven under his breath.

"I appear to have tripped," said XB. Jack grinned.

They walked down the street, noticing the hustle and bustle of the city, and when they reached the Renaissance Center, they saw the Viceroy, with seven guards walking towards a pickup truck, restored and operational. Then Jack saw Grenn, Miko, and Tricks behind him, working their way through the hustle of what now, as Jack saw, was guards. The four of them got to Grenn and the others, and the Viceroy, who looked up and saw Jack, Kato, XB, and Marven.

"Where were you?" snapped Miko, seeing them melting out of the crowd.

"Long story," said Jack, "What's going on?"

"Someone is outside the gate. A Black Priest and more of those wolfmen we ran into."

Jack's stomach dropped, and Kato, remembering the bites from his last encounter with the wolfmen like Otherkin, began to snarl in rage, revealing the feral side all Otherkin had inside them. Marven looked stunned, and mutter, "I thought we had more time."

Jack and the others didn't catch that, and the Viceroy stepped forward and said, "I gathered the city guard to the front gate. I already have sentries on the towers and have sealed all entrances to the other gates. They won't be coming in that way."

"Have they made demands?" asked Jack.

"No," said Harris, "But we are about to find out."

3 Black Priests, Dark Kin, and Lovecraft up in here

Jack, Kato, Grenn, Miko, and Tricks were back on their bikes, escorting Harris per his request on their bikes. They reached the gates, and they all dismounted. The market was being evacuated, and two thirds of the city guard was here. Not just soldiers, but armored vehicles, police cars, fire trucks, and civilian models repurposed for combat. Around 16,000 guardsmen and five hundred vehicles were in place, with half the men going to the gate.

The remaining guards were at the docks, prepared for an invasion of the waterfront. Harris was not taking any chances.

A Black man wearing the blue of the city guard met with Harris and said, "Sir, we have about two thousand hostiles outside the city. They seem to have no guns but are armed with knives and other bladed weapons. They appear to be dog-type Otherkin, but I say they are more wolf-like myself. There are also two men in black with them, seeming to lead them. We evacuated the outlying farms, and the city is on lock down."

“Good,” said Harris, “What is the enemy doing now?”

“Nothing,” said the guard, “They're just standing there. They didn’t even stop us evacuating the farms. But one of the men in black demands to talk to you, and sir, I just have to say, his voice, it, it’s strange. It was as if it was pulling my head, demanding me to obey whatever it said.”

“We have encountered that,” said Jack. “Viceroy, I strongly suggest you just take them out now.”

“We’re protected by walls,” said Harris. “They can’t get in, and we outnumber them more than ten to one. I won’t just go out there and slaughter them.”

“Viceroy,” began Jack, but Harris cut him off.

“That’s final, rider,” said Harris, then to the guard, “I’m going to the wall to try to reason with them. Get six thousand men on the wall, and the remainder at standard formation throughout the city.”

Harris began to head for the gate, Jack, the other riders, and guards trailing behind. Jack came to his shoulder and said, “Sir, I strongly urge you to reconsider. These priests don't care what you have to say. They are only loyal to their leader, who they think of as a god. I urge you . . .”

“I will not start killing indiscriminately just because of ideology,” snapped Harris. “The Ancients did that throughout history and killed millions. Do you wish to see that in this time?”

Jack went silent, but he had his hand on his gun, ready to fire at a moment's notice. They reached the gate's ascending steps and started climbing up the stone and metal wall. They climbed as quickly as they could, until they reached the top, and stood at the top of the wall, looking out towards the Green, then down below at the two thousand Wolfmen. They were just standing there, looking up at the wall. They didn't move, they didn't even yell, they just stood there.

Jack grabbed binoculars from a guard next to him and looked down, scanning the group below. He found them at the head of the formation of monsters. Two men dressed all in black, from hat to boot stared up at the wall, watchful and angry at the city's defiance. A surge of rage flooded Jack, rage he hadn't felt since Niki's death, and with that rage came memories. With those memories came an extreme wave of despair that made him want to pull out his gun and fire down at the two Black Priest's necks. This was one of the few times he wished he carried a rifle instead of a shotgun, the two too far down for the buckshot to do any good.

"Get me the megaphone," said Harris.

"I've heard of those," said Kato excitedly. "Supposed to increase the volume of your voice by a factor of . . ."

"Kato," said Grenn, "Now's not the time."

A guard brought the device, which looked to Jack like a

combination of a blow horn and gun. Harris grabbed the handle and aimed it down to the crowd of monsters below.

"This is Harris, Viceroy of Detroit," Harris said, his voice booming clearly over the wall. "You are ordered to disperse, and for motivation, over six thousand guns are aimed right at your heads. Any movements that can be considered hostile to the city will end up with you dead in front of the gates. I have no wish to do this, so withdraw."

One of the Black Priests stepped forward. Looking like specks down there, he looked like an ant almost. Then the voice came, not amplified, but somehow seeming to travel through the air and enter their ears. The same, familiar pulling in his head hit Jack with an all too familiar ring. The guards began to focus on the priests, and even Harris seemed speechless for a few moments.

"This city must be cleansed till only the worthy stand and make the journey to Etam. Your faithlessness and oppression of the people's true hearts, which you suppress and kill with false religions and false hope, has been blackened and twisted. Only through faith in the Golden Lord can they be saved."

Jack put a hand on Harris' arm, shook it, and then said, "Remember Traverse and Jackson."

Harris shook his head, then his eyes cleared, and yelled, "Snap out of it guys, we are loyal to Detroit, not these bastards."

Most of the guards shook their heads. Others were still

dazed, their battle strength helping them to focus. Harris raised the megaphone, and yelled, "You will leave this city; you are barred from entering. Leave now."

"The engine of your doom comes from the south and will soon be upon you," said the Black Priest. "And when it comes, your walls will be rubble, your city torn down, and all heretics will be ash."

Jack saw the priests walk away, but their Wolfmen stayed. Jack turned to Harris, who looked confused.

"The engine of our doom," said Tricks. "So cheesy."

Jack looked at Kato, who shrugged, as did Grenn and Miko.

"What's south of here?" Jack asked Harris, "Directly south?"

"Nothing but the Green," said Harris. "No cities, nothing."

"Kato," said Jack, "You and Tricks come with me. The rest of you, stay with the Viceroy."

Jack ran back below with the other two riders. They ran and saw who they were looking for - Marven and XB. XB was in a duster, blue jeans, black shirt, boots, goggles, with a bandana where a human mouth and nose should be, shaded goggles, and a wide brim hat. Marven suggested with all going on, they should disguise XB. XB was not happy about it.

"They said something is coming from the South," said Jack. "I don't know how far, but according to Harris, there is nothing but Green."

"We can use the satellite network to see what they are talking about," said XB.

"Huh," said Jack.

"The Tokahama Corporation controlled several satellites in orbit for their real-time traffic updates but can also map the world in real time. I can access it through the Cloud."

"Well, do it," snapped Kato.

"Of course," said the robot. XB went still. Five minutes passed, then ten, then fifteen. At twenty minutes, XB went, "Oh dear."

"What," said Jack, "What do you see?"

"You can observe by connecting your phone via Bluetooth," explained XB.

"What?"

"Go through and go to the Bluetooth setting."

Jack did, finding the strange icon.

"Now press it, and then look for XB 7889-1203, that will allow you to see what I see."

Jack did, and the picture changed. He saw the Green from above, and he couldn't help but gasp. He was seeing the world from above. There was a vast sea of Green covering it, endless and unbreakable. The only breaks he saw were water spots. He couldn't even see human settlements above, it was just too dense, too alien.

The screen zoomed in, and the Green filled the screen even more. But then he saw it, a path, a path that cut through the Green, and the camera followed it until . . .

"Holy fuck," said Jack, as the others joined him. It was a monstrous, black ooze of a monster, its body shifting, forming large tentacles that cut through the forest, felling the mighty trees. It rolled through, a horrible mass of shifting mass, destructive, and deadly. It was horrible to look at and observe as it cut through the Green.

"What the fuck is that?" asked Kato, baring his Irish Setter's teeth in fear.

"I cannot say for certain," said XB, "But it appears to have a similar appearance to a Hellmaker from Etam Kingdom."

"What?" asked Kato.

"In the game, Hellmakers are a large creature that are created by dark wizards in the land of Etam. It requires a virgin and a potion, according to the game rules. Once that is finished, the creature is unleashed, and sent to destroy whatever it was made to destroy."

"This is a fictional character?" asked Jack, "from the game the Otaku mentioned back in the Cloud facility?"

"Yes," said the robot, "this appears to be a full-size replica."

"It's the real thing," said Marven, gravely.

"How?" asked Jack.

“I don’t know how, but it appears the Golden Lord has somehow turned his territory into an exact replica of the game.”

“Okay, I’m confused,” said Kato.

“That doesn’t matter,” said Jack. “How do we kill it?”

“There is no method to kill a Hellmaker,” said XB, “according to the game.”

“This isn’t a game,” said Jack, “If it’s alive, it can die. XB, how long until it gets here?”

“I estimate ninety-two hours.”

“Four days,” said Kato. “We have time.”

“We need to get the others back here,” said Jack. “XB, can we reach the others with the phones now?”

“Yes,” said XB, “The city defense might help as well.”

They all stared at the robot for a long moment.

“What?”

“What city defenses?” asked Marven.

“The Tokahama Corporation installed retractable weapons inside the city's walls in case of terrorist attacks. If we can access the mainframe, we may be able to keep the creature coming at bay or kill it.”

“You say this now?” asked Jack, irritated.

“You didn’t ask.”

Jack took a deep breath, “How long does it take to activate them?”

"A full system check will take five days; however, I can do it in a hundred hours."

"I can help," said Kato. "If something goes wrong, I can fix it as we go."

"I'll get back with Harris and come up with a plan to hold it off till we can get the defenses up."

"I'm going back to the coven," said Marven. Jack nodded.

They all ran, Jack heading up the wall, Kato, XB and Marven heading back to the coven. There was a lot of work to be done and little time to do it.

Chapter 8

Journey to the Waste

---

1 Jerimiah's Choice

Jerimiah worked in the barn alone. He enjoyed working with his children, but today wasn't a day for that. He'd been feeling guilty lately about Ara. She had refused to leave her room at all for the past few days. She hadn't worked, barely ate, and at night, he could hear her through the floor, pacing and cursing in Spanish. Jerimiah knew they were making the right choice to protect the baby, but he felt certain that Ara wasn't feeling that way.

Jerimiah finished feeding the goats and headed back to his home when he saw the bishop's carriage coming up the path. Jerimiah smiled. He had asked the bishop to come to talk to Ara a few days ago, to help her cope with what was happening, though he knew it would take from the bishop's other duties. He felt the girl needed the strength of God, and the bishop could act as a guide.

The bishop stopped his buggy in front of Jerimiah and smiled, the two men shaking hands, and saying, "It's good to see you," and whatnot, but Jerimiah saw a strain on his old friend's face, and a discomfort that glinted in his eyes.

"My friend, what is wrong?"

The bishop shifted for a moment, and then said, "A Black Priest came here a day ago."

Jeremiah blanched, "Is he still here?"

"No, he left the same day, but he was looking for the girl."

Jeremiah was shocked. "What did you tell him?"

"The girl is being protected by us."

"Good."

"But if we release her to their custody, the priest has promised to help open trade with us and Etam."

"What?" asked Jeremiah, "You're not considering this, are you?"

"Jeremiah," said the bishop, "Our only trading partners are the Navajo, and they live deep in the Wastelands. It cost us much just to get there."

"The Navajo have always been fair to us," Jeremiah said coolly. "Etam has done nothing but threaten us, and you're considering making a deal with the devil, just for better trade?"

"It's not just access to Etam," said the bishop. "We could gain their knowledge and trade with communities that are currently unknown to us. We could move out, colonize, spread our influence all for the glory of God, and our people."

Jeremiah was shocked, unable to believe this. "You would sacrifice a girl, who suffered in the land that seeks her, that raped her, all for profit?"

"How dare . . ." began the bishop, but Jeremiah interrupted.

"This is not our way, we can't."

"It is decided, Jeremiah," said the bishop, coldly, "and unless you wish to suffer the shunning, I suggest you do not continue."

Jeremiah paled. The bishop looked at him gravely, then said, "Bring the girl to my house in six days. I must be off now."

Jeremiah watched him leave, too angry to speak, then he walked into his field.

He returned to his house a few hours later and joined his family for supper. Again, that night Ara didn't join them. Tonight, Jeremiah couldn't blame her. This wasn't right, what the bishop was doing, and nor was it moral. How could God want this, it was a virtual paganistic sacrifice for what, more bread? His conscience was against it, as was his heart, but if he did anything to prevent it, it would mean shunning, and he and his family would be cut from their community of New Haven.

Lilith didn't miss her husband's look of concern. After they cleaned the kitchen, she tucked in Emma, Mary, the two boys, and kissed Jeremiah junior good night. She joined him in the sitting room where he sat in front of the fireplace, his hand resting under his chin and beard.

"What is it, husband?" asked Lilith.

He was silent for a long time, but Lilith waited until he said, "Have you ever been faced with an ultimatum, Lilith?"

"No," she said, "All of my choices were of a clear mind. Why do you ask?"

Jeremiah explained everything the bishop said to him. When he was finished, a look of horror came to Lilith's face.

"We can't do this, Jeremiah. We'd sacrifice the girl. This is not moral."

"I know," said Jeremiah, "But if I interfere, we could be shunned."

"Damn the shunning," snapped Lilith, shocking her husband. "I will not let us stoop to that level. Etam wants us to abandon our god. I'd rather be shunned by man than dishonor the lord."

"But our family . . ."

"We can survive," she snapped. "The shun won't affect Mary or Emma. Jeremiah Junior will be fine as well. I will not allow Ara to be used in business. It is not our way."

Jeremiah looked in the fire for a long moment, then determination was painted on his face. He stood, looked at his wife, and said, "Get Jeremiah and Emma. We are sending Ara to the Wastelands."

2 The Road to the Wastelands

Ara sat on the bed, anger still infecting her soul like a plague. She was a prisoner again, and in many ways, it was a prison worse than being kept by the Golden Lord. This was not cruelty, but a blind adherence to faith, one which stripped others of that which should not be taken from any: A freedom of choice. In the room she was kept in by the Golden Lord, she had wanted to die, for she hated the creature that held her. He used her, abused her, invaded her, and now she was carrying his child, but chose to live on. She had to find her brother, and that was it, the reason she chose to endure her tormentor.

But now, the choice to help was taken away from people she'd grown to trust. They didn't let her move around alone, with both Jeremiahs watching her, and made sure she couldn't harm the baby. Anger kept her burning and planning to escape. She was going tonight, when the father slept, she'd find her way to the Waste . . .

The door opened, and Emma walked in, holding a candle in the dark room.

"What?" began Ara.

"Come with me," said Emma.

She grabbed Ara's arm, and they moved downstairs and out the front door, heading to the barn. There she saw Jeremiah Sr. and Jr., along with Lilith, loading down two mules. She saw food, water and other supplies being loaded quickly.

"Emma, what . . ."

"No time," said Emma, "Just move."

They got to the mules, and Lilith hugged Ara, saying, "Dear, it's time."

At first Ara didn't understand, but then . . . "I'm free."

"Yes," said Jeremiah Sr. walking up to her, "I do not agree with your decision over wanting to terminate the baby, but my conscience won't allow me to keep you here."

"What changed?"

"Better not ask or dawdle, only move. Emma and Jeremiah will escort you to the entrance to the Wastelands. Once there, you have to travel on your own. Stay on the path and the Navajo will find you. Do not leave the path if you value your life."

Overcome with gratitude, Ara hugged Jeremiah Sr. and said, "Gracias, Senior, gracias."

He returned the hug, then said, "Hurry, get on the mule."

She got on the animal and Lilith walked forward and said, "Please, reconsider termination. All life is a gift from God. Promise, please."

Ara nodded, tears in her eyes. She had no wish to lie to Lilith, so she only nodded.

Jeremiah Sr. walked to his daughter and son on the other mule and said, “Keep her safe, and stay on the path.”

“We promise,” said Jeremiah Jr.

“Now go,” said Jeremiah Sr.

With that, the two mules started to trot, back towards the Green, and towards the Wastelands.

Chapter 9

Revelations

---

1 Restoration

In the city of Dearborn, on the third day of talks, when Doug thought the talks were not going as good as they hoped, the overhead lights came on. At first Doug didn't notice, nor did Omar, Fahda, the Iman Simion, or the Sultan for several moments, and then, they noticed in the late evening lights, that it was still bright in the room. Then Fahda looked around, then up, seeing the lights recessed in the ceiling glowing a soft light. Electrical light.

"What on earth," he said. Then the others looked up. Doug's eyes looked at the lights in amazement, and the Sultan said, "Did you do that?"

"No," said Doug, suddenly feeling a buzz in his left pants pocket, and heard a sound like falling chimes. Then he remembered the phone he got from the Otaku. How was it working? He pulled it out of his pocket and looked at the phone. A name was on it. Jack.

"What's that?" asked Omar.

"It's a cell phone. We got several on our travels. Jack must have . . ." He petered off, and when he touched the green icon at the bottom of the phone, a voice Doug knew well came out of it.

"Hello, God damn it! I hope this works."

"Jack?"

"Doug, God damn it, it worked. How is it going?"

"It's going good," said Doug, and seeing the surprised but annoyed look on his host's face, looked at the phone for a moment. He saw an icon that reminded him of sound waves. He pressed it and Jack's voice came out of the phone as clearly as if he was in the room. The Sultan, the princes, and the Iman gasped in amazement.

"A working cell phone," said Fahda, "Amazing."

"Man, I can't believe this, what's going on?"

"Umm," said Doug, "Well, the power came back on."

There was a silence over the line, one which made Doug fear he had lost Jack.

"Jack?"

"Sorry, misheard, I thought you said the power was back on in Dearborn."

"Actually, most of the locals call it New Mecca, but, yeah, overhead lights recessed into the ceiling turned on."

"One second," said Jack. After a moment, he returned, and said, "XB says it's because of the Cloud network. Something about digital power."

"Huh?"

"I don't get it either, but basically, the station is giving De . . . I mean New Mecca, power."

"What about the other cities?"

There was silence, and then, "Doug, give me a few minutes, okay?"

"Ok."

The phone went silent for about five minutes. During that time, Queen Tarfa, Iman, Raina, and Salma all walked in, with Iman speaking first: "Father, the light, by Allah, the lights in the city, those still intact, they're on. By Allah, they're on."

"We know," said the Sultan, pointing to the ceiling.

Iman smiled, and Princess Raina walked to Doug, knelt before him, and kissed his free hand. Salma and Tarfa did the same, and even Iman stood before him and bowed.

"Great rider," said Raina, "You have brought a miracle to our city. Thank you, thank you."

"I don't think it was him," said Omar, "his . . .cell phone . . .the device in his hand contacted another . . .umm, Jack is also a rider right . . .right, and said the power is coming from Detroit."

"What," asked Iman, and he turned to Doug in sudden anger, "You have indebted us to Detroit? How dare you?"

"Calm yourself," snapped the Sultan. "I think this wasn't intentional. By the sound of it, they didn't know this would happen."

"What were they attempting to do in Detroit?" asked Salma.

At that moment, voices came back to the phone, which caused the newcomers to jump.

"This better work," said the voice of Thug.

"Thug?" asked Kshea's voice.

"Kshea?"

"Guys."

"Jack?" asked both Kshea and Thug.

"Hey," said Doug.

"Doug?"

"What's going on?" asked the Iman.

"Be silent," said the Sultan, but even he looked confused and annoyed.

"Thug, Kshea, what's going on in the other cities?"

"Power came back," said Kshea.

"Same," said Thug, "Everyone thought I had something to do

with it. I've had three marriage proposals from three different women and two from men. I mean, they are handsome, but . . ."

"The same thing happened here," said Kshea, "The Raj's were tearing at me with their words, talking about empty promises, then the lights came on, and they were all singing my praises."

"Listen," said Doug, "Get each guy who is in charge of the cities together. We need to get a council going here."

"We do," said Jack. "It's more important than you think. There are Black Priests outside of Detroit. And more of those Wolfmen."

"What," yelled Doug, Thug, and Kshea at the same time while the Iman and all the royals looked at the phone with fear.

"Yeah," said Jack, "Two thousand arrived behind them, but now their number has nearly tripled."

"Why hasn't Harris attacked?" said Fadah. "He still has far more men."

"At first, he didn't want to slaughter them," said Jack. "But now, there is something else. Another creature is on its way. I'm sending a video that we got from XB."

"Who?" asked the Sultan.

"Long story, but get your leadership together before I send it."

Three minutes later, the untouchable and the Maharaja came to the line. They and the Sultan gave cold but cordial greetings. When that was done, Jack sent the video. The image he saw made Doug's blood freeze. The black, shining creature was breaking through the Green, heading towards Detroit. It made everyone in the room have a look of pure horror on their faces.

"They're bringing it to break Detroit's walls," explained Jack. "We have a plan, but it will take time, and that thing will be here in three days. As for Harris, he sealed the main gate and has begun evacuating the City from the water. Every boat is being filled as we speak, but it won't be enough."

"There are over two million people in Detroit," said Queen Tarfa. "If that thing breaks through . . ."

"Not just that," said the voice of the Untouchable "If Detroit is destroyed, we lose the power we have."

"And our cities are even more exposed than Detroit," said the voice of the Maharaja, "If Detroit falls, we fall."

The Sultan stood and said to the phone, "My fellow leaders of Plymouth and Canton, I can put together a force of about a thousand men in a short amount of time."

"As can I," said the Untouchable.

"I have an expeditionary force of about five hundred men and women, plus another thousand I can have ready in a day. It will take two days to reach Dearborn on foot, and a half a day to get to Detroit," said the Maharaja.

"If you can draw the Black Priests and the wolfmen away from Detroit," said Jack. "The others here can distract the big ugly, buy Detroit more time as we try to enact our plan."

"We'll be outnumbered," said Iman. "What are they armed with?"

"Blade and speed," said Jack.

"That's it?" asked the Maharaja.

"And teeth, claws, long arms, and very bad tempers."

"Fun," said Omar, and stood. "I will begin to gather the men together. Colonel Algizer and Major Hussan will help me gather some of our best."

"Then it is decided," said the Sultan.

"Agreed," said the riders, one at a time.

"Hurry up," said Jack, "You're already outnumbered. If you can pull back these wolfmen, me and the riders here can keep that beast busy for a while."

Doug stood, "Gather your forces; it's time to ride. May the road guide us."

2 The Wait

Jack stood on the wall, cigarette in hand, smoke puffing out of his mouth. He was looking down at the Black Priests as they stood like gargoyles in the setting sun, wondering if they ever slept. His hand rested on his pistol, wanting them to move and give him an excuse to shoot them in the throat. Wolfmen were around them, snarling in the dusk, as the last rays of the sun slowly disappeared.

Jack sensed somebody behind him, and he turned slowly, seeing Marven and Watu behind him. How they came to this section of the wall unnoticed was unknown to him, but he was grateful for their company. But he also had a thing he needed addressed.

"You knew about the Hellmaker, didn't you?"

"Yes," said Marven, "But I thought we had more time. I saw it in an echo."

Jack nodded, remembering his experience with time echoes. He puffed a smoke ring and said, "We have three more days. Three days, and God, I hope that wall holds."

'Time is a fickle thing,' said Watu. *'I concern myself with it very little.'*

"Ironic," said Jack, "From a being who can see into the past."

The bear chuckled, and Jack puffed another cloud of smoke. After a moment of this, Marven said, "So, any research into these creatures or Etam?"

"I skimmed through a few, and yes, the Hellmaker is a creature in the game. This game, no matter how long I don't think about it since I discovered it back with the Otaku, seems to pop up now and then. The Black Priests, the Hellmaker, the wolfmen, they all are parts of this game. How this is possible, why this is happening, I know not, but there's something here that seems like fiction and reality are becoming one."

"Somewhat," said Marven.

"Did this Golden Lord and these Great Old Ones base their entire society on a game, Marven?" asked Jack.

"What do you think?"

Jack shrugged, "I suspect it, but the question is why."

"That is something you have to learn," said Marven.

Jack sighed, "So what have you been doing?"

"Talking to the coven we met."

"Anything interesting?"

"A few things, nothing you need to worry about."

"Now I am worried."

They chuckled, and Jack threw down the butt of his cigarette, the cherry glowing orange in the coming darkness. He grabbed another from his pack and lit it again. Marven indicated he wanted one, and Jack obliged, handing him the smoke. They stood overhead, smoking their cigarettes, the smoke forming a cloud around them.

"You should sleep," said Marven.

"I will," said Jack, "Soon, for now, I need to know more. It's this time, the waiting, when I feel the most at peace, before a fight. I can see the scenarios in my head, and how they will end. I see it, and yet, I still feel the failures at the edges, like wrinkles, and with seeing them I can smooth them out. It's calming."

"Arthur had the same sort of tradition when he went to a battle," said Marven, with a grin. The plants woven into his dreadlocks glowed in the night, and Jack almost sensed Marven's true power from it.

"What was he like, Arthur?"

"He was wise, kind, a bit of a player, but he loved his people," said Marven. "He saw much magic. He saw what happens when witches and warlocks would put their magic to good use. He also saw the destruction it could cause if left unchecked. He was wise, and a great warrior. In the end, he became a legend, a folk hero for all times."

Jack smiled at that thought. "He sort of reminds me of the Hooded Rider, from when our order was still young. He was a great rider, who instead of wearing a bandana would always wear a hood. He slew and captured many beasts of the Green and bandits when he rode the great roads on his bike. He was a great leader among the riders and one of the greatest warriors. But there was one mission he said was the one he most thought defined him as a rider. There was a little girl, stuck in a tree, and she was scared. The Hooded Rider climbed up the tree and helped her down on his back. That was what defined him as one of the greatest riders, being willing to treat a small child in distress on the same level as he would by fighting a cave bear. I don't know if the story was true, but it was one of our best legends."

"Do the riders have more legends?" asked Marven.

"Yes, Yury, the rider who never used a gun. Jakava, the first Otherkin rider, and so on."

"Maybe one day you'll be a legend, like the knights of old, or the riders of now. I see much of the knights of the round table in the Order of the Riders. They stood for much of the same things - justice, freedom, equality. Arthur never believed that a man's skin or the land he was born on made him any more or less than who he was. No, that was all the other kings and prissy noblemen who came after. Women on the other hand, well, he liked them, often in his bed, but he did like them, just didn't think much more of them outside his prick."

Jack snorted. "The fuck is a prick?"

"His cock."

They laughed.

'The night grows older,' said Watu. *'The day is being born.'*

Marven nodded. "Goodnight, Jack."

"Night."

Jack walked down about a half hour after the two left. He went to his room and slept almost immediately.

He dreamt of Niki, and this time, they were in the cabin on the beach near Marquette. She was in the bathing suit that Jack's mother had made for her before their honeymoon. It was a one piece, but it fit her form in a way that made Jack feel desire in the pit of his stomach. He stood and walked towards her as she lay in the sand, putting a hand on her shoulder. She turned and smiled.

"Is this real?" asked Jack.

"As real as it was those years ago," said Niki.

"Are you, as Marven said, a ghost?"

"I couldn't leave you," said Niki. "I didn't want to move on without you."

He kissed her again, feeling her lips on his, her flesh in his hand.

"Stay," said Jack, as she pulled him towards her, "Stay, please, I can't . . ."

"I'm here," said Niki, and in the sand, they made love again, and when Jack awoke, that cloud in his mind, reminding him so much like the cloud that was always over Detroit, was lifted for a short time.

3 The Gathering

Two days after the call, three armies gathered. For the first time since the Green, Muslims, Hindus, and Sikhs of America came together in one common cause. There were misgivings, mistrust, and a little fear in the group of men and women brought to fight, but they were united in a cause, to keep the power. Guns, swords, spears and three motorcycles gathered. The riders looked over the soldiers.

Colonel Algizer led the Muslims, armed with rifles, and in gray uniforms. The Raj of the Kshatriyas led the Hindus in blue, armed with swords and rifles as well. The Maharaja Kynel led the Sikhs while Sati and Cody stood with them. The elite soldiers stood behind them in blue uniforms, blue turbans or head coverings, armed with swords and spears, but short shotguns on their backs. The Sikhs rode their strange sheep mounts, while the Muslims and Hindus rode on horses. Twenty-five hundred men and women, ready for war.

For the riders, they looked at a distance as the armies formed columns and ranks, ready to march to Detroit.

"So far so good," said Kshea, looking at the forces before her, kissing the cross she carried per her faith.

"It's like fireworks down there," said Thug, "One wrong match and we all go up in smoke."

"Keep faith, brother," said Doug.

"Think we have a chance?" said Kshea.

"A good chance," said Doug, "We just need to buy the city time."

"Well then, let's ride. Looks like they are ready," said Thug.

They looked and saw the army begin to march with hooves pounding in the ground. Revving their bikes, Doug, Kshea, and Thug rode to join them.

Chapter 10

The Battle of Detroit

---

1 Hellmaker

Jack saw it on the horizon, a patch of black that broke through the Green like a man going through grass. It was unholy, a being not entirely solid, forming, reabsorbing and reforming tentacles, each one then the size of large trees. The beast had no eyes, no mouth, yet it made huge, unholy roaring sounds that vibrated through the Green, even as far away as it was. It was coming with only one thing on its mind - if it has a mind, that is - destruction.

Jack watched the horror that approached then looked down at the Black Priests, who he swore were smiling in pleasure, such evil beings as they were.

Harris came up, seeing the monstrosity that Jack told him

about several days ago. He didn't fully believe it till now, even as he evacuated the city. He now watched, fear on his face, now seeing the true power of his enemies.

"I should have killed them when I had the chance," said Harris.

"You should have," said Jack. "But even if we had, we'd still have to face that beast."

"You think you and your riders can stop it?"

"Just give us time, and we will take it down."

"How?"

"We are Riders. We can do anything."

At that, Harris walked away, and Grenn, Miko, and Tricks came up. Jack showed them the beast on the phone but seeing it in real life made them realize what they were up against. As they stood there, Jack dialed up Kato. He answered his phone on the third ring.

"Hello?"

"Kato, how much longer?"

"Need a few more hours, but XB is working overtime."

"Good. Kato, listen, if we don't come back, and something happens to Doug and the others, you'll be the last rider here. Defend the facility at all costs. With any luck, it won't come to that, but if it does, seal the facility, keep XB inside, and get out of Detroit."

"It won't come to that," said Kato, then, "May the great road guide you to the right path."

"And you," responded Jack, he clicked the phone off, and turned to Miko, Tricks, and Grenn, whose skin was patterned into oranges and yellows, giving the effect of fire on his skin.

"Let's get to the side gate," said Jack.

They nodded. The side gate was a smaller gate about five miles or so down from the main gate, only large enough to admit a truck. It was all part of the plan.

When they got there, they mounted their bikes, loading magazines into rifles, shots into shotguns, and pistols with as many rounds as they could hold. Jack and Tricks, as pathfinders, were in the front, while Grenn and Miko, being truck clan, mounted behind them. All part of the plan. There they waited, Grenn using his phone to track how much time till the Hellmaker arrived. Closer and closer it got, and Jack could almost sense the anticipation from the Black Priests and the Wolf-type Otherkin. They waited, still.

Soon, Jack began to feel the ground tremble, and a foul odor filled the air, but still they waited. It grew stronger and stronger, and still they waited. They began to hear its roars closer, still waiting, and waiting.

Jack screen lit, and he answered it. It was Doug, and he had connected with Kato as well. Jack answered.

"You ready?" asked Jack.

"Yeah," said Doug, "Kato, how much time do we have to hold it off?"

"About an hour," said Kato, "XB and I are almost done."

"Ok," said Doug, "We have our rifle men in position. Once you hear the shot, take off like a bat out of hell, keep that Hellmaker busy. Thug will join you as soon as he can. Kshea and I will help our forces against the Wolfmen."

"Got it," said Jack, and hung up. They sat and waited, for ten, long, agonizing minutes. The beast had to be close enough to the gate, where it wouldn't just turn around, yet far enough to keep it busy. Doug was waiting for . . .

A volley of shots came down the front gate. There were several loud hollows in the air, and Jack knew they got the Wolfmen distracted. He dialed one number as a second volley came, and it was answered from Trick's phone, which was in the hands of Harris.

"Hello," said Harris.

"Now, do it NOW!" yelled Jack. A second later, the gates were open, and the four riders took off.

They were at top speed, following the gate and the horrible smell that hit Jack's and the other's noses. Probably would have killed Kato, his sense of smell being better than a human's.

A few minutes later, they saw it up close about three fourths of a mile away from the walls of Detroit. The Hellmaker. Behind it, Wolfmen were charging into the cliff where the trucks were hidden, but also where men in blue and gray were firing down at them, drawing them away from the Hellmaker and paying no attention to the four riders charging in on it.

Jack and the others charged it, motors roaring in the air, and raised their guns. Jack had his shotgun slung on his back, instead he used a P90 that he borrowed from the Detroit defense force, and they opened fire, the bullets sinking into the huge beast. It roared, whether in pain or annoyance, Jack couldn't tell.

They were within a thousand feet of it when Grenn and Miko veered off to the left and right while Jack and Tricks continued to charge in the front of it, unwavering, and battle ready. Tentacles continued to form, melt into the mass, and reform as they charged. At three hundred feet away, Jack saw his opening as a tentacle began to form on the ground, extending out like a tree root, the tip of it feeling for its prey. Jack hit the accelerator and got on the tentacle, thick as a tree trunk. The substance was not entirely solid, but the bike's tires were able to grip on and Jack took the bike and rode up the tentacle, his tires ripping up it. Using the P90, he fired into the mass as he rode up it, the bullets ripping through its mass. Tricks, right behind him as they rode up it, the smell powerful as they climbed and peppered it with bullets. Down below, Grenn and Miko circled it, firing up into the mass, avoiding hitting the two pathfinders. The creature roared as it was peppered, but for a terrible moment, it didn't slow. But eventually it did, and soon it stopped, roaring as the two riders on its body and circling it began to piss it off.

It began to form more tentacles, trying to crush the riders, but they darted around it like flies. It kept missing, making the beast roar again, trying to smash the little creatures causing it pain. Over the sounds of the engine, Jack heard a combination of shooting and roars of pain in the distance, and hoped the troops were holding the line.

Fifteen minutes passed, and the riders continued to harry the Hellmaker, once in a while making a move to the gate when they had to reload or re-mount it, but it made little headway as it batted at the four riders. It roared and screamed, and Jack knew that there were over three thousand soldiers on the wall, ready to shoot it down at a moment's notice. If it got within a certain distance of the wall, they had orders to shoot, even if the riders still fought on it. So far, the riders had kept it back. For how much longer was unknown.

Jack was about to make another run when he heard the shots of a new rifle. Jack looked up and saw Thug, barreling down at the creature, his weapon aimed at a tentacle that was batting at Miko. In a few moments, he managed to mount it with Jack and the two riders circled on top of it, burying bullets into the top of the Hellmaker.

The beast screamed, and then a tentacle came out and clipped the front tire of Grenn's bike. He spun out of control for a moment, but managed to regain his balance, and charged back in, the fender intended to protect his front tire bent up.

Twenty-five more minutes passed, and Jack hoped they could keep this up just a little longer.

2 Into the Woods

Before Jack and the others left the gate, Doug, Kshea, Thug, Maharaja Kynel, the Kshatriyas' Raj, and Colonel Algizer looked down as the Hellmaker was moving towards the city. The dark cloud over the city seemed to be thick with fear. That seeped into all of them, like death and fear, overwhelming them for a moment. But they had a plan, and they were ready. They had positioned their thirty-five hundred men carefully the previous night.

What was said over the phone was already said and needs not be repeated, but when the time was right, Doug nodded to Algizer and the Kshatriyas Raj, who both waved flags at a distance over the cliff that two companies of riflemen stood on. Almost two hundred troops armed with rifles aiming down and the Wolf-type Otherkin. Major Hussan, seeing the flag, along with a

Kshatriyas Hindu named Devonro, raised their hands. The soldiers took aim, the commanders lowered their hands, and the soldiers fired. Shots rang out, and over two hundred bullets hit the six thousand wolfmen below. Hundreds fell in an instant, and in the confusion, they turned and saw the rifle companies. Their teeth bared even as their brothers fell, and the shorter Black Priest turned and yelled, "Get them."

The wolf men charged at amazing speed, teeth bared and ready to fight.

"Now," yelled Doug, as he, the riders, and the commanders headed back into the woods, the two companies still firing and drawing the wolf men to the trap.

Doug, Kshea, and Thug reached their bikes as the commanders headed back where the trap was, ready to do their duty.

The riders revved up and Doug led them towards where the retreat point started. The men that had taken the shots were falling back, the wolf men right behind them, snarling and growling, claws and knives at the ready, thousands of them. Doug, Kshea and Thug charged them, firing rifles and a pistol into the furry mass, their bullets ripping through them. But that was just the beginning. The wolfmen didn't know that the riders had already fought them; they didn't have their bikes then, yet still held their own. Now they had their bikes, armed and ready, and they would see the true power of a rider.

Thug was the first to reach them, his monster bike plowing through their numbers like a stone through glass. He jumped and in his hands were a rifle and a pistol. Flipping in the air above his still running bike, Thug hit at least thirty of them with his combined weapons before landing on his bike's seat, pulling the accelerator at top speed and then the brake so his back wheel sent dozens more flying as he used his front wheel as a balance. As this finished, he reloaded his rifle in a second, taking out ten more before riding through them again.

Kshea's smaller, leaner bike dotted through them. She stabbed out with a knife, cutting them in the necks as she passed, her arm like a blur, stabbing into the mass of beasts with the trained eye of a killer, stabbing at the beast like a dolphin stabbing a shark with its snout, too fast for them to catch. One tried to jump and tackle her, but she put the brake on, leaning to the side, sliding under it and cutting the beast from throat to groin, then came back up, continuing her dance.

Doug's bike weaved through them using his shotgun in the mass, flipping it at top speed to reload a shot and taking out five at a time with each one. When it ran out, he drew a machete and began to slash at them, breaking through their ranks with ease, blood spraying out from the fur.

The riders plowed through the mass, not to stop the horrid

beast, but only to buy time for their army to reposition and to break through so Thug could help reinforce the riders. Hundreds fell before them, as they were invincible on their bikes, breaking through the tide of Wolfmen.

Soon they reached the cliff, the Wolfmen pursuing their foes into the Green, leaving hundreds dead in their wake. They reached it and without a word, Thug took off and headed down the path, and Doug and Kshea whirled, turning to rejoin the battle that was soon going to take place in the Green.

They weaved through the trees, killing each Wolfman they encountered, shooting their way towards their goal. The sounds of fighting grew on their ears as they reached the dead point and saw the chaos before them. Thousands of Muslims, Sikhs, and Hindi were engaging the Wolfmen, firing weapons into their mass, or engaging them with sword and spear. Sikh hunters, including Sati, danced among them, stabbing and slashing. The Hindi warriors, led by the Kshatriyas Raj, both shot at and engaged the wolf men. Muslims darted through the trees, killing dozens at a time when they took shots. But the army was taking casualties, too. Dozens fell to claws and fangs, slashing knives and pure strength. Men and women mixed in with the dead wolves. Doug and Kshea, seeing this, charged in, their bikes and weapons killing dozens at once, reinforcing the army and turning the tide. Hopefully it was enough.

3 The Wall Awakens

Forty-five minutes had passed and the five riders had kept the beast at bay, but they were only slowing it down. Soon it would be at the point where the wall guard would open fire. Jack didn't know how much longer they could keep this up. His P90 was out of ammo, and his pistol only had three mags left. Thug's bike was banged up a little and slower than it usually was after it fought through the Wolf-type Otherkin. Grenn's bike was also damaged, and Miko was starting to tire. They were all starting to tire.

A tentacle shot out as Tricks came around for another pass. It was a thin, whip-like one that hit her chest and sent her sprawling. Jack and Grenn disengaged to tend to her while Thug and Miko continued to harass the Hellmaker, but it began to move again as the attacks on it had lessened somewhat.

Grenn reached Tricks first, his skin going cloud gray with concern, checking her over as she moaned in pain. Jack pulled up next.

"She okay?" asked Jack.

"I think so," said Grenn, "But she might have broken a rib."

"Get her back inside," yelled Jack. "Get her to the hospital and then get with Kato. Protect the Cloud facility. We will handle the Hellmaker."

Grenn nodded as he and Jack first got Trick's bike to a safe distance, and then Grenn got Tricks on his bike, taking off to the side gate.

Jack remounted his bike and went back to engage, horrified to see how much distance the Hellmaker had made. It was almost at the sweet spot.

"Miko, Thug, get out of there!" yelled Jack, firing his pistol to get their attention. It worked, and seeing where they were, they drove off. Jack looked at his cell phone. They had ten minutes left before XB could get the defense system up. Even with the bullets raining down on the beast, it seemed to sense its goal was close and prepared to strike.

"No," said Jack, horror gripping him as the largest tentacle yet had risen from the top of the Hellmaker, and began to come crashing down on the wall, with Jack, Thug, and Miko, helplessly watching.

It fell even as bullets peppered at it and then, twenty feet away, it struck something, stopping it dead in midair then slid off harmlessly. It attacked again with the same results. Jack watched and as it happened a third time, Jack realized what it was. Magic. Marven must have had something to do with this, but how? It didn't matter, it was buying time, and the guards, not questioning the miracle, began to shoot with renewed vigor.

Then the loud sound of engines hit the three's ears, and they turned, and what they saw made them gasp. A hundred motorcycles and twenty trucks were coming in, all mounted by men in leather jackets and bandanas. It was the second rider party. They were charging in, ready to fight. Jack and the others turned, riding to them, seeing a rider named Daxter, a white man with blonde hair and blue eyes, and a Doberman-Dog Type Otherkin named Ragvan, leading the party.

When they reached them, the party had stopped, for one, to stare at the beast before them, and two, to figure out what was going on with their fellow riders, covered in dust, smelling of gun powder, bikes dented and damaged slightly.

"Jack," yelled Daxter, "What the fuck is that?"

"Just shoot it," yelled Jack, "And get some men up that trail. Doug and Kshea are battling the enemy in the Green, and they need reinforcements."

Daxter nodded and looked at Ragvan, who waved his hand and said, "Riders, to me, all who travel with me, up the path and to the Green. Who is our enemy, brother?"

"Wolf-type Otherkins, from what we can tell," said Jack.

Confused, but not questioning, Ragvan and twenty-five other riders headed to the path on the cliff, while Daxter yelled, "Hit that fucker with everything you got."

Hundreds of bullets went flying towards the beast, and the two groups hitting it managed to push the Hellmaker back. Its screams echoed through the Green, roaring and moaning in pain. Its tentacles flailed in the sunlight.

Suddenly, a large, grinding sound activated, and the wall in front of the main gate where the Hellmaker was open, with two of the largest guns Jack had ever seen coming out of them. They aimed at the Hellmaker, and with an earth-shattering crash, they fired. Chunks of the Hellmaker went flying off, melting into the ground without the main body sustaining it. It screamed and roared, and it was slowly taken down into pieces. Then Jack saw something. A white dot in the middle of the black mass. Jack revved up by instinct, not knowing why. Thug tried to stop him, but he was driving off, avoiding the bullets flying all around him.

Jack reached the slowly dying mass and saw what the dot was. A human leg. Revving the engine, Jack rode up the beast, timing the cannon shots. He saw the leg, and, reaching out with one hand, grabbed it, nearly dislocating his shoulder as he did so. Out of the mass came a girl, barely a teenager, naked, and covered in a wet, gooey substance. Swinging her onto the back of his bike, Jack flew off the beast as it let out one last shriek of pain and began to melt away, its host no longer keeping it intact.

4 Turning Tides

Doug and Kshea darted throughout the battle, taking out

dozens of wolf men at a time, with bullet and blade, lead and steel taking out their enemies' lives in an instance. The men of Dearborn, Canton, and Plymouth fought with skill and grace and power that caught the wolfmen off balance, gun, blade, and blood pushing against the tide.

But the fact was they were still outnumbered, and at least a third of their men had died. Doug and Kshea helped where they could. Doug saw Kynel with Sati and Cody, surrounded by twenty wolf men. Doug managed to get seven, and the three were reinvigorated. The Kshatriyas Raj's great sword slashed away into several Wolfmen, but Kshea was able to help by using her knife and beheading five at a time. Algizer and a platoon of rifle men were about to be overwhelmed by two hundred wolf men when both Doug and Kshea charged them, killing half and giving Algizer time to pick off the rest. It still wasn't enough.

Eight more minutes passed and then a sound of engines cut the air, and Doug turned, and saw them. Twenty-five Riders, all on bikes, all charging in. Human, Androgenans, Otherkin, and Skin-Changers, charging in on their bikes, firing guns and killing hundreds more as they swept through the ranks of wolf men. The men and women of Dearborn, Canton, and Plymouth, screamed in hope and watched these living legends take form and kill without mercy.

Doug cheered with the others, covered in blood and filled

with despair, now with a new hope and wonder. He was so absorbed, he didn't see the Wolfman flying at him, tearing him from his bike and slamming him into a tree. Choking under its great claw, the beast opened its jaw, hot breath hitting Doug hard. He stabbed it in the neck with his knife, but it seemed not to notice, instead stabbing him in the chest with its claws. Doug screamed in anger and then half the beast's head blew off. Kshea came to him, holding a large rifle in her hands.

She looked at the holes in Doug's chest, and held him close to her, crying, "Thank god, you are alright."

"I'm fine," said Doug, looking into her eyes, and their lips brushed against each other. For a moment, the battle melted away from them, and nothing was more exciting than them.

They didn't know the battle was about to end, the wolfmen would be routed, and the Black Priests would be captured. All there was for them was that moment, that time, and it was that which saved their hearts for the battles to come.

Chapter 11

Aftermath

1 Ending of a Battle and the Beginning of a New Hope

Jack held the naked girl in his arms, protecting her, like a father over his daughter. She wasn't conscious yet, but she was breathing and alive. Jack looked at her, cradling her, and was soon joined by Thug, Miko and Daxter. The battle was over, the guns were back in the walls, and the riders were helping the army from the three cities that had aided Detroit in gathering the dead. It was over.

"She was inside that beast," said Thug, looking at the girl with pity.

"Yeah," said Jack, "she was. She was the key, the engine that drove that unnatural, unholy monster to the wall. So much pain."

"Why?" asked Miko.

"To kill us in the most horrifying way imaginable."

They stood there until they saw two figures coming towards them. A man in robes and dreadlocks and a bear, large and lumbering.

Marven knelt by the girl and stroked her head as a loving father, looking at Jack, he said, "Give her to me."

Jack nodded and gave the girl to him. He picked her up and put her on the back of Watu, and the two walked away, disappearing into the day. Daxter and Miko gasped. Jack and Thug said nothing.

There was a clamoring of voices and motors. Jack saw two riders in a small pickup, followed by an injured Doug and a bloody-but-in-one-piece Kshea following them. In the back, bounded by iron, were the two Black Priests.

Jack stood, Thug, Miko, Daxter, and twelve other Riders joined them. They dismounted as the two riders driving the truck opened it and pulled out the two priests and the guards followed.

"Unbelievers," said the tall one, "How dare you defy the will of the Golden Lord? You might have stopped his beast today, but he will bring forth a darkness even greater than the one you face. He will destroy this city like Babylon. He will . . ."

"Shut up," said Jack, just annoyed by the pull in his mind by now, "Or I'll stab you both in the throat."

The tall one glared, but the shorter one had a flash of

nervousness on his face.

Jack walked forward and said, "I couldn't arrest your brother, Kal, so I'll just settle for you two. Have fun in prison, bastards. Let's see how your voices affect others in solitary."

The tall Black Priest continued to curse them, but they ignored it, the voice no longer affecting them as it once did. Logic won out.

Jack walked to Doug, seeing blood on his side.

"You're hurt."

"A flesh wound," said Doug. "I'll be fine."

"I got him," said Kshea, as she put her arm under him, and walked him to the main gate, which was opening. Jack noticed the tender way she helped Doug.

"Something is different between them," said Thug.

"Yeah," said Jack.

"Can't put my finger on it."

Jack was about to laugh when he saw three men walking towards him. One was in a turban of white and wore a blue combat uniform, flanked by two people, a woman in blue, blood-stained clothing, and a head covering. The other a bearded man in a blue turban and blue combat uniform. The second was a shirtless man in a thin white turban, with no shirt, a cape, and an orange wrap around his waist. The third was a completely hairless man in black overalls, having a strong military bearing.

Out of the gate came Harris and his own guards. The two parties faced each other, with the riders in the middle, waiting, then . . .

"I have medics ready to treat the injured," said Harris.

"Good," said the man in the thick turban.

"I'll take you to them," said Thug quickly. "I know the way."

The medic, who was in a van, followed Thug on his bike to the path up the cliff and headed for the battlefield.

Harris walked forward and said, "Maharaja, Raj Taylor, Colonel Algizer, we must speak."

All three nodded and followed him into the city. Jack followed on his bike with Miko and Daxter. The other riders remained behind.

2 Wizards and Dragons

Three days passed and Jack found the bar he was going to meet Marven in. To Jack's surprise, though, it wasn't that much of one, Marven was already waiting for him, and he followed the man as he started walking after seeing Jack.

Jack followed him to a coffee place called "The Raven." It was an old coffee bar in the city, but it also served some of the best beer Jack had ever had in his life. The two entered the bar. In his robes and with his hair with grass-woven dreadlocks, he somehow seemed to match this mixed crowd of drinkers, writers, scholars, idealists and so many more. They were people of ideas, future, and hope. That was somewhat embodied by Marven and his ways.

The two sat and a woman got them drinks. Jack got an oatmeal stout and Marven got something called chai. The drinks were brought, and they thanked the waiter.

"How is the girl?" asked Jack, "I'd like to see her."

"In a moment," said Marven. "I feel you have more questions for me."

Jack nodded, but before he could start, Marven asked, "How are Tricks and Doug? I heard they were injured during the battle."

"They are fine," said Jack, "Doug only had flesh wounds and was stitched up. He will be good in a few days. Tricks had a few fractures, but she will recover, and be back to riding before we leave."

"That's good."

For a moment, Marven seemed to stare off into space, but then looked at Jack and nodded, giving him permission to ask questions. Jack asked the first one that he needed to know.

"When the Hellmaker was at the wall, it was about to attack, and then it stopped, like something was holding it back. That was you, wasn't it?"

"In a way," said Marven. "I still can't use magic the way I used to without risk. However, the coven could. I used their power and acted as a lens for them, shaping the spell into my desire without using my own power."

"So, some kind of cosmic loophole?"

"Basically. Magic is a very powerful force, but when learned, it can be very useful."

Jack decided not to go back along this line of questioning. Instead, he asked the one that was most important.

"Can we use the path the Hellmaker took to get to Etam?"

Marven sipped the chai and said, "No. You use that road, and there will be worse things than Hellmakers waiting for you. You saw that beast, and while it didn't break you, it did show you what Etam is capable of. You've seen the Golden Lord, at least an avatar of him. That being is what you are facing, and you need time to prepare for him. The tunnels are the first step. Where they will lead you, well, you will see, but they will prepare you and help you get past the worst the Golden Lord and the Great Old Ones have to offer."

Jack shuttered inwardly, imagining what horrors waited for them.

"Well, Daxter wants to try and take it. He thinks it's the best way."

"For him, yes. But for you, I see you are going to need more time. Take Etam from both directions, travel through the Green to the Tunnels of Night, and along the way, find the answers to stopping what the Golden Lord has planned."

"What are his plans?" asked Jack.

"To be honest, I know not what his final goals are, and I also think he doesn't know either. He seemed to be more playing a part than actually having some end game plan, he and the others. I don't know what he wishes outside domination, which concerns me. Nobody dominates for the sake of domination alone. There is a goal in mind, good or ill, there is always a goal. But what it is I don't know, it is almost as if they are only playing parts."

"Like, trying to make a story?" asked Jack.

"A story of their design."

"Marven, what are they? I saw them in the echo before they transformed. Are they kids, or are they something else?"

"I don't know. They are clearly no longer children, but they also seemed not to be beyond childish things. Perhaps they are a mixture of such things."

That scared Jack the most. The fact that Merlin himself didn't know what they were facing.

"The girl should be ready to talk," said Marven, standing. Jack followed.

"Remember," said Marven, "She is traumatized, and has been through something no child should. Give her time."

At this same time, two more riders were in a hospital in a

private room. Doug lay in bed, his side stitched. Kshea was holding his hand, having arrived only a few moments earlier.

"How do you feel?" she asked.

"Sore," said Doug, "But alive. Kshea, about what happened . . ."

"I know," said Kshea, blushing and looking away, "It was stupid."

"No," said Doug, "I . . . I think it helped me when I was hurt."

Blushing, the tattoo girl with pink-dyed hair turned to him.

"But," said Doug, "we can't do anything else until after we reach Etam, and stop the Black Priests at the source."

Kshea looked away, a tear in her eye, but Doug pressed on, "However, when we get back home, I'd like to explore it. Gives us a reason to keep alive."

Kshea turned back and smiled, "A reason to keep alive. I think we all need that."

Doug grinned, and then went pale. Seeing this, Kshea turned around, seeing the white bear in front of her.

The bear sat on its haunches and surveyed them with something bordering on indifference. Then in their minds, the bear said, *'Come,'* his voice vibrating.

"Where?" asked Doug.

'To see the dreamer,' said the bear.

The bear got on all fours, walked over and said, *'Put your hand on my fur.'*

Doug and Kshea did and in a moment, the world melted around them and they were somewhere else, dark, but with an odd light and a large body of water in the center. Kshea looked around with eyes of confusion and fear, but Doug knew where they were.

"It's Dreamer's cavern," said Doug.

"Who?" asked Kshea. After she said it, the great power Doug knew touched him, and he guessed, Kshea. They turned and saw the water ripple as a great serpentine body came out. The great dragon looked down at them. Kshea screamed and grabbed Doug's arm, reaching for a gun that she didn't have on her.

"Kshea, it's ok," said Doug.

"Ok!" yelled Kshea, "It's a dragon!"

"It is," said Doug, "But I think he is an ally too."

"You know that thing?"

"That thing has ears, you know," said Dreamer.

Kshea stared dumbfoundedly at Dreamer. Doug grinned, but there was something on his mind. Doug looked up at the dragon. "You knew about the Hellmaker."

"I knew your enemies were planning something, and I knew it would strike the Dark City first. The ones calling themselves Black Priests believed that it was the center, the key to make this land fall. They were wrong. They sent the Hellmaker to the wrong place. Marquette and the riders are now their biggest threat, and realizing this, they will do whatever they can to destroy you."

"Why didn't you stop it?" asked Doug.

"The concerns of men do not concern my kind. However, if the priest completed the bidding of their masters, then our desires would be blunted."

"What are they, your desires? And if this is so important to you, why don't you stop them yourself?"

"I would have done it centuries ago, but I was needed here to ensure the other dragons slumbered. Like your bear friend, I am the only one of my kind that kept his mind. However, where his kind could live in the wild without magic on instinct, if my kind did the same, it would cause chaos and destruction. There was a time it happened after magic was cut off from the world that my kind only damaged the world, forcing man to kill mine out of desperation. Those that survived I brought here, where they wait, wait for the day magic moves as naturally through this world like the wind. I could kill the Golden Lord, and the Great Old Ones with ease, but they are not the ones restricting what magic has returned to the world. I don't know what is, and until I do, my kind must slumber."

"That's why you are helping us, to free your race?" asked Doug, as Kshea continued to stare.

"Yes, we have similar goals that both benefit our designs."

"Well, we will be in Etam in a few weeks at most," said Doug. "That beast they sent left a path straight to them."

"You cannot follow the Hellmaker's path, or at least, your party cannot. There are beasts on that path that will not spare you an instant of thought before they kill you. In fact, there are some that will destroy you utterly without even noticing you."

"But it's the quickest way," said Kshea, finally breaking through her fear.

"Quickest does not mean the safest. You must travel to the tunnels of night. There you will find the next stages of your journey and how to defeat the Golden Lord."

"How do you know that?" ask Doug.

"If you are going to defeat the Golden Lord, you will need more than the cities you have allied yourselves with and your order of riders. You need more allies, and in following the tunnels, you will find the ones you will need the most."

Doug was silent for a moment. He was going to have to talk to the other riders before he started out again. But he had another question.

"You told me I have to let Jack lead after the battle of Detroit. Why?"

"Because in the tunnels, you will see much, and only he will fully understand. You will see once you enter."

"Not very clear."

"I cannot always give you clear answers, for there isn't always a clear path. I can give you the best answer I can, though, with what knowledge I do have."

Doug knew it was almost time to go, but he had one last question.

"What will we find in the tunnels?"

"Answers."

3 Healing, Hope

Jack walked into the coven. It was as it always was, dark but lit by candles. They went to the sanctuary where the girl was being kept. Three people, two women and the Rabbit-type Otherkin, were watching her sleep. The Otherkin had her against his fur, keeping her warm, and comforted. She was dressed in a black robe, clean, and sleeping.

Marven knelt in front of her. Jack stood in the back, and he watched the wizard survey the girl with a look in his eyes of a man watching his daughter desperately. Stanel came in a moment later, looking at the scene, and looking at Marven like one who is looking at a divine being, with absolute reverence and hope on its face.

"He is strong," said Stanel.

"He is something," said Jack, watching.

"I never felt that much magic in my life. In a way, I see now what it is, and how much my coven has to learn."

"We all have to learn if we are going to survive," said Jack.

"What do you mean?"

"You will see." Jack walked away from a confused Stanel as the girl began to stir. They knelt next to her as the Otherkin stroked her heir, and said, "She is very weak. We are doing what we can for her physical body, but the mental mind is fragile."

"Can we take her to the hospital?" asked Jack.

"They won't know what to do," said Marven, "And I barely have a clue. What this girl went through, the pain was constant."

The girl stirred, and for a moment, Jack saw her eyes, blue as robin eggs. But they were tragic eyes, eyes having suffered pain beyond what any human should, and she began to sob and shake. Jack put his hand on her shoulder, and said, "Hey, it's okay. It's okay."

But the girl continued to shake in fear, the memories of how she was used and assaulted raging in her mind. They were shadowing her, overwhelming her, but she had one memory, one she had to share.

"Voynitch!" she screamed, and she kept screaming it, again and again until the Otherkin put a furred finger on her head, and she fell asleep. Marven touched her softly on the cheek, making sure she was resting, and smiled at the Otherkin, saying, "You learn fast."

"Thank you, High One."

"They are all learning fast," said Marven, looking over at Stanel, who smiled.

"We can send the girl to Marquette," said Jack. "She will be safe there."

"No," said Marven, "This place will heal her, even with that machine beneath the surface."

That reminded Jack, and he stood. "I've got to go to the Cloud Station. Take care of the girl."

"We will," said Marven.

Marven and Stanel nodded, and Jack walked to the staircase. After the long journey down, he found the station. XB 7889, Kato, and a dozen people were inside the station. Kato was near the door, watching XB instruct the new Otaku who just arrived from the substation three days after the attack. Doug had called Rick and sent Otaku to Detroit to watch over the Cloud Network and learn its wonders. They were all excited, in their white, puffy robes, memorizing all of XB's words. Around them, more robots were moving around, over twenty. They, too, were brought from the substation.

It was funny, the Otaku arriving on their plushy road, and demanding access to the city, talking about the Cloud network and the importance of preserving human knowledge. Finally, the guard had reached a level where he couldn't stop laughing and just let them in. They got to the coven next, following directions of XB over a phone and tried to evict the coven. What ended up happening when the riders arrived, seeing one of the Otaku getting a wedgie while three more were getting noogies for trying to remove them. In the end, XB had to give them another entrance about ten miles down in an old warehouse where the Otaku set up their sanctuary. In a day, they had turned into a combination of tech house and house of worship, until the Guard came and tried to evict them, but were stopped when a chest of gold fell into their laps. So they left them alone, on the agreement that the Otaku pay taxes on the building they were "renting."

Jack looked up at Kato and asked, "Well, will the power stay on?"

"They are shutting down the power plant for a week to see how effective this power from the Cloud is," said Kato, "Apparently, cities across Michigan are getting lights back. People are happy. I have heard that Detroit is being given so much attention, they agreed to let researchers from Dearborn, Canton, and Plymouth access to the Henry Ford Museum just to give them room to breathe."

"The talks are good," said Jack, "They're slow, but they are progressing. Should be off in a few days."

"Doug and Tricks going to be up for it?" asked Kato.

"They should."

"We're still taking the tunnels?"

"I think we should," said Jack, "They'll be ready for us on the path."

"I was thinking the same thing," said Kato.

"I've got to go for now, Kato. Let me know how things are going here."

"Will do. I'll be back tomorrow."

"See you, Kato."

Chapter 12

Entrance to the Wastelands

1 The End of the Green

Ara stared out into the sand, scrub, and stunted plants that faced her, and saw for the first time, the true end of the Green. So much sky was above her, Jeremiah Jr., and Emma. It was a dead land, a land where none but the strongest could live. It was not just a desert, dry, or sand. It was a sun-soaked, deadly, evil thing she was facing. But the sky. So free and so blue it was. So alive, unblocked by the endless forest of her home, it made her heart weep, and so dry it was, it sucked the moisture right out of her skin. They stared, seeing the line between the Green and the Wastelands. Sand versus grass, tree versus dune, flowers versus scrub. It was impossible to know if this was where the Green ended or where the Wastelands began.

"How large is it?" asked Ara.

"No Amish has ever been to the other side," said Jeremiah, "The Navajo might know, but we do not."

"It's so dead," said Emma, clutching at her brother's arm.

"It looks dead," said Jeremiah. "But there is life. Lizards, snakes, birds, insects. There is water, though little. You best save what you have, for the water you do find is harsh and metallic."

Ara looked out, and her eyes set on the path. It was like a giant snake trail through the sand, beaten in by hundreds of years of Amish traders traveling it.

"Stay on the path," said Jeremiah, as he followed it himself. "There are creatures in the Wastelands far more deadly than any you will find in the Green."

Ara nodded and hugged them both. "Gracias."

"De nada," said Emma.

They smiled at each other, and Ara, on the back of the mule, took her first step into the Green. Emma and Jeremiah watched as she started through, hoping and praying she would turn back. But on and on she went until they couldn't see anything but a speck on the trail.

"Will she be alright?" asked Emma.

"She will," said Jeremiah, his sister missing the look of longing on his face, wanting with everything in his soul, for her to turn back. He wanted . . .

"We better get back to New Haven," said Emma, interrupting his thoughts.

"You're right," said Jeremiah, "We better hurry. If we ride hard, we can be back in two days."

They turned their mules, and both with one last hard stare, one of concern and one of longing, they turned back to the Green.

2 The Blood of Choice

Jeremiah Jr. and Emma were back in two days. Those two days will be covered later for the rest of the men and women who travel the Green, but those two days were uneventful for the siblings. What was important was the night of the second day.

The two saw the Green soften around them, and knew they were almost back to New Haven. There they'd reunite with mama and papa, be safe again. Jeremiah believed he would stop thinking about Ara and find the girl chosen for him by God. Emma just wanted to be home. It had been a hard trip for her. She'd never rode that hard before, and her brother's teasing didn't help.

It was when they reached the willow, the large one that told them that home was close, that was when they saw the orange light. Jeremiah knew that light well. It was the light of fire.

Quickly, he grabbed the reins of his mule to stop the beast of burden and leaned over to do the same for his sister's.

"What is it?" asked Emma.

"Don't know. Hitch the mules. I don't want to scare them. Let's go."

They hitched the mules to a low-hanging branch and began to tiptoe forward. Silent as shadows they went, fearful of what they would find at the end.

The Green thinned near the house, but there were places to hide. The siblings chose a large bush where they often hid during hide and go seek when they were children. They looked through the flickering shadows and leaves and saw a sight that made fear course through them.

Two figures, who they recognized as their parents, were on their knees, in front of a man in black robes and a black wide brim hat. He stood above their parents. Behind this man who looked like a priest was a pair of men in golden and red armor, with capes flowing behind them in the wind. Mary was held by the back of the neck and crotch by one. Behind these two knights were a pair of creatures like werewolves, each holding the baby boys in their claws. On the side, the house, barn, fields . . . they were all on fire. The smell of burning livestock was in the air in the form of charring meat and burning hair.

The two were paralyzed with fear, unable to move, and

watched as the priest knelt in front of his father again.

"I ask you again, peasant," said the priest. "Where is the girl? The one from New Spain." Jeremiah felt a pull in his head that rooted him and Emma to the ground; they had to listen and know what his man said. However, there was another voice, one like his father's saying, "Don't move, for the love of God, don't move."

"I cannot tell you what I do not know," said the father, his voice harsh, angry, but had weakened much.

The priest walked to the father and pulled his head up. "I don't believe you. Tell me, or you will suffer."

"I am always suffering to serve my god," said the father, "You cannot make me fear to the point of my abandonment of faith."

"Oh, I think I can," said the priest, and then pointed to one of the wolves, who lifted Samual, screaming and balling over his wolf-head, and jaws open wide.

"No," yelled the father, trying to stand, but was unable to due to his bonds. But he struggled mightily, yelling and screaming, "No! Leave him alone. Leave him alone!"

"You have already sealed his fate," said the priest, who then looked at the wolfman and said, "Feast."

"Nooooo!!!!!" screamed Lilith, fighting hard against her bonds as well, as the Wolf lifted the screaming child over his head and dropped the baby into his open jaws, swallowing Samual whole. Emma felt Jeremiah put his hand over her mouth to stop her screaming. She was going to scream, but she didn't. Instead, she gagged, and it stopped at the hand over her mouth, spewing out between the fingers. Jeremiah didn't notice, only watched in horror as his brother was killed as easily as he would kill a pig. He wanted to scream, in pain, in horror, in loss. Instead, he was frozen like a statue.

Both their parents were devastated, unable to save their boy. The priest came back and said, "Where is she?"

"Wastelands," sobbed their father, "The Wastelands."

"Thank you," said the priest, who stood and looked at his soldiers, then said, "Kill them."

Jeremiah pulled his sister back, turning away as they heard the screaming of their family. The children and the parents screamed and screamed, and Jeremiah dragged his sobbing and silently screaming sister back to the Green.

They got back to the mules, where Jeremiah finally let go of his sister. They both started puking and sobbing. They would never be the same after that. They were both broken inside in a way none could repair. No faith, no word, no kind would be able to.

"They are dead," said Emma, "Mary, the boys, mama, and papa. Oh God, why?"

"It's the bishop's fault," said Jeremiah, rage replacing the sadness. "He was going to trade Ara like he would sheep, and our father refused to do so. He should have stopped them, but he didn't. He betrayed our people. He betrayed what it is to be Amish. I will kill him."

"Where are we going to go?" asked Mary.

"The Wasteland," said Jeremiah, "We are going to the Navajo. We are going to plead and with them, get our revenge."

He picked up his sister, still sobbing, but anger also entering her heart. They got back on the mules, and took off again, riding them harder than they ever had before.

3 The Price of Blood

The killings of the other boy happened the same way as with the baby, with no further need to be described. The soldiers sliced off the adults heads. The wolves were about to feast on the girl when a voice yelled, "Stop."

The Black Priest turned and saw Blaine, his fellow Black Priest walking forward, sword in hand.

"What is wrong, brother?" he asked in confusion at Blaine's rage.

"Why did you kill them?" yelled Blaine, "And put down that girl."

The wolf men dropped Mary, who had fainted, thank God.

"Evert," said Blaine, "Why did you kill him, and where are the boys?"

"The wolves needed meat," said Evert, "And the soldiers needed the sword practice."

In one swift stroke, Blaine beheaded his brother and one of the soldiers of the Golden Lord's army with the sword he carried. The last soldier and the two DarkKin moved in, claws extended and sword drawn. They died at Blaine's sword. Then he turned back to the corpse, the fire making it glow, knowing what was coming.

The corpse split as the Golden Lord's avatar came out of it, the mass of organs forming from Evert's body. It saw Blaine and the horror the Lord created from the priest's corpse made him want to scream, but he stood, sword in hand, ready to face this beast.

"Blaine," said the Golden Lord, "Why have you betrayed me?"

"I have never cared for you, father," said Blaine. "As you have cared for none of us. You have power, but this," he indicated the carnage around him, "This is an evil nobody should condone. I have always worked against you in the shadows, but now, here in the light of the flame, I reveal myself to you and show you that you have no power over me. I will stop you however I can, and I won't stop until Etam is free, and you and the Great Old Ones are dead."

"I strip you of your powers," said the Golden Lord, and Blaine felt a lessening of himself, "No longer will you have the Voice. No longer will your body be protected."

Blaine went to his knees, weakened, but also knowing he was free, looked up, and said, "Fuck you."

The mass of viscera lunged at him, but the time limit was up, and it fell apart.

Blaine stood, thinking, "So this is what it's like to be free of the Golden Lord. I like it."

He went to the girl. She was stirring. He picked her up, and she opened her eyes. Seeing the man who was wearing clothes like that of her parents' killer, she screamed, but Blaine hugged her and held her, turning her away from the bodies.

"It's okay," he said, "It's okay, you're safe."

It lasted for over an hour, and when it ended, the girl still cried softly, but held Blaine desperately.

"Do you have any family here in New Haven I can take you to?" asked Blaine.

"My brother and sister were in the Wasteland," she said, face caked with tears.

"Then we will head there," said Blaine. "We will find them."

He stood, "Which way?"

She pointed, and carrying the girl, Blaine grabbed one of the horses the party brought and after mounting the mare, started to gallop into the Green. He had faith that Slavern would reach the other girl and protect her. Now, his redemption had started, and it started with this girl.

"There was another girl," said Blaine, "A pregnant girl. Is she with them?"

"Maybe," said the girl. "She was heading for the Navajo."

"We will find them, child," said Blaine, "What is your name?"

"Marry."

"I'm Blaine, I got you."

"You promise?"

"I promise."

They rode into the darkness.

Chapter 13

The Ride to the Cave

1 The Deal

Jack, Kshea, Thug, Kato, Grenn, Miko, and Tricks were sitting in Jack's room, passing cigarettes and the bottle of hard whisky around. They sat and waited, waiting for what was to come. The treaty of the Five Cities was being signed. What it meant for their journey, they were going to wait and see. They all knew they were heading for the Tunnels of Night. Jack and Doug argued that having two separate parties of riders coming in both directions was both a technical and tactical move. For one, there was a chance they could find more allies, and two, seeing Etam from all sides and not just one was a wise move so they knew what they were dealing with.

They waited for another hour until Doug and Daxter entered

the room. They all looked up, nervous.

"The deal has been signed," said Doug, "Plymouth, Dearborn, and Canton will get free access to Greenfield village in exchange for support on Marquette and Detroit's stand on Etam, the Black Priests, and all factions connected to them."

Jack sighed, relief entering his body.

"Anything else?" asked Miko.

"Marquette is going to train Riders down here as well," said Daxter.

Silence fell upon all in the room. This news, this was . . .

"New lodge in Detroit?" said Grenn.

"And in all the cities," said Daxter, "Twelve riders from Marquette will help them set up. There are a few motorcycles collected over the years in Detroit, so they will supply them."

Then Doug smiled and said, "We also have a replacement for Samantha. Came by boat last night."

"Who?" asked Tricks.

Doug went to the door, and said, "You can come in now."

Through the door, her skin patterned to look like a raging volcano, evident of her excitement, came in the long brown-haired skin-changer, Meg, the Keeper of Ironwood Lodge. She smiled and they all stood.

"Meg," said Jack, standing, walking over, gave her a hug, which she returned, her skin patterning after that of a waterfall.

"It's good to see you, Jack," she said.

"How?" asked Kshea, surprised, "Keepers can't leave the lodge grounds."

"I argued for this leave," said Meg. "Keepers are supposed to keep the rider's home and hearth, but you are going to be without home and hearth for months or even longer, so I argued a Keeper should be there to give you home and hearth while you travel these unknown roads. I've been replaced for now, and the lodge is in good hands. If you will have me, I brought my bike and am ready to ride the roads."

All the riders hugged her and welcomed her and decided to celebrate. They drank and talked happily over this, smoking, drinking, and just having a good time. When Jack woke up, he had a headache. He didn't dream of Niki that night.

He walked with Kato and Meg the next day to the Cloud Station and found XB waiting for him at the new warehouse entrance. Meg came along to get caught up on the dealings and plans the riders had and learned all the events of the battle of Detroit. She was amazed and fascinated by the stories, and by XB.

"Hey XB," said Jack, "Just coming to say goodbye."

"Are we leaving?" said XB.

"What?" asked Jack. "I thought you were staying here."

"There are other Cloud stations that must be addressed, and I am the only robot to be able to travel outside the service network," explained XB. "Besides, I feel the Cloud needs much updating, and I feel I can get much information from traveling with you. And if we find other stations, we can activate them as we go."

Jack smiled, "Well, come on, I know Kato will be happy to have you."

Jack was about to turn, but stopped and asked, "What about the Otaku?"

"The organic employees are too busy learning about Detroit's operation."

Jack shrugged. Kato grinned and said, "You just couldn't get enough of us, could you XB?"

Meg walked forward and said, "It's good to meet you, XB. I am Meg, Keeper of the expedition. My duties are to give the riders home and hearth on their travels as they make it through the Green."

"Fascinating," said XB, "I would like to learn more of this as we travel."

"Of course," said Meg with a smile, her skin patterned like snowfall.

2 The Caverns of Night

A Hindu guard man stood before the entrance to the cavern

on horseback. It had been three days since Meg joined the party on her large Chopper. It, like all the bikes, was packed on the newly supplied truck, along with XB. He was powered down for now, only his retina eyes on, collecting information to be added to the Cloud network later. The fuel truck was filled with both diesel and gasoline for the vehicles.

Before them stood the cave entrance to the Tunnels of Night. It was beautiful in the dense part of the Green, even this early in the morning, there was a soft blue glow about it. It was like looking into a tunnel of star light. It was so beautiful, all the riders were mesmerized by it, and both Grenn and Meg's skin patterned the image before them. The Guard stood and said, "This is the main central tunnel. It goes hundreds, if not more, miles. We never got to the end of it, but we know this tunnel the best. There are many side tunnels we also mapped as well. Some are small caves, while others are new paths we found. Stay on this one as much as you can. We think there is an exit, but once you stray from the path, you can become lost in it."

Doug nodded, and said, "You can go."

The guard nodded and rode off.

Doug looked at Jack, remembering Dreamer's words, and said, "Jack, you take point. Your instincts are the best. Kshea, Grenn, you stay on the fuel truck and guard it. Jack, what do you think we should do next?"

Jack looked into the tunnel and said, "Those not driving the trucks should stay on the supply truck. We have no idea how far this goes, and we need all the caution we can get. Kato, you drive with Tricks on the supply truck. Grenn and Kshea, you will be with Miko. Meg, Thug, Doug, and I will stay in the back of the supply truck with XB and guard it. We have no idea what's in there, so we have to take it slow."

They all nodded and mounted up. Kshea looked at Doug. He looked back, both feeling something in their stomachs, but moving on, knowing their duties. The Trucks started, and the tires began to roll. The two large trucks entered the tunnel, the walls covered in glowing crystals that resembled starlight.

Jack raised his gun, checked it, but knew they were ready. Under his usual tarp hid Watu. With him, Jack knew that Marven would join them when he could. The nine riders, one robot, and one magical bear lay in wait, ready to move on with their journey, and ready to face the secrets of the Tunnels of Night.

Jack looked down at his phone and decided to open the Cloud network. He suddenly remembered to look up the word the girl used while screaming. He looked it up and found it.

"Voynich; A handwritten manuscript written in the 15th century. The language used to write it is unknown and . . ." Jack scanned through until . . .

"What the fuck?" asked Jack, reading.

"The Voynich manuscript was also a central spell book in the fantasy game, Etam Kingdom, and was fictionalized to be the central spell book in the game."

Jack stared and yelled for the others. Thug, Doug, and Meg all looked at the information.

"The girl," said Jack, "The one I pulled out of the Hellmaker, she mentioned this book."

"What does that mean for us?" asked Thug.

"Not sure yet. I'm going to read for a while. You guys keep guarding."

And so, Jack went back to reading all he could. He was going to absorb every bit of information. He knew there was a connection to this book and the Golden Lord, he just needed to find it.

The tunnels closed in around them, and in that Darkness, a new hope and a new wonder had entered the rider's hearts. It was time for the next adventure to keep their home safe.

Epilogue

Slavern and his men had kept their arms in their camp. They had just reached the village called Ironwood. All forty were with the resistance, and he hoped that they wouldn't be killed on sight. They needed allies in this fight, not enemies, and Slavern was ordered to go unarmed in the hope they would listen. Blaine had convinced the Golden Lord they would retrieve the mother of the child of Kal, assuring their loyalty to him. It was a lie, but they were sent since the Great Old Ones believed them. Kal would go find Ara and help her escape as well. Slavern hoped he would succeed.

Slavern and his men entered the town, still in their Golden Lord Army finery, but unarmed. Villagers saw them and went to get the authorities. They came, ten men armed with billy clubs, wearing blue uniforms. One walked forward, a white-skinned human, pudgy and pimply, but glaring at Slavern.

"Halt," he said, "Who are you?"

"Soldiers of the Golden Lord," said Slavern, "We come from Etam with a warning and to parlay. We were sent by our leader, who is part of the resistance, with a warning. We need to talk to you and the riders."

The guard stood there for one moment, then looked at one of his men and said, "Go get Hendricks and a representative of the Riders.

He then ordered Slavern to go to his knees, which he did, and they waited. An hour later, Slavern gasped as three riders came to them on motor bikes, bandana and leather-clad, armed with firearms, riding giant, roaring bikes. Slavern, never having seen a motorized vehicle before, was amazed.

Ten minutes later, a man came to them, Hendricks. An old man in his seventies, with wispy hair, and glasses, but scowling at the soldiers. One of the Riders, a large, Doberman Otherkin, wearing a leather vest over a white shirt, walked with Henndricks.

"Why have you come?" asked Hendricks. "We don't welcome any from Etam."

"We came to seek aid," said Slavern. "And protect someone."

"Who?" asked the Otherkin rider.

"The Black Priest who came here; I'm guessing he had relations with someone."

"What makes you suspect that?" asked Hendricks.

"Because Kal was connected to the Golden Lord, and anything from the Golden Lord, he can sense. He knows about the child and wants to make it a Black Priest. He cares not for the mother, save for maybe his own carnal pleasure, but she is in danger."

Hendricks and the rider looked at each other, and then the rider looked at one of his companions, a small, Androgenan rider named Umar, and said, "Send a message to the Marquette Lodge."

The Rider took off. Hendricks looked down at Slavern and said, "You will be put under house arrest, but will be provided with food, water, and medical attention. You will not go outside. My friend here will have someone take your statement. Do you understand?"

"Yes," said Slavern. This was the first step for the resistance. The first step to taking down the Golden Lord and freeing the people of Etam. He would tell them everything. It would take a long time, but he would not fail, for Blaine's sake, the child's sake, and the people of Etam's sake.

www.ingramcontent.com/pod-product-compliance
Lightning Source LLC
Chambersburg PA
CBHW051059030726
47504CB00006B/1704
* 9 7 8 1 9 6 0 1 0 4 3 3 5 *